Seneca Falls Library
47 Cayuga Street
Seneca Falls, NY 13148

GOLDEN SPIKE

THE IRON HORSE CHRONICLES, BOOK 3

GOLDEN SPIKE

ROBERT LEE MURPHY

FIVE STAR
A part of Gale, a Cengage Company

Farmington Hills, Mich • San Francisco • New York • Waterville, Maine
Meriden, Conn • Mason, Ohio • Chicago

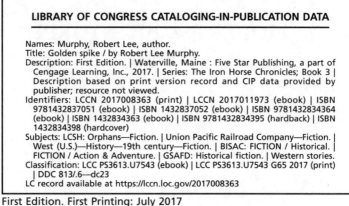

LIBRARY OF CONGRESS CATALOGING-IN-PUBLICATION DATA

Names: Murphy, Robert Lee, author.
Title: Golden spike / by Robert Lee Murphy.
Description: First Edition. | Waterville, Maine : Five Star Publishing, a part of
  Cengage Learning, Inc., 2017. | Series: The Iron Horse Chronicles; Book 3 |
  Description based on print version record and CIP data provided by
  publisher; resource not viewed.
Identifiers: LCCN 2017008363 (print) | LCCN 2017011973 (ebook) | ISBN
  9781432837051 (ebook) | ISBN 1432837052 (ebook) | ISBN 9781432834364
  (ebook) | ISBN 1432834363 (ebook) | ISBN 9781432834395 (hardback) | ISBN
  1432834398 (hardcover)
Subjects: LCSH: Orphans—Fiction. | Union Pacific Railroad Company—Fiction. |
  West (U.S.)—History—19th century—Fiction. | BISAC: FICTION / Historical. |
  FICTION / Action & Adventure. | GSAFD: Historical fiction. | Western stories.
Classification: LCC PS3613.U7543 (ebook) | LCC PS3613.U7543 G65 2017 (print)
  | DDC 813/.6—dc23
LC record available at https://lccn.loc.gov/2017008363

First Edition. First Printing: July 2017
Find us on Facebook– https://www.facebook.com/FiveStarCengage
Visit our website– http://www.gale.cengage.com/fivestar/
Contact Five Star™ Publishing at FiveStar@cengage.com

Printed in the United States of America
1 2 3 4 5 6 7 21 20 19 18 17

In Memory of My Parents
Harold and Helen Murphy
Who instilled in me a love of history and an appreciation
for literature

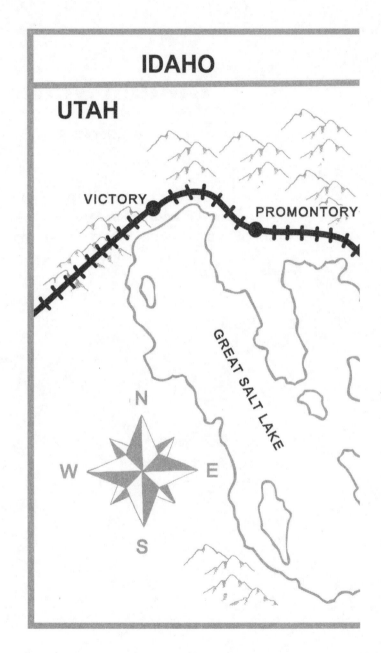

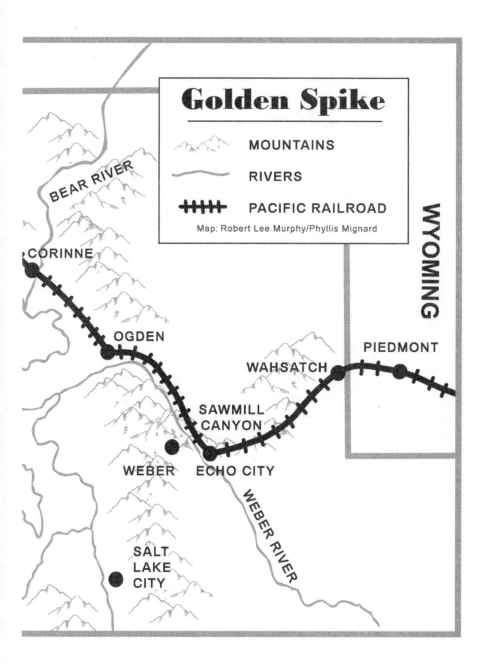

ACKNOWLEDGMENTS

Marianne Babal, Historian, Vice President, Wells Fargo Historical Services, provided important information about the company's stagecoach operations in 1869. Katherine Santos, Archivist, California State Railroad Museum's research library, provided excellent assistance with their microfilm files about Leland Stanford. I am indebted to Charles Trentelman of Ogden's Union Station research library for pointing me to the University of Utah's digital newspaper site. My special thanks to Carol Reed, Assistant Registrar of the Carbon County Museum in Rawlins, Wyoming, for assisting me in identifying the commanding officer of Fort Fred Steele, Wyoming, during January 1869. Wendell Huffman, Curator of History, Nevada State Railroad Museum, in Carson City, provided me with a floor plan and a rare photograph of Governor Stanford's special passenger car used at the driving of the golden spike ceremony at Promontory Summit, Utah. The actual, unrestored, car is part of the Nevada State Railroad Museum collection. Peter A. Hansen, Editor, *Railroad History,* assisted me in identifying the passenger who rode the cowcatcher on the locomotive *Jupiter.* As with previous books, my writing has been improved by the constructive criticism offered by my fellow members of the Society of Children's Book Writers and Illustrators and by my compatriots in Sun City Anthem Authors. Once again, I express my appreciation to Hazel Rumney, Editorial Developmental Coordinator at Five Star Publishing, for spotting the errors in my draft and for guiding me toward a much improved result. Thanks to Erin Bealmear, Content Project Editor, for providing a thorough copy edit of the book. I thank my wife, Barbara, for giving me the freedom to travel while doing research and to spend hours huddled at my computer writing.

PROLOGUE

The driving of the Golden Spike at Promontory Summit in Utah on May 10, 1869, almost didn't happen. None of the history books documenting the facts encompassing the joining of the two halves of the first transcontinental railroad mention this crucial event. Only five people appear to have been aware of the incident. Will Braddock knew. He was one of those five.

CHAPTER 1

The black Morgan's hooves skidded on the icy surface, and his forelegs almost buckled. Will Braddock leaned back in the saddle to help the horse regain his footing.

"Easy, Buck, don't need you breaking a leg." Will Braddock bent forward, pressing his cheek against the horse's neck to shield his face from the bitter crosswind blowing down off the mountains. "We have to be close."

Will strained to see ahead, but couldn't make out the buildings of Echo City. It shouldn't be much farther, though. He'd ridden out of Weber two hours earlier for what should have been an easy trip back to Union Pacific's end of track in Utah Territory. Before he'd ridden far, storm clouds scudded down the slopes of the Wasatch Range and engulfed him and Buck in driving rain that turned to sleet.

Twenty minutes later, Will slid a boot out of a stirrup and kicked on the door of Echo City's livery stable. A sheet of water cascaded off the brim of his slouch hat and splattered across his legs and Buck's withers, adding to the horse's already soaked coat. The stable door swung open, and he tapped his heels into the horse's flanks urging him into the dim confines of the barn.

"Evening, Zeke," Will said.

Ezekiel Thomas, the stable attendant, grasped Buck's bridle and whisked the water off the white star emblazoned on the horse's forehead. "Evening, Will. Nasty out, eh? Been expecting you."

"Expecting me?" Will stepped out of the saddle.

"Sure thing. Your uncle's over to the Chinaman's café having supper. He said you'd be returning this evening."

Will had ridden to Weber earlier that morning, at his Uncle Sean Corcoran's direction, to pick up a package from Samuel Reed, the Union Pacific's construction engineer, who'd telegraphed that his plans for Ogden were ready. The Mormon city would become the last major rail yard for the UP on its march westward to join with the Central Pacific and complete the first transcontinental railroad.

With tracklaying nearing its end, General Grenville Dodge, the chief engineer, had disbanded his Uncle Sean's survey inspection team, which Will had joined two years earlier. Will's uncle, being a capable engineer, had switched from surveying to supervising the construction of roundhouses, depots, and maintenance sheds. Will's job as the team's hunter had been discontinued, and his uncle gave him a part-time job as an errand boy. Will accepted the cut in pay, because it was better than being unemployed. What the fifteen-year-old would do after the railroad was finished remained a mystery he tried not to contemplate.

Hee-haw!

The braying of a mule in one of the stalls drew Will's attention. "That Ruby?" he asked. The dim light made it difficult to see the mule clearly.

"Yep," said Zeke. "That's Ruby. Contrary animal, if ever I seen one."

"She can be ornery. I can vouch for that." Will chuckled, remembering the times he'd wrestled a packsaddle onto the back of the sturdy mule. Ruby had served as the pack animal for Homer Garcon, who'd been the survey inspection team's cook. The former black slave now rode Ruby as his mount when he accompanied Will's uncle on his rounds. Homer had taken an even steeper cut in pay when he, too, accepted the demotion from cook to errand boy.

"Homer with my uncle?" Will asked.

"Yep."

Will lifted his saddlebags off the Morgan's rump. "Buck needs water and feed. Can you take care of him for me?"

"That's my job. Your uncle done paid for his stabling."

"I'll leave my Winchester with my saddle. Won't need them in the café."

"I can see not needing a saddle in the café," Zeke said. "But that fancy rifle might be handy, what with the likes of them customers eating at the Chinaman's place."

"Too wet out, Zeke. Troublemakers like dry weather."

Zeke shrugged his shoulders and threw up both palms. "If you say so."

Will threw the saddlebags over his shoulder and ducked back out into the rain. The poncho the railroad provided kept his upper body reasonably dry, but his buckskin trousers were wet from mid-thigh to the tops of his calf-high, Wellington cavalry boots.

He sloshed up the main street of the latest iteration of the Hell on Wheels town that had quadrupled the size of the small Mormon community of Echo City when the tracklayers had arrived. Will's boots crunched through the thin layer of ice on the dirt road and squished in the mud beneath the cracked surface. He hunched the poncho up around his neck to keep the biting wind from whistling down his buckskin jacket collar. He rubbed his left bicep briskly. The old arrow wound ached in cold weather.

Opposite the livery stable, the two-story, false-fronted Lucky Dollar Saloon dominated the line of ramshackle buildings and tents comprising the temporary town. The tinkling of a piano inside the saloon accompanied the warbling of a lullaby. A shadow moved behind closed curtains lining a front window of the Lucky Dollar. From the figure's heavyset outline, Will knew it was Mort Kavanagh. The self-proclaimed mayor of Hell on Wheels controlled all aspects of the gambling and drinking establishments that followed the railroad's construction in order to entice the tracklayers into spending their hard-earned money on whiskey.

Beyond the Lucky Dollar, Will passed Abrams General Store. The Jewish merchant had closed up shop already. The miserable weather would have yielded few customers at such a late hour. Will planned to visit the store tomorrow. He'd chewed the last of the jawbreakers on the ride in from Weber, and he wanted to buy another poke of his favorite candy.

Lantern light glowed from the bay-windowed office that jutted onto the Union Pacific depot's platform. Will could see the stationmaster hunched over his telegraph key. Normally, the depot would be dark and silent this time of evening. Must be a train coming in. None had arrived from the east for almost a week.

The current snowstorm was the latest of several that had blown through, creating drifts in Wyoming too deep for the 4-4-0 locomotives to push through. Passenger and freight traffic ground to a halt. If it weren't for this bad weather, a person should be able to travel nonstop on the Union Pacific a thousand miles from Omaha, Nebraska, to the end of track in Echo City. From here, travelers rode the stagecoach to connect with the Central Pacific's end of track, which was advancing eastward from beyond the Utah-Nevada border. Passengers then continued their journey to California by rail.

A few paces farther down the street brought Will to Wells, Fargo & Company. He opened the station's front door and stepped inside.

Jenny McNabb turned from the woodburning, iron stove

where she worked at preparing the meal for the passengers who would arrive on the train. They would enjoy a hearty, hot meal before boarding the stagecoach. The fourteen-year-old girl had gained the reputation a year ago as being the best cook on the Wells Fargo line.

"Will," she said. "You're soaking wet. Close the door, and don't come any farther. You're tracking up my clean floor."

Her blue eyes flashed gray, a sure sign to Will that Jenny meant what she said. He closed the door behind him and didn't move.

Jenny had coiled her waist-length, black hair into a tight bun on the back of her head. She reached up and pushed a loose strand back into place.

"This storm's bad," Will said, "but from the activity at the depot, it looks like a train's finally going to make it through from Wyoming."

"I know. Papa said we'll have to keep the passengers here until morning, though. He and Duncan are out back trying to put all the horses under cover. That old barn was only built for six teams, not nine."

Echo City was the latest in a series of stagecoach stations that Jenny's father, Alistair McNabb, had managed for Wells Fargo. The former Confederate officer had lost his left arm during the war, but he did the work of men who had both. Duncan, Jenny's ten-year-old brother, served as the stage station's telegrapher, when he wasn't helping with the horses.

"Want a cup of coffee?" Jenny asked.

"Can't stay, Jenny. Have to meet Uncle Sean and Homer over to the Chinaman's café."

"You given any thought to what you're going to do once the railroad is finished?"

"Some. Haven't decided, though. Try not to think a lot about it. You?"

Jenny raised her eyebrows. "Head on to California, I suppose. That was our original goal when we left Virginia two years ago. Once the UP joins up with the CP there won't be any need for a cross-country stagecoach service."

Will couldn't think of anything to say. It was sad to realize his friends also faced an unknown future.

"Stop by later," she said. "Might have a piece of pie left over if the passengers don't eat it all."

Will left the station and continued to the end of the street, where the Chinaman was required to erect his café. The other businessmen in Hell on Wheels tolerated the old Chinaman because he provided a meal at a decent price, but they certainly didn't want him locating his eating establishment in the center of their town.

Entering the café, Will nodded to his uncle and Homer who sat at a table near the single window set into the wooden front of the canvas-roofed structure. Will dropped his hat and saddlebags on the floor and hauled the rubber poncho off over his head. He shook the water from the heavy rainwear and hung it on a peg beside the door. He slapped his hat against his thigh and hung it atop the poncho. Retrieving the saddlebags, he walked to the table.

He shivered when he sat down. "It's as cold in here as it is outside," he said.

"Old Chinaman's too stingy to buy a stove for the customers," his uncle said. "The only heat comes from his cookstove in the back."

"And that sure don't do much," Homer added.

Will tapped a dark patch of ice on the tabletop. "Coffee?" he asked.

"Freezes as soon as you spill it," his uncle said. "Want some of the stew? If you eat it fast, it stays warm enough."

"Need something. I'm starved . . . and cold."

Will's uncle motioned to a young Chinese waiter who hurried over with a bowl and spoon and placed them in front of Will with a polite bow, causing his pigtail to swing over the front of his shoulder.

Homer pushed a plate of cornbread toward Will. "Can't butter it." Homer whacked a chunk of butter resting on a tin plate with his knife. The blade bounced off the top of the frozen lump.

Will dragged a thick bundle of papers out of his saddlebags and handed them to his uncle. "Sam Reed's plans," he said.

While Will tackled the bowl of stew, his uncle sorted through the documents.

"I see Sam even had *Colonel* Seymour sign off on the plans." Will's uncle uttered the title in a sneering way.

Silas Seymour had bestowed the honorary title upon himself, much to the disgust of many former Army officers who now worked on the railroad. Thomas "Doc" Durant, the Union Pacific's vice president and general manager, had sent Seymour to Utah to spy on Sam Reed, Sean Corcoran, and others. Seymour always thought he knew a better way to build the railroad, even if it cost more money and took more time. Seymour's meddling earned him the nickname of "the insulting engineer."

"How did Mr. Reed get Seymour to sign off?" Will asked.

"My guess is Sam pointed out that Durant wouldn't be happy if Seymour antagonized Brigham Young any more than he already has. When Young bought out the Mormon settlers' farms along our right-of-way and donated their land to the UP for our Ogden yards, Durant knew he'd saved a lot of money."

"That ought to make General Dodge happy, too," Will said.

"Yes, but I wish General Dodge could wrap up his business in Washington City and get back out here. He's the best at keeping Seymour in line."

Dodge had recently completed a two-year term as a United

States congressman, but he'd remained in the nation's capital to negotiate with Collis Huntington, the Central Pacific's lobbyist, on where the two railroads should join tracks.

"In the meantime," Will's uncle said, "we'll have to do the best we can. Fortunately Jack Casement's on his way back. He telegraphed he was leaving Ohio this morning. He wants to review these plans as soon as possible and not wait until he returns. Wants me to meet him at Fort Fred Steele on his way back."

"Can't you give the plans to Dan?" Will asked.

"Jack's brother has his hands full keeping the tracklayers from walking off the job because the payroll hasn't been met for weeks. Doc Durant has no intention of sending any more money than necessary from New York, and this storm is giving him the excuse he needs not to do so. Besides, Dan Casement doesn't know anything about estimating the kinds of materials required to do the job."

Jack and Dan Casement held the contract with the Union Pacific for laying the tracks. Jack had taken a few weeks off during the winter downtime to return to his home back east for a vacation with his family. He'd left his younger brother, who was the company bookkeeper, in charge of looking after their warehouse and construction train, presently idled in Echo City.

The back door of the café banged open, and Will glanced up when the chilling blast of air reached his face. He dropped his spoon into the bowl of stew, and his mouth fell open. Staring back at him from across the room was Paddy O'Hannigan.

CHAPTER 2

Will pushed away from the table. The back legs of his chair caught in a crack in the crude, wooden floor, and he toppled over backward. He reached down to lift the flap on the Army holster he wore buckled on his right hip over his buckskin jacket. From where he lay sprawled on his back, he kept his eyes locked on Paddy, who raised the tail of the woolen coat he wore, reaching for his own pistol.

Paddy sneered, exposing a mouthful of rotten, broken teeth. He spat a stream of tobacco juice onto the café floor. The skinny Irishman's smirk caused the scar running down the left side of his face to twitch visibly.

Will's holster flap resisted lifting. The freezing weather had stiffened the leather. He reached across his body with his left hand to hold the flap up so he could grasp the butt of the Colt .44-caliber revolver with his right.

Paddy beat him to the draw. He pointed his pistol at Will's uncle, double-cocked the hammer, and pulled the trigger. The explosion filled the room with a boom. Smoke rose from the end of the barrel.

Will's uncle groaned and slumped forward in his chair.

"Sure, and I told ye Major Corcoran," Paddy said, "I'd get ye for killing my pa."

Paddy double-clicked the hammer again and aimed at Homer.

Will still struggled to free his revolver from its holster.

"And, sure it is, nigger, I'm going to kill you, too."

Out of the corner of his eye, Will could see that Homer seemed to be paralyzed.

Paddy pulled the trigger. The hammer snapped against the percussion cap with a metallic clunk. No explosion followed. Paddy looked at the gun.

Will knew any number of things could have caused the revolver to misfire. Maybe the cylinder was empty, perhaps the percussion cap had fallen off the chamber's nipple, or the wet weather had dampened the powder charge.

Will freed his revolver from the holster, double-cocking the hammer as he raised the Colt.

Paddy turned and bolted out the back door.

Will got to his feet and kicked the chair out of the way. He leaned toward his uncle, who sat up at that moment holding his left shoulder. "Uncle Sean? Where're you hit?"

"In the shoulder. Think it broke my collarbone."

"Homer," Will said, "take Uncle Sean over to the railroad doctor. I'm going after Paddy."

He headed across the dining area toward the rear door, which Paddy had left open.

"What are you doing?" his uncle demanded.

"Going after him." Will paused in the doorway and looked back at his uncle and Homer. "I thought he was dead. I'm going to finish this."

"That's not a good idea," his uncle said. "You're not using your head, Will."

"This won't take long, Uncle Sean." Will stepped into the alley, pulling the door closed behind him. The sleet blew into his face, making it difficult to see. He'd left the café without his poncho or hat, and he felt the cold settle through his thick hair and cling to his scalp.

A shot exploded, and a bullet smashed into the wood of the doorframe beside him. Will ducked behind several barrels lined up along the back wall of the café. A second shot, fired from a little farther away, smacked into one of the barrels. Pickle brine sprayed out the hole.

Will peered around the side of the barrel and spotted a figure running toward the far end of Hell on Wheels. The runner's bowler hat confirmed he had Paddy in sight. Will rose and raced down the alley after his nemesis.

He hadn't seen Paddy since last summer in Wyoming, when they had their gun battle atop the freight train as it rolled across the bridge over Green River. Will shot Paddy twice then, hitting one or perhaps both of the Irishman's legs. Paddy jumped into the river before Will could finish him. The act had surprised Will, because he'd known from a previous experience that Paddy couldn't swim. When Will searched the riverbank the next day, he found no evidence Paddy had lived.

Now, in the dimming light of the evening and the haze created by the slanting sleet, Will barely kept Paddy in sight fifty yards ahead of him. Opposite the canvas warehouse of the Casement brothers, Paddy stopped and snapped another shot in Will's direction. The whiz of the bullet sounded loud as it whipped past Will's ear. Either Paddy had become a better shot since Will had last confronted him, or maybe it was the luck of the Irish.

Will raised his Colt and aimed at Paddy's back. He paused. If he had the Yellow Boy Winchester he'd left at the stable, the shot would have been guaranteed. He lowered his pistol. No matter what weapon he used, he refused to be labeled a back shooter. Once last year, while leading Count von Schroeder's hunting party in Wyoming, Will had a chance to shoot Paddy in the back with the Winchester rifle, but he'd held off.

The double doors of the canvas warehouse swung open, and Dan Casement emerged. "What's going on out here?" he shouted.

Will trotted up to Casement and stopped. "Paddy O'Hannigan's trying to kill me, again." Will pointed to the figure disappearing down the slope, heading toward the bank of the Weber River.

"O'Hannigan, eh." Casement at five feet tall had to look up at Will who towered over him. "We fired that rascal a couple of years back for stealing railroad property, you know. What's he still doing around here?"

"I'm pretty sure he's a henchman for Mort Kavanagh."

"Wonder why that doesn't surprise me. Kavanagh's giving your uncle fits over property right now, and he's always creating trouble for me by enticing my workers to get drunk and not show up the next day."

"I'm tired of having to fight Paddy," Will said. "I'm going after him. But where can he run tonight, in this storm? He can't cross the river."

"Some Irish workers are holding a wake down that way. One of the gandy dancers was crushed to death under a load of iron rails today."

"I'll check out the wake, sir. See you later." Will stepped off the trail to follow in the direction he'd seen Paddy heading.

"You be careful, Will," Casement called after him. "The Irish are usually rip-roaring drunk at one of those wakes. Hard to tell what they might do when they're all liquored up."

"I'll be fine, sir. What could they do to me?"

CHAPTER 3

Paddy stumbled as he made his way down the slope toward the Weber River, away from the Casements' warehouse tent, which was located on the outskirts of Echo City. He paid careful attention to where he stepped. He didn't want to slip on the icy bank. The bullet wounds Will Braddock had inflicted on him last year in his left leg caused him to limp, making it awkward to balance on the slippery surface. He paused to look back up the slope and saw that Braddock had stopped to talk with Dan Casement.

"Humph," he grunted. "Sure, and I'd be better off without either of ye two!"

Will stopping at the warehouse gave Paddy the needed time to increase the distance between himself and the strapping youth who continued to interfere with his plans. What a time for his revolver to misfire. All three of his enemies had been right in front of him in the Chinaman's café. He knew he'd put a slug into Corcoran. He'd seen him slump over from the impact. If the percussion cap hadn't been missing from the next cylinder, he could've killed all three of them before they would've been able to raise a gun in response. Paddy didn't really care for guns, and he seldom drew his Colt .36-caliber revolver. Because of his dislike of firearms, he'd failed to check the piece to ensure it was in proper working order. He needed to be more careful about that in the future.

The angle of the bank steepened. Paddy turned sideways to

reach down with the strength of his right leg to take the force of his weight. He used his gimpy left leg on the upper side to steady himself. He stomped down hard with the instep of his right boot, breaking through the icy covering to ensure a solid footing before he took the next step. Even taking these extra precautions, he moved downward rapidly.

With the increased angle of descent, he'd dropped out of sight of the Hell on Wheels town. That meant Will couldn't see him, either. That was a good thing.

Paddy sidestepped down twenty or thirty yards until the ground leveled out close to the water's edge. He paused to take a deeper breath. The exertion from maintaining his balance caused his thigh muscles to tremble. He took another breath, then struck off downstream toward where he could see the glow from a bonfire and hear drunken singing at the Irish wake.

One of these days he'd finish what he'd sworn to do five years ago when he'd held his dying father in his arms on that dock in New York City. Sean Corcoran, who'd been a major in the Army then, had stabbed his father to death with a saber. Paddy reached up and rubbed his left cheek, massaging the scar running from his ear to his lip. Corcoran's saber had sliced across Paddy's face on its journey into his father's chest when Paddy had stepped in to intervene. The trouble had happened because his father and his Irish crew of dockworkers had tried to hang that no-account former slave, Homer Garcon. The free blacks had been taking the jobs the Irish wanted to keep for themselves, and the Irish immigrants were determined to do whatever it took to frighten any competition away from their waterfront employment.

The singing grew louder as Paddy approached the wake. He spotted a wagon and team parked not far from the circle of mourners clustered around the bonfire. In the bed of the wagon a swath of canvas covered a hump that was undoubtedly the body of the man they planned to bury.

It was two years ago, when Paddy had tried to steal General Dodge's prized Morgan horse from a stable in Omaha, that he'd made his first contact with Will Braddock. Braddock had managed to thwart that attempt, and had also foiled a second attempt when Paddy later arranged an Indian raid on Dodge's train. Twice Braddock had caused Paddy to fail to steal the horse, and that had not set well with Paddy's boss and god-father, Mort Kavanagh. Kavanagh had wanted to give the horse as a bribe to a Cheyenne chief to entice the Indians to raid the railroad and slow down construction so he could sell the tracklayers more whiskey.

He smiled to himself when he recalled the third, successful attempt at taking the Morgan away from Braddock. Paddy and Black Wolf's band of Cheyenne Indians had waylaid Braddock during a horse race a year ago celebrating the founding of the new town of Cheyenne. Paddy wanted to kill Braddock then, but that half-breed Lone Eagle, a member of Black Wolf's band at the time, had stepped in and prevented it. At least, Paddy had finally been successful in stealing the black horse.

Paddy wasn't worried about eventually fulfilling his vendetta. Sooner or later the odds would turn in his favor, and he would kill all three of his enemies. For now he had to get away from Braddock. He knew he wouldn't do well in a fair fight against Braddock, who'd earned a spot on the railroad as a hunter because of his marksmanship. Paddy preferred knife fighting—a preference that extended to approaching his opponent stealthily from the back. He could feel the rub of his Bowie knife sheath against his right ankle, where he kept it tucked inside his boot.

He needed to find Collin Sullivan, the gang leader who'd organized this wake. Paddy had worked for Sullivan two years ago, before General Jack had fired him. Stepping into the light reflected from the roaring bonfire, Paddy searched the faces of the dozen Irishmen seated on railroad ties around the blaze. Directly opposite, he spotted Sullivan. Paddy eased around the back of the encircled tracklayers, who sounded more like carousers than mourners.

"Collin," Paddy said. "Sure, and I be needing yer help."

The burly, redheaded Sullivan looked back over his shoulder at Paddy. "And just what do ye mean by that, laddie?" He raised his bottle of Irish whiskey and chugged a swig.

"Well, now, sure, and ye know ye would've paid twice the price for that case of whiskey if I hadn't arranged a deal for ye and the boys." Paddy had convinced Kavanagh to let the Irishmen buy a case of poor quality whiskey at half-price, pointing out to his boss that after the wake the drunks would stagger back to the Lucky Dollar and spend more at the saloon's inflated prices.

"Aye, and we thank ye for that. What is it ye be wanting?"

"Sure, and there be a young lad following me who wants to kill me. He'll be showing himself here in a few minutes. All I'm asking ye to do is to delay him a mite, so's I can get away."

"Delay him?"

"That's all. Don't kill him. I plan to do that meself by and by."

CHAPTER 4

Will reached the bottom of the slope and stopped where the ground leveled off near the edge of the river. He heard the roar of the mountain stream rushing past, but he couldn't see the surface of the water. The waning crescent of the moon would not appear until hours after midnight, and if the snow didn't stop it wouldn't provide any illumination even then. Darkness engulfed everything around him. In the distance, a faint, flickering light revealed the location of a fire. That must be the Irish wake Dan Casement had mentioned. It would make sense for an Irish thug like O'Hannigan to seek solace among his cronies.

With limited visibility to reveal his footing, Will relied on his hearing to keep him a safe distance from the rapidly flowing waters of the Weber. He knew the course of the stream meandered through a narrow plain as it descended northward on its journey to the Great Salt Lake, and he found himself swinging away from the fire for a time. It would be shorter to cut straight across toward the light from the flames, but he wasn't sure what surface he might encounter. He decided it best to following the curving river.

Drawing nearer the fire, he first heard the thumping of a small drum, then the screeching of a fiddle, and the twittering of an Irish whistle. The clapping of the participants almost drowned out the sound of their voices singing, or rather shouting, a familiar tune.

In Dublin's fair city where the girls are so pretty
I first set my eyes on sweet Molly Malone
As she wheels her wheelbarrow
Through the streets broad and narrow
Crying, "Cockles and Mussels alive alive O!
Alive alive O! Alive alive O!"
Crying, "Cockles and Mussels alive alive O!"

He counted a dozen men clustered around a bonfire of railroad ties. If the Casements knew the Irishmen were burning their precious ties, heads would roll.

Will approached the gathering without anyone seeming to notice his presence. A few paces from the backs of the men sitting closest to him, he realized he still held his revolver in his hand. Probably not a good idea to step into the light with a weapon. The tracklayers might take exception and blaze back at him with their own firearms. He returned the pistol to his holster.

When he stepped into the view of the men sitting on the opposite side of the fire, he extended his hands away from his body with his palms up. A burly man holding a whiskey bottle in one hand, raised his other, and the musicians ceased playing. The singers turned together to look at him.

"Good evening, gentlemen," Will said.

"Evening, son," the burly fellow answered. "And what is it we can be doing for ye?"

"I'm looking for a skinny Irishman, named Paddy O'Hannigan. I believe he came this way."

"Oh, do ye now?"

"Yes, sir."

"And who be asking?"

"Will Braddock. I work for the Union Pacific. Same as you."

"And what is it ye do for the grand ole railroad?"

"I work for my uncle, Sean Corcoran. You probably know

him. The leader of the survey inspection team."

"Aye, that we do."

"And what is your name, sir?" Will asked.

"I be Collin Sullivan, foreman of this lot."

A loud pop from within the bonfire, created by an exploding knot in a tie, caused several of the men to shift on their seats, revealing axe handles that seemed to be within reach of each of them.

Will cleared his throat and raised his hands higher to show he hadn't reached for his gun.

Sullivan laughed. "Well, we all seem to be a bit jumpy, now. Why don't ye join us while we conclude our wake for our dear friend Fagan who departed us unexpected-like earlier today?"

The foreman waved a hand in the direction of a wagon parked on the other side of the bonfire from Will. In the bed of the wagon, Will could see what must be a body draped with a canvas tarp.

"Thank you, Mr. Sullivan. But I really must be on my way. I have to find O'Hannigan."

The tracklayers rose one by one from their seats, each picking up his axe handle as he did so. Will surveyed the men as they stepped away from the fire toward him. He decided his best course of action was to run. He turned to head back the way he'd come, but felt the blow of an axe handle that'd been thrown at his back. His knees buckled and he toppled forward.

"Don't kill him, boys." Will heard Sullivan's voice through the ringing in his ears. "Ye heard what Paddy said. He reserves that right for himself."

Will tried to push himself up from the ground, but another blow thumped him in the back of the skull. His vision blurred, he gasped, and collapsed.

★ ★ ★ ★ ★

Will shook his head to clear the cobwebs. Where was he? Why was he bouncing up and down and back and forth on a hard surface? How long had he been here?

"Drive closer to the river, Higgins!" Will recognized Sullivan's shouting voice.

Wherever Will was, he lay on his back and everything around him shook.

"Aye, that I be trying, Collin. But it's steep along here, to be sure."

The answer to Sullivan's order came from above where Will lay. Opening his eyes and rolling them as far back in his head as he could, he saw the back of a man sitting on the seat of a wagon. He heard the slapping of reins and the stomping and snorting of horses. Will now realized he lay in the bed of a wagon.

"Easy, boys, easy," the driver said. "Sure, and I don't want to wind up in the river."

The wagon abruptly titled sharply to Will's right. Something bumped hard against his side, and he glanced left. A canvas-covered lump rolled against him as the wagon slid sideways.

"No, boys! No!" the driver shouted. "Pull!"

Wheels grated across rocks. The wooden bed of the wagon heaved up beneath Will.

"Jump, Higgins! Jump! She be going over!" Sullivan's warning sounded far away.

Will looked up in time to see the driver drop the reins and bail off the seat to the uphill side of the tilting wagon. The horses neighed in loud screams. The wagon flipped on its side and crashed down the slope.

The body of the Irish corpse slammed into Will, pinning him against the sideboard.

The wagon flipped upside down. Will's back slammed onto

cold, hard ground beneath the overturned wagon, a heavy weight on his chest. The clouds parted, and moonlight filtered through cracks in the wagon's wooden bed. The wide-open eyes of the cadaver stared into his.

CHAPTER 5

The long, wailing locomotive whistle announced the arrival of Union Pacific's train from the east. Jenny lifted her eyes from the iron pot of stew she stirred and looked to where her father and Duncan sat at the long, wooden table that ran down the center of the Wells Fargo station. "They're finally here, Papa," she said.

"They're running late all the time, it seems. The shoddy condition of the tracks up toward the head of Echo Canyon is making the engineers proceed with extra caution. Not to mention the snowstorm that's blowing through here tonight." Jenny's father swung his legs back over the bench seat and used the stump of his left elbow to push himself up from the dining table.

"I was about ready to add more water to this stew," Jenny said. "It's been simmering so long the broth's almost boiled away."

"The passengers will be so hungry after their long journey today, they'll eat anything you throw at them. They will love your cooking, Jenny. I know that." Her father wrestled his coat on with his one good arm and slapped his old, gray Confederate officer's hat onto his head. "Come on, Duncan. Let's go help our next stagecoach passengers transfer their luggage from the depot."

Jenny's ten-year-old brother joined their father, buttoned his heavy coat up around his neck, and pulled his own hat down over his unruly hair. When Duncan opened the front door, a blast of cold air and flurries of snowflakes rushed into the station. "Hurry up, Pa. It upsets Jenny when her floor gets all wet and dirty."

After her father and brother closed the door, Jenny picked up a mop and swabbed the entry. She didn't know why she bothered in such bad weather. But, at least the arriving passengers would have a fresh floor to track up when they straggled in out of the storm. She supposed she had learned the habit of cleanliness from her mother, God rest her soul. Jenny shook her head as she recalled the futile efforts of her mother trying to keep the entrance to their Virginia plantation home clean when the Confederate Army had commandeered it for use as a field hospital. Then, it was blood, not snow, that soiled the floor.

Jenny sighed, returned the mop to a peg on the rear wall, and gathered a stack of plates from a shelf to set the table. The telegraph message Duncan had received from the Union Pacific earlier in the day provided the information that twelve passengers arriving on the train desired tickets for the journey over the Wasatch Mountains to Salt Lake City. The Concord stagecoach, scheduled to depart in the morning, could accommodate nine inside the cramped cabin. Three passengers would have to be brave enough to ride outside on top of this coach or lay over a day for the next one.

By the time Jenny set the table and changed into a fresh apron, the door opened and a rush of people descended on the dining table. Eleven men of various ages and demeanor crowded into the room and removed their coats and hats, which they hung on pegs that lined the front wall. They quickly occupied the two bench seats extending along opposite sides of the table. One woman stood alone by the door collapsing an umbrella and brushing snow from her traveling coat. Jenny decided the woman was not attached to any of the men because none of them offered to help her find a seat.

"Ma'am," Jenny said. "Please sit over here." She pointed to an old wicker rocking chair sitting beside a potbellied stove in a corner of the room. "It will be more comfortable than the benches."

"Merci, mademoiselle."

A French lady. Jenny glanced at her from time to time out of the corner of her eye while ladling the stew from the pot onto the plates in front of the men. The lady, who appeared to be approaching middle age, removed her woolen coat, the color of which matched her dress, and hung it on a peg near the stove. She propped her umbrella against the wall. Extracting a long hatpin from the back of her hair, she lifted a wide-brimmed hat, also of a color matching her dress, and hung it above her coat. With a sigh she eased herself into the rocker.

Jenny set two platters of biscuits in the center of the table beside crocks of butter she'd placed there earlier. She handed pitchers of buttermilk to the men who occupied the positions on one end of each bench. After filling his own glass, each man passed the pitcher to the next man on his bench.

"Madame, voulez-vous quelque chose à manger?" Jenny asked the seated lady. "Would you like something to eat?"

"Vous parlez français," the lady replied. "You speak French."

"Un peu. A little. I learned basic French at the academy in Virginia . . . when I was young."

"When you were young." The lady smiled. "You are still young, child."

Jenny felt her face flush. "Perhaps. But, I am almost fifteen, madame."

"You may call me Madame Baudelaire . . . Madame Angelique Baudelaire."

"Yes, ma'am. I mean, Madame Baudelaire. My name is Jenny

. . . Jennifer McNabb. My father manages the Wells Fargo station here."

"*Mais, oui.* He greeted us at the train station."

"*Ragoût est acceptable?*" Jenny asked. "Is stew acceptable? I made it myself."

"*Certainement.*"

Jenny filled a plate with a portion of stew, and placed a buttered biscuit on the edge. "Madame." She handed the plate to the lady, then returned to the main table and offered seconds to the men. As each man finished his meal he placed the standard fare of a dollar and a half beside his plate. Two of the men were gracious enough to add a dime to that amount.

Gathering up her mop again, Jenny cleaned the entrance floor and beneath the benches. After which, she cleared the plates and utensils from the table.

Jenny's father and brother entered the station. She shook her head as they once more tracked up the entryway.

"Gentlemen, and lady," her father said. "Your luggage has been loaded aboard the coach. However, because of this storm, we will not dispatch the coach to Salt Lake City until morning. The mountain pass is difficult enough in daylight when the road is covered in snow. I wouldn't want the coach sliding off the road because the driver cannot see the way. Until then, make yourselves comfortable. There is a hotel, if you can call it that, down the street a bit. You may apply there for a room, or you may make yourself comfortable wherever you can here in the station."

Four of the men put on their coats and hats and headed out the door, obviously deciding to try the hotel. Four men claimed spots on the benches, and the remaining three spread out on the table. All of them left their boots on. Jenny would have a mess to clean in the morning.

Jenny washed the dirty dishes and stacked them away quietly, so as not to disturb the sleeping passengers. When she'd finished, she returned to Madame Baudelaire. "I'm sorry we have no beds here. I can escort you over to the hotel if you like."

"*Mais, non.* If I may, I can sleep in this chair."

"You are welcome to it, Madame Baudelaire. My mother, God rest her soul, used to sleep in a chair just like that."

"*Votre mère est morte?* She is dead?"

"Yes, almost two years ago."

"Why do you live out here on the frontier, instead of in Virginia?"

Jenny told the French lady about the McNabb's journey along the Overland Trail until her mother died two years ago and they had buried her at Virginia Dale Station in Colorado. Jenny attempted to describe the ordeal in French but soon gave up when the conversation demanded more complex vocabulary than she recalled.

"So your sister did not stay with the rest of the family, then?" Madame Baudelaire spoke excellent, although heavily accented, English.

"No, she went on to Sacramento."

"Ah, but that is my destination. I go there to open a millinery shop."

"Oh, my," Jenny said, "that's what my sister did. She has a millinery shop there."

Madame Baudelaire drew back her head and frowned. "A Virginia girl has a millinery shop? How can a girl from Virginia know anything about the fine art of the millinery?"

Jenny bristled at the challenge. "My sister is quite artistic, I'll have you know. She is very talented."

"Humph!"

How dare this prissy French lady accuse Elspeth of not knowing enough to design ladies' hats! Jenny hadn't seen her sister's shop, but she was sure it would be a nice one. Her sister was ambitious, and she had been clever enough last year to impress a German count with her evident talent. The count had even financed Elspeth's new store in Sacramento.

"Good night, Madame," Jenny said. She brushed in front of the lady and entered the side door into the private portion of the station where she and her father and brother shared the bedroom. She hoped the French wench didn't sleep a wink!

The next morning the stagecoach departed at first light, taking the passengers on their journey to Salt Lake City. They would then travel onward by another stage to connect with the Central Pacific's trains somewhere out in Nevada at its end of track. Wells Fargo would soon cease operating its east-west stagecoach line.

Jenny's father and brother were out back tending to the horses while she tidied up the station. She took a last swipe with the mop to clear away the remnants of mud and snow. She was in the process of hanging the mop back on its peg when the front door flew open.

A gust of wind drove another pile of snow across the threshold. A disheveled figure staggered into the doorway and collapsed on the floor. Jenny's mouth dropped open. Will Braddock looked up at her.

CHAPTER 6

"Will!" Jenny shoved the door closed, knelt beside him, and removed his slouch hat, tossing it aside. She slid an arm under his shoulders and lifted him to a sitting position. "What happened to you?"

"Got whacked on the head." He reached up and felt behind his left ear.

Jenny pushed on Will's chin to turn his head away from her and ran her fingers through his matted, brown hair. When her exploration encountered a large lump on the back of his skull, he winced.

She separated the locks of his wavy hair so she could examine the spot. "No blood. A good-sized goose egg, though."

Will sighed and pushed himself to his feet. Muddy water dripped from his clothes onto the floor. He looked down at the puddle expanding around his boots. "Sorry for the mess."

Jenny waved a hand in the air. "Oh, don't worry about the floor. I can always mop it . . . again."

She grinned at him and was pleased when she noticed the blush spread across his cheeks. She grasped his elbow and guided him to the closest bench. "Remove those wet clothes. They're filthy. I'll wash them out for you. Take them off."

"Undress? Here? Why don't I go into the back room?"

"You don't think I'm going to let you track up the rest of my floor because you're modest. Remember, I've seen you in your underwear before. This isn't the first time I've had to clean you

40

up after one of your escapades."

Will shrugged out of his buckskin coat and handed it to her.

"Pants, too," she said.

He sat on the bench and tugged off his boots, then stood and dropped his wool trousers. He lifted them upward with a foot, grasped them, and held them out. "Satisfied?" he asked.

She shook her head. "You're going to have to take off those wet underclothes, too. Come along into the bedroom now, and I'll give you a pair of Papa's underdrawers to wear while I clean your things."

"I thought you didn't want me to go into the bedroom."

"You've taken the muddy stuff off. What's left is only wet. Move!"

Jenny pushed him into the family's bedroom. The shared sleeping quarters provided little privacy. A blanket, draped over a line, divided one corner from the rest of the room. That small space served as her bedroom. The larger portion held the two beds her father and brother used.

She lifted the lid of a battered trunk, took out a pair of folded woolen underdrawers, and handed them to Will. "Here, put these on, then bring the rest of your clothes out to me. Take a blanket off Duncan's bed there. You can wrap it around your shoulders to keep warm."

Jenny returned to the main room of the station. The potbellied stove held coals from the breakfast meal she had prepared for the passengers before they'd departed on the morning stage. She opened the stove door and fed a handful of kindling in on top of the glowing coals. She waved a pie pan in front of the open door to create more draft to rekindle the fire. Once the kindling flared up, she laid two small logs on top of the kindling and closed the door. Filling a wash basin with water from a bucket, she placed the basin on top of the stove.

The door to the bedroom opened. Jenny turned as Will

entered the main room holding his underwear and socks with one hand while he clasped Duncan's blanket around his shoulders with the other.

"Sit over here by the fire." She pointed to the bench on the side of the table nearest the stove and handed him a rag. "You can clean your boots while you tell me what happened."

While Will worked on his boots, he told her about Paddy O'Hannigan shooting his Uncle Sean. He described pursuing the thug and being waylaid by the Irishman's pals.

"And how is it that you're so wet?" she asked.

He told her about the wagon accident and the tumble with the corpse. Will visibly shivered while describing the wide-open eyes staring back at him.

Jenny laughed at the face he made. "You become involved in some of the most comical situations."

"Humph! I didn't think it was funny."

"Sorry," she said. "You have to admit it was weird."

Will shrugged. "Yeah, I guess."

Jenny turned back to the stove and continued stirring his clothes in the basin with a long-handled wooden spoon. "What do you plan to do now?"

"I have to go see about Uncle Sean. I hope he's all right. Homer was to take him to the railroad's doctor. Didn't you hear the shooting last night?"

"Of course, I heard it. But there's gunfire going on all day and night around here." She swung around and wagged the spoon at him. "Why would I take special notice of one shooting over another?"

He shrugged, and because he still held a boot and the rag in his hands, the blanket slipped off his shoulders.

"Will, there are more holes in you than in your socks."

Her eyes surveyed his upper torso, taking inventory of the wounds he'd sustained since he'd come west. She'd been involved in patching most of them. Where the arrow had passed through his left bicep, he still bore ugly scars at both the entrance and exit wounds. On his left shoulder, the slashing scar was evident from the time Paddy had tried to stab Will when he'd stepped in to keep the Irishman from killing her. Stretching around his left side from high on his rib cage to his waistline were five wicked, parallel scars left from his encounter with the grizzly last year, when Will had shielded the German count from attack by the bear.

Will set the boot on the floor and gathered the blanket back around his shoulders.

Jenny returned her attention to the stove, fished each article of clothing out of the basin, and wrung the excess water out over it, then she hung the items on a line stretching along the wall behind the stove.

"How long until those things are dry enough to wear?" he asked. "I want to go check on Uncle Sean."

"An hour or so. While you wait, you can eat some of the passengers' leftover breakfast."

"Thanks. I am hungry. Paddy attacked us before I could finish supper."

The front door banged open. Jenny swung around from the stove to see her father and brother enter the station.

Her father stopped, shifting his gaze from Jenny to Will, who had turned to look over his shoulder toward the front door.

"What's this all about?" her father asked.

CHAPTER 7

"I can explain, Mr. McNabb." Will gathered the blanket more closely about his shoulders as he stared at Jenny's father, who removed his hat, shook the snow from it, and hung it by the door.

"I hope so." McNabb unbuttoned his coat and added it to the peg beneath his hat.

Duncan stood in the doorway, his mouth open. He looked from his sister and Will back to his father.

"Close the door, Duncan," Jenny said. "We're losing what little heat we have in here."

"Oh . . . sure." Duncan closed the door, removed his own hat and coat, and hung them on a wall peg beside the one his father had used.

"Would you like some coffee, Papa?" Jenny smiled. "I'm sure you're cold, and it will help warm you up." She poured the black liquid from a pot on the stove into a tin cup and handed it to her father.

"Thank you, Jenny." He took the proffered cup and sat on the bench on the opposite side of the table from Will. "Now, young man, let's hear this explanation about why you are sitting here alone with my daughter wearing no clothes."

Will stammered out the story about chasing after Paddy and winding up being clubbed by the Irish tracklayers. He left out the part about the cadaver's eyes, but he did describe the wagon overturning while riding with the corpse.

44

McNabb sipped his coffee, grasping the tin mug with both hands to warm them while he drank. When Will finished his tale, McNabb nodded slowly. "Show me the lump on your head and maybe I'll believe you."

Will turned his face away from Jenny's father. She stepped closer and gently brushed Will's unruly hair up and away from his shoulders. She touched the spot on the back of his skull causing Will to wince.

"All right," McNabb said. "When will his clothes be dry, Jenny?"

Jenny reached above the stove and felt the clothes. "They're dry enough now, Papa."

"What are you going to do, Will?" McNabb asked.

"I'd like to go find Paddy O'Hannigan and throttle him once and for all, but I have to go check on Uncle Sean. Maybe I should have gone there first, sir?"

"That probably would have been a good idea," McNabb said, "but since it appears my daughter's virtue is still intact, get dressed and get out of here."

Five minutes later, Will stepped into the large wall tent that the Union Pacific's doctor used as the railroad's hospital. Along one sidewall a row of cots served as the ward. Will's uncle occupied the last bed in the row. Homer sat on a stool on the far side of the cot and raised his head when Will approached.

"Uncle Sean?" Will removed his slouch hat and crushed it against his chest.

Will's uncle opened his eyes, turning his head slightly, a lopsided grin appearing on his lips.

"Uncle Sean, how are you?"

"Been better." His uncle sighed deeply.

Will looked at Homer. "What's the doctor say?"

"Doc say he gonna make it. But he ain't gonna be working

45

for a while."

"Did you stop Paddy?" his uncle asked.

"No, sir."

Will told his uncle and Homer about his pursuit of their mutual enemy and his run-in with the Irishmen at the wake. He grimaced when he reached up with his left hand and tested the bump on the back of his head.

"We'll all three have to stay alert." Will's uncle shifted on the cot, generating a groan. "That foolish Irish boy is determined to carry out his revenge."

"Can I do anything to help you, Uncle Sean?" Will asked.

"Yes, you have to take Sam Reed's plans to General Jack. Doctor says I can't travel right now without reopening this wound. Wants me to stay in bed and rest."

"All right," Will said. "Where are the papers?"

"Homer has them. He'll go with you."

"I can go by myself, Uncle Sean. I thought I'd already proved I'm no longer a boy."

"You have. But, one of the men overheard Mort Kavanagh talking about getting his hands on those plans so he could buy up adjacent land. I don't want that, and I know General Dodge doesn't want that. Kavanagh might send Paddy out to ambush anybody he thought might be carrying the plans. Two sets of eyes will be better than one to keep a lookout. Besides, Homer would be bored sitting here all day."

"What if Paddy tries to attack you here?" Will asked. "What if you need help?"

"Doc will take care of me. He's not going to let any outsider in here."

"All right, Uncle Sean."

"Homer," Will's uncle said, "take enough money out of my saddlebags to pay the livery stable to keep our horses and Ruby while you're gone. And take enough for food for yourselves. I know you two haven't been paid for a long time. Fortunately, I have a little extra."

Homer dragged a pair of saddlebags from beneath the cot and counted out several paper bills, showing his boss how much he'd withdrawn from the roll of money he'd extracted from one of the pockets.

Will's uncle nodded. "Give me my notebook and a pencil, Homer."

Homer dug into another pocket and located the items.

Will's uncle scribbled on a blank sheet of paper, ripped it out of the notebook, and handed the sheet to Will. "Take this to the stationmaster. He'll give you passes to ride the train."

Homer returned the notebook to the saddlebags and placed them back under the cot.

"Better take that Yellow Boy with you, Will. You may need the firepower." His uncle used the nickname that folks out west had affixed to the Winchester that the German count had given to Will the year before. "Now, off with you both. And don't get into trouble."

CHAPTER 8

"Will Braddock, welcome aboard." Hobart Johnson, the conductor, punched a hole in the pass that Will held out.

"Hello, Mr. Johnson. You remember Homer Garcon?" Will took back his pass and returned it to his haversack, which lay under the seat in front of him.

"Of course, I do." Johnson reached across Will and took the pass Homer extended. "I rode your mule into Benton from the train wreck site on the North Platte last year."

"Yes, sir. You surely did." Homer beamed from where he sat by the window on the wooden bench seat of the passenger car.

Will saw Homer's pleasure at the conductor's recollection of their first meeting.

"Where you gents bound for?" Johnson asked. "Your passes indicate free rides up and down the line."

"Uncle Sean is sending us back to Fort Fred Steele to meet up with General Jack Casement. He's returning from his vacation back east, and we're taking him the plans for the new yard in Ogden so he can get a head start on ordering the materials."

"Ah, General Jack's on his way back. That's good. He can whip these unruly gandy dancers back into shape. Mark my word, there's going to be trouble if they aren't paid soon."

"That's what Uncle Sean is worried about, too."

"By the way, why isn't your uncle with you?"

Will told Johnson about the shooting.

"That bloody O'Hannigan sure causes a lot of trouble."

Johnson shook his head. "I believe it was decided he most likely set the nitroglycerin charge that caused that wreck I mentioned."

"Yes, sir. That's what we believe."

"Well, you two can spread out if you like." Johnson waved a hand across the aisle. "We have lots of room on this run back to Wyoming. Only you two and a dozen others boarded here at end of track. This recent storm must have held up most eastbound passengers in Salt Lake City. I was hoping we'd have a full car."

"Jenny McNabb said the stagecoach was delayed because of the snowdrifts in the Wasatch passes."

"That's easy to believe," Johnson said. "The snow this winter has played havoc all the way along the line. Been really tough in Wyoming's Red Desert."

"Any problems in Utah?" Will asked.

"Not too bad. The snowplows have been able to keep the drifts off the tracks. Only thing slowing us down is the 'Zig-Zag' around Tunnel Two. The Mormon crew has their hands full trying to blast through that hard rock. And we have to tiptoe through the 'Zig-Zag,' since 'Colonel' Seymour insisted that track be laid on ice."

"Ice?" Will asked.

"Yes, the 'insulting engineer' was in such a hurry to push tracks down through Echo Canyon that he wouldn't wait for the ground to thaw."

Conductor Johnson tipped a hand to the brim of his cap and took a step away, then turned back.

"By the way, how is Miss McNabb? She was with us on that ride into Benton last year, too."

"She's fine. Still cooking for Wells Fargo."

"Well, you give her my best next time you see her."

"Sure thing."

Two short blasts from the lead engine's whistle, followed by another from the helper engine, signaled the train was ready to pull out of Echo City. The grade eastward was too steep for a single locomotive to haul a train up Echo Canyon. A single passenger car had been attached to the rear of a string of a dozen empty flatcars on their way back to Wyoming where they would be reloaded with ties, rails, and joiners for the continued construction of the Union Pacific.

Will jolted on his seat as the locomotives' actions yanked the passenger car into motion.

Homer rubbed the heel of his hand across the pane of glass next to him to clear the frost that had accumulated on the window from their breaths. "There's a heap of snow out there," he said.

Will looked through the circular clearing Homer had made. The drifts reached the bottom of the windowsill a few feet from the side of the car. "That snow's four feet deep, at least," he said, "and I hear tell it's even deeper in Wyoming."

"Must be, if the trains haven't been able to get through for so long."

"I expect it'll melt soon," Will said. "The weather this morning's much warmer than yesterday. Hardly a cloud in the sky . . . and that awful, cold wind has stopped blowing."

The train gathered speed and the steady clacking of the wheels over the rail joiners soon had Will nodding.

Will awoke and stretched his back. "Why are we slowing?" he asked.

The train moved along the tracks at a crawl. The clicks and clacks of the wheels passing over the track joiners occurred less frequently. The sound of excess steam blowing from the locomotives' cylinders, and the grinding of wheel rims on iron rails, accentuated the reduced forward motion of the train.

"We's entering the 'Zig-Zag.' " Homer nodded his head in

the direction of the window off his right shoulder.

"Guess I fell asleep."

"You sure did. Done you some good I 'spect. You needed a little rest after your latest run-in with O'Hannigan."

Will leaned across Homer to look out the window. The frost had disappeared from the pane and no longer obscured the view. With the concave curve of the track, Will could see the locomotives, their tenders, and the string of flatcars, easing around the first side of the wye. Then the track straightened, bringing all the cars into line and making it impossible for Will to see the complete train.

The forward momentum abruptly ceased. The engines had reached the end of the straight leg of the wye. Two quick blasts of their whistles signaled a crewman to throw the switch. The locomotives chuffed blasts of steam and the train lurched backward, being pushed in reverse out of the straight leg and onto the second curved side of the wye.

By looking across the car, and out the windows on the opposite side, Will watched the train ease back along the curve and onto the mainline. Two more sets of whistle blasts, another jolting stop, and the train cleared the switch. More chugging and whistle blowing, and the engines dragged the train into forward motion.

"Look at the water flowing out of the side of the embankment, Homer," Will said.

"Where's all that coming from? Ain't raining."

"The ice beneath the tracks is melting."

The wooden-sided passenger car groaned and swayed pronouncedly from side to side as the train crept across a two-tiered trestle. When it emerged on the earthen embankment on the opposite side of the overpass, the train slowed even more as the weight of the locomotives and railroad cars sank into the mushy roadbed.

Everyone on board, including Will and Homer, opened the windows in spite of the cold, and leaned out, trying for a better look at what was happening around them. Chattering voices from the male passengers and concerned squeals from the females spoke of the danger sensed by everyone.

With a jolt, the entire train careened sideways. Nails and screws holding the passenger car together screeched as the torquing motion pulled them loose from the wood and steel comprising the coach's structure.

Will looked at Homer. His companion's eyes opened wider and his mouth dropped open.

A groan erupted from the disintegrating coach generated by the snapping sounds of breaking glass and splintering wood. Passengers yelled and screamed. The car slid off the tracks and down the embankment.

CHAPTER 9

Will grasped the armrest of his seat and reached across to the empty, facing seat where he'd laid the Yellow Boy. Count Wolfgang von Schroeder had given him the lever-action, Winchester rifle last year for saving the nobleman from an attacking grizzly. Will grabbed his most prized possession by the barrel before it could slide down the seat and fly out the open window of the coach.

The railcar tipped onto its side. Will's whole weight shifted to rest on Homer, who was pinned against the outside wall of the coach by Will's body. From behind him, Will heard the screams of ladies mingled with the shouts of men, all accentuated by the crashing of bodies falling out of seats and tumbling to the downside of the sliding passenger coach.

Smoke filled Will's nose. The potbellied stove had tipped over, and its hot coals spilled out, setting fire to the wooden coach body.

Window glass continued to crack and shatter, sending shards flying through the air. One piece stabbed into the seat cushion beside him. An inch or two to the left, and it would have made an ugly wound in his arm—or worse.

The body of the coach ripped away from the undercarriage when the iron wheels of the trucks dug into the gravel of the embankment and refused to move farther. The lighter, wooden superstructure sheared free of the heavier, metal underpinnings. The body of the coach accelerated down the forty-five degree embankment.

A final, thudding crash brought the passenger car to a jolting halt at the bottom of the slope.

Groans and cries replaced screams and shouts as passengers slammed into the side of the coach and came to rest against broken window frames, now buried in the mud in the ditch. Water from melting ice flowed into the car through open windows, broken siding, and demolished flooring.

The fire, fueled by the varnish used to preserve and decorate the wooden interior, traveled rapidly along the walls and ceiling of the car. The dry material of the seat cushions exploded, row by row, as the fire spread forward through the car.

Homer moaned. Will peered at the older man's face, whose cheeks were drawn up in a grimace with his lips pulled tightly back over his teeth.

"Homer," Will shouted. "We have to get out of here. The fire's coming this way."

"I can't."

"What do you mean, you can't?"

"I think my collarbone's broke."

"Oh, no. I did that when I slammed you against the side."

"Not your fault."

"Come on, I'll help you."

Will shifted the Yellow Boy to his left hand and rolled off Homer. He stood up, his feet coming to rest on the side of the car, which was now the bottom of the box formed by what remained of the passenger coach. He fished his haversack, containing the Ogden plans, out from under the ruined seat in front of him, and slung the strap over his head and shoulder.

Will helped Homer to his knees, then to his feet. The heat from the approaching fire caressed the back of his neck.

Calls for help came from the back of the overturned car.

"You should help them other folks," Homer said. "They's

hurt worse than me."

"I'll get you outside, then I'll come back."

Will guided Homer in taking steps along the side of the car that now lay beneath their feet. The seats, bolted to the floor, ranged along their left side. The overhead package shelves, protruding from the side of the car, formed their right wall. Every other step they dropped through an open, broken window, where their feet sloshed into icy mud.

When they reached the rear of the car, Will faced the closed door that led to the rear platform of the coach. The hinges ran along what was now the top of the door instead of the side. The door, though slightly sprung, remained closed.

"Brace yourself against the frame, Homer, while I push this door open."

"That door has to be pushed up to get it open, Will. It's going to be heavy. I can help with my good arm."

Will nodded, realizing he probably didn't possess the strength to lift the door by himself. He stepped forward and heaved against the door with his shoulder, using his back muscles to force the barrier up. Homer moved in behind him, reached over Will's shoulder with his good left hand, and added his power to the lifting motion. The door gradually rose.

Will climbed through the opening, reached across the floor of the platform, and stepped onto the railing's iron rail. He could use it as a ladder to step down from the car. It was awkward with only one free hand, but he wasn't going to drop the rifle.

"I'll hold the door, Will, while you fetch a timber to prop it up. We's got to keep it open for them other folks to pass through."

"You sure you can hold it?"

"I 'spect I can." Homer stepped into the open doorway and braced his raised arm against his chest in order to transfer some of the weight to his body. "Hurry, Will."

Will tumbled off the damaged rear platform and landed on his knees in the mud. Freezing water soaked his trousers, jolting him back into action. A corner post of the coach swung in the air. He hated to do it, but he laid the Yellow Boy on the ground so he could grasp the post with both hands. He twisted and wrenched the top of it free from where it was still attached to the body of the car, then he wedged one end of the post against the wooden door, which Homer held above his head, and kicked the bottom into position in the soggy dirt of the embankment.

"I think that'll hold it, Homer."

Homer eased out of his position. The door settled with a thud against the top of the post, quivered momentarily, then rested in an open position.

"Let me help you away from the coach," Will said, "then I'll go back and help the others."

"Here, I'll take him." An Irish brogue spoke from behind Will.

Will sighed and transferred Homer's weight to an old friend, Grady Shaughnessy.

"Am I glad to see you, Grady."

"Sure, and it's been a long time, Will."

Half an hour later, all the passengers and Conductor Johnson had been helped from the demolished coach. They sat huddled on a pile of ties at the base of the embankment, which still gushed water down its sides. The passenger car lay smoldering in its own pile of ashes before them.

Will wiped the mud from the Yellow Boy with his bandana. "You showed up at the right time again, Grady," he said.

Grady Shaughnessy, the muscular Irish, track-grading foreman, grinned. He and some of his crew had fended off a Cheyenne raiding party who had ambushed Will and Homer two years before in Nebraska. Will rubbed his left arm, where the arrow had pieced his bicep during that encounter. That injury had almost cost him the chance to work for the Union Pacific.

" 'Tis my pleasure, as always," Grady said.

"Homer and I thank you, again," Will said.

"So, ye have the plans for the Ogden yard?" Grady asked. "That'll be the last major facility before we hook up with the CP, to my way of thinking."

"I believe you're right. Now, I have to find a way to get these plans back to General Jack at Fort Fred Steele."

A locomotive whistle caused Will and the others to look eastward.

"That be the evening freight coming south," Grady said. "She'll be having to head right back to Wahsatch. Won't be no passing through the 'Zig-Zag' until me and the boys can rebuild this embankment."

"How long will that take?" Will asked.

"Oh, two days, at most. We'll dig this mushy mess out and replace it with good gravel. Lots of that's coming out of Tunnel Two from the Mormon's blasting."

"All because of that fool 'Colonel' Seymour." Conductor Johnson spoke up. "If he hadn't insisted on laying track on frozen ground, this would never have happened."

"Sure, and that be the truth," Grady said. "Fortunate, it is, that no one's hurt worse. One of these ladies was burned some when her dress caught fire. Mostly scrapes and bruises, though. Only one serious hurt is Homer, here."

Will and Grady had rigged a temporary sling for Homer's arm and strapped it against his body to constrain the motion that caused the most pain.

"Homer, I think you'd better stay in Wahsatch until you're better," Conductor Johnson said. "The railroad doctor there can look after you."

"But, I'se supposed to go with Will."

"If you don't avoid using that arm for a time," Johnson said, "you'll never heal."

"He's right, Homer," Will said. "I can go on alone. Can't anything worse than a train wreck happen."

CHAPTER 10

Paddy approached the rear of the large tent structure that formed the dance-hall portion of the false-fronted Lucky Dollar Saloon. The Utah sky above Echo City stretched cloudless from horizon to horizon. The snowstorm of the past several days had left drifts piled against the backs of the string of temporary buildings that comprised this version of Hell on Wheels. Horse and foot traffic up and down the alleyway had plowed a path that extended from one end of the portable town to the other.

Paddy lifted the canvas-flap back door, shook remnants of snow from the thick material to keep the cold, white powder from tumbling down his collar, and stepped into the vast empty space covered by the circus-style tent. At this early hour, the dance floor was empty. Only two of the dozen tables held occupants engaged in faro. One drunk leaned against the far end of the extensive wooden bar that ran the length of one side of the tent.

"And a fine morning to ye, my good man," Paddy said. He doffed his bowler hat and executed an exaggerated bow toward Randy Tremble, the bartender, who ignored the greeting and continued to polish the glasses lined up in front of him.

"Is it that his honor has requested my presence?" Paddy asked.

"You might say that," Randy answered. "All he told me was to send someone to find 'the wee runt' and tell him to get his butt in here pronto."

Paddy snorted and continued across the compacted dirt floor of the saloon to the raised wooden one that was a part of the false front of the building. He stepped up and knocked on the door that led to the office built into one corner.

"Enter!"

Paddy opened the door at the command and took off his bowler hat when he walked into Mort Kavanagh's office. "Ye sent for me, Mort?"

"That I did." The heavyset owner of the Lucky Dollar Saloon pulled a long cigar from his mouth and blew a smoke ring across the desk.

Sally Whitworth, who sat in one of the two chairs facing the desk, waved her hand in front of her face and blew out her breath. "Mort, for goodness sakes, find some better cigars. That thing stinks!"

Kavanagh turned the cigar sideways and blew on the tip, causing the coals to glow brightly. "Ah, you're probably right, darlin'. Next time you visit Abrams General Store you ask that Jewish peddler if he's received any of my favorite cigars, yet. This was all he had last time."

"You can be sure I will."

"In the meantime, Sally, my dear, fetch a bottle of that good rye whiskey from Randy while I converse here with this Irish no-account."

Sally rose and brushed her flowered skirt smooth with her hands. "How many glasses, Mort?"

"Make it three."

Paddy felt the slight grin spread across his lips and crease the scar on his left cheek. Mort was going to treat him to the special rye he kept for himself.

Sally approached the open doorway, which Paddy continued to occupy. He stared at the beautiful redhead, but did not move. She turned up her nose and slid sideways past him. Paddy grinned when she shuddered as her sleeve brushed against him.

"Close the door, Paddy, and sit," Kavanagh said.

Paddy sat in the chair vacated by Sally, relishing the warmth she'd left behind. He laid his hat in the other chair and drew his Bowie knife from his boot top. He extracted a plug of tobacco from a vest pocket, sliced off a chaw, and dragged it into his mouth with his lips from the side of the blade. He grunted and winced when he bit down on the chaw.

"What's that all about?" Kavanagh asked.

"Toothache."

Kavanagh shook his head. "You haven't enough good teeth left to have a toothache. You ought to have the barber pull the rest of them and buy yourself a set of false ones."

"With what, Mort? Ye ain't paid me in weeks."

"Well, I'm about ready to offer you some new employment. I'll even advance you a little bit of cash."

Paddy shifted the chaw to the backside of his mouth to avoid biting it with his aching front tooth. He certainly wouldn't be spending any of the money Kavanagh might give him on having his teeth pulled. He had to save his money to send to his mother and sister who continually hounded him from Brooklyn to supplement the meager amounts they took in as laundresses. No, the tooth would fall out on its own, soon enough.

The door opened and Sally reentered with a tray on which she balanced a bottle and three glasses. She placed the tray on the end of Kavanagh's desk and dropped into the chair beside Paddy, squashing his bowler. Paddy had been distracted wetting his lips in anticipation of the drink and had forgotten to remove his hat from the chair.

Sally jumped back up and pulled the flattened hat from beneath her with the tips of her thumb and forefinger.

"Ah, darlin', now look what ye've done."

Mort laughed. "I've heard tell it's bad luck to put a hat on a bed, Paddy. Guess you proved it's also not so good to put one on a chair."

Sally grimaced as she held the hat out to Paddy. "I hope that dirty thing didn't ruin my dress."

"Humph!" Paddy slammed a fist into the hat and pushed the crown back into shape. This was the fourth hat he'd had to buy in a little over two years. Will Braddock had shot three off his head, causing Paddy to part with money he didn't really want to spend replacing headgear.

Sally sat again and poured two fingers of rye into two of the glasses. Paddy watched her hold the bottle poised over the third glass as she looked at Kavanagh. His boss nodded, and Sally poured two fingers into the remaining glass. She handed one glass to Kavanagh and took one for herself. Paddy had to reach out and pick up the third glass himself.

Kavanagh raised his glass. "Here's to success with your new mission." He nodded to Paddy and sipped the amber liquid.

Paddy returned the salute with his own glass, then inhaled the aroma of the rye whiskey. He tucked the tobacco chaw farther into the side of his jaw with his tongue, touched the rim of the glass to his lips, and slurped a gulp of the fiery liquid. "Ow!"

Sally looked sideways at Paddy and frowned.

"He has a toothache," Kavanagh said.

"How can he have a toothache?" she said. "He hasn't got anything left except rotten stubs. Not to mention the foulest breath of anyone I know."

Paddy glared at Sally as he tilted his head to allow the alcohol to slide down the side of his mouth away from the tobacco wad, which he kept pinned to the opposite jaw with his tongue. He wasn't going to let a toothache stop him from enjoying this good rye. He swallowed the fiery liquid and grinned.

"Mort," said Paddy, " 'tis good whiskey, that is."

"Glad you like it," Kavanagh said. "Now, let's proceed with business. Paddy, I have to admit I was impressed when I heard how you convinced those tracklayers to waylay that Braddock fellow so you could get away from him the other night. That gave me the idea for your next assignment."

"Yeah, Mort?"

"It's no secret that the two railroads are about to join up. Soon as that happens, the Lucky Dollar Saloon will be out of business. Hell on Wheels will cease to exist. Hundreds of tracklayers will be out of work and head off to other parts. But before they do, I want to get my money back from them. I've been extending credit to these workers for a long time. The Union Pacific hasn't paid their wages in months."

"Aye, and just what is it ye be wanting me to do about that?" Paddy asked.

"You are good at stirring up trouble, O'Hannigan. I want the workers to stop construction work until they're paid. I want you to incite them to strike."

CHAPTER 11

Will could hardly believe his eyes. Each side of the tracks was strewn with piles of trash, but there were no buildings. No shacks. No tents. Bits of scrap iron, shards of broken pottery, and heaps of splintered wood showed briefly through the snow cover that the wind whirled over and around the wreckage.

"Mr. Johnson?" Will called out.

The conductor, who had been checking passengers' tickets near the front of the coach, walked down the aisle and stopped beside Will.

"What can I do for you, Will?"

"Mr. Johnson, I thought this was where Benton should be." Will pointed a finger toward the expanse of ruin the train rolled past.

"Was here. When the rails moved on, Benton dried up and disappeared."

"Why? It was a thriving community last time I was here."

"No water. They couldn't find any potable water by drilling wells, and it became too expensive to haul it from the North Platte by rail, so everybody gave up and headed west."

"Huh." Will shook his head and watched the last of the rubble disappear behind the train.

Conductor Johnson patted Will on the shoulder, smiled, and returned to the front of the car. When he reached the door he turned to face the interior of the passenger car. "Folks. Next stop is Fort Fred Steele . . . twenty miles. Be there in less than

half an hour. There are no meal facilities at the station. If you get off, I suggest you don't wander far from the train, unless this is your destination. Train will stop for only fifteen minutes . . . time enough to take on water and fuel. We're behind schedule, because of all the snowdrifts we've had to plow through. I know you are all as anxious to reach Cheyenne as we are. The UP will get back under way as fast as we can."

Will heard numerous comments that seconded the conductor's desire.

A half-hour later Will gathered up his haversack and Winchester and exited the coach. No other passengers followed. He had left Homer Garcon in the care of the Union Pacific's doctor in Wahsatch yesterday, almost twenty hours ago. Will entered the small station to shield himself from the gusting wind while he waited to seek directions to Fort Fred Steele's headquarters building. He had to wait for the train to depart before the sole station attendant came back inside.

After having his destination pointed out, he crossed the tracks to walk the two hundred yards that led past a row of officers' quarters and several enlisted men's barracks on this newest Wyoming fort the Army had built the preceding year to provide protection for the railroad. Will was reminded of Fort D. A. Russell outside Cheyenne, because there was no encircling stockade. From the number of barracks, and lack of stables, he assumed a sizable contingent of infantry occupied Fort Fred Steele. As with Fort Russell, there were too many troops for any Indian band to want to attack.

"Will Braddock!"

Will turned his head aside at the sound of a familiar Italian accent. Lieutenant Luigi Moretti approached from one of the officers' quarters.

"Hi, Luey," Will responded. He grabbed the brim of his slouch hat when a gust of wind threatened to blow it off.

"What are you doing here?" Moretti asked. The Italian-born first lieutenant twirled his mustache to sharpen its point.

"Uncle Sean sent me to deliver some plans to General Jack Casement. Have you seen him?"

"Yes, he arrived on the westbound train early today. I saw him go into headquarters about an hour ago. I imagine he's talking with Colonel Stevenson. They knew each other during the war."

Will nodded. "And what are you doing here, Luey?"

"I'm waiting for General Dodge to return west from Washington City. I'm still assigned to protect him until this railroad construction is finished. My men and I have been biding our time here at Fort Fred Steele during the winter months. By the way, how is Major Corcoran?"

Will told Luey about Paddy shooting his uncle.

"My heavens," Luey said. "The major went all through the war without being shot and then that crazy Irishman puts a bullet in him."

Luey had served as a major himself during the war and had known Will's uncle. Luey still referred to Sean Corcoran as "major," even though Will's uncle preferred that people not use the title when addressing him. Some former officers insisted they be addressed by the highest rank they had attained during the war, whereas most were addressed that way out of respect for their former service. Such was the case for Generals Dodge and Casement.

"Come on, Will," Luey said, "I'll walk with you. Let's get out of this cursed wind that never seems to stop blowing here."

Will and Luey crossed the parade ground and mounted the short porch that fronted the headquarters building. Inside, a sergeant manning an orderly desk asked them to state the purpose of their visit. When the sergeant heard that Will had a package to deliver to General Jack Casement, he asked them to

wait and said he would see if Colonel Stevenson would receive them. Although Stevenson had been brevetted a brigadier general during the late war, he preferred to be addressed by his current rank as the commanding officer of the Thirtieth Infantry.

The sergeant returned and said they could go in, but he told Will to leave his rifle beside the orderly desk. Then he escorted them to Colonel Stevenson's office.

"Good morning, Colonel," Will said. "I don't mean to disturb you. My uncle asked me to deliver some papers to General Jack."

The commanding officer sat behind a large desk, and General Jack sat in a side chair in front of the desk.

Colonel Stevenson stuck his head forward and wrinkled his brow. "I know you. You're the lad who was waylaid during the horse race a couple of years ago."

"Yes, sir. I'm Will Braddock."

The colonel stood and walked around from behind his desk. He held out his hand, and Will reached to shake it.

"It's good to see you again, Will," Stevenson said. "If you had been a soldier then, I would have arrested you for desertion."

Will grinned, and Colonel Stevenson laughed.

"I don't think I've heard this story," said General Jack.

Stevenson returned to his desk chair and related the incident that happened at Fort D. A. Russell in 1867. After being clubbed over the head by a band of Indians who ambushed him and stole the Morgan horse Will was riding in a race celebrating the founding of the new city of Cheyenne, some soldiers had brought him to the fort's hospital. When Stevenson refused to send troops to apprehend the horse thieves, Will had climbed out the window of his hospital room, slipped away on foot from the fort, and stole the horse back from the Cheyenne's camp.

"Ah," General Jack said, "so that's how you wound up with that black Morgan."

"You have the horse?" asked Stevenson.

"I do now, sir," Will replied. "General Rawlins rode Buck until he left to return to Washington. He gave me the horse, then."

"He may wish he had that horse to ride in the inaugural parade in March," Stevenson said.

"I'm sure as President Grant's newly appointed Secretary of War," General Jack said, "John Rawlins will have his pick of any number of horses the Army has in Washington."

"Rawlins will be good in that job," Stevenson said.

"I hope his health holds out long enough for him to perform it," General Jack said. "I understand his tuberculosis is worse. His trip out west didn't seem to help him."

"Well," Stevenson said, "enough about that topic. You came here looking for General Jack, not me."

Will lifted the flap of his haversack and withdrew the bundle of drawings and specifications and handed them to General Jack. "These are the plans for the new railyard in Ogden, sir. My uncle thinks you will need to order special materials right away in order to not slow down construction."

"Your uncle would know. I'll review these this afternoon and send telegrams to the suppliers before I head on to Utah tomorrow. Thanks for bringing these, Will."

"If it's all right with you, General Jack, I'll travel back with you tomorrow. I have a pass."

"Certainly. We'll take the morning train. I'll see that we have seats."

"If you have no need for me this afternoon, sir, I'd like to borrow a horse and ride down to Bullfrog Charlie's old cabin. I think his son, Lone Eagle, may be living there now. I would like to see him."

"Lone Eagle Munro?" Colonel Stevenson asked. "I have a voucher here from General Dodge to pay him for services rendered last year as a scout on that hunting expedition you led for Count von Schroeder. He's never collected it. You want to take his pay to him? I'll get the money for this voucher and have it for you before you take off."

"Sure thing, sir. I advised Lone Eagle last fall to seek employment here as a scout. Guess he didn't do it."

"If you don't mind, sir," Lieutenant Moretti said, snapping to attention. "I'll ride along with Mr. Braddock. I'm in need of a good scout for my detachment. Perhaps I can convince Lone Eagle to join up."

"Fine. Lieutenant, take Will over to the corral and find him a horse. Those bloody savages stole all of our mules the other night. A mule would do better in these snowdrifts, but there aren't any left."

CHAPTER 12

Will and Lieutenant Moretti crossed the North Platte River at Fort Fred Steele on the ferry near the railroad bridge, turned south, and rode up the east bank of the river. Will knew they could have ridden down the west bank and then used Bullfrog Charlie Munro's personal ferry to cross the river directly opposite the old mountain man's cabin. But, that would have meant the horses would have to swim the frigid river since that ferry wasn't large enough to carry animals.

Will had tied a bandana over the brim of his slouch hat and cinched it beneath his chin to keep the cold wind from blowing his headgear away. His breath hung beneath his nose in a spidery cloud each time he exhaled. He rode in silence beside his military companion for most of the dozen miles after crossing the river because it hurt his teeth when he sucked in air to speak.

He glanced sideways and grinned at the sight of icicles dangling from the tips of Moretti's long mustache. "You better be careful, Luey. You'll snap the ends off that mustache if you bang it on something."

"I know." Luey laughed. "It happened once last year. Had to cut the opposite side down to match the shorter one. Took two months to grow back."

"I don't see how you maintain it, even during the summer months."

"Problem then is the heat. They droop and blow into my

mouth, and I have to be careful not to chew them off." His laughter sprayed a stream of ice crystals ahead of his face.

Will pulled up on the reins and brought his horse to a standstill. Luey paused beside him. The trail they rode emerged from a stand of cottonwoods at the edge of a large clearing adjacent to the river.

"That's the cabin, on the far side of the clearing. Best we go slowly in case someone's there other than Lone Eagle." Will carried his Winchester rifle in his left hand, and he now levered a round into the breech.

The lieutenant reached across his waist, flipped up the leather flap on his pistol holster, and withdrew his revolver. "Best to be prepared," he said. He cocked his Remington handgun and held it upright in a ready position.

The two of them sat at the edge of the woods and surveyed the clearing and the distant cabin. Will's horse snorted and shuffled. "Easy, fellow," Will said. He tightened the reins, pulling the gelding's head back.

Pinned on the wall of the cabin a large bearskin covered most of the wall to the right of the door leading into the structure. Unless Lone Eagle had created an additional entrance, Will remembered this door as the only way into the cabin. The grizzly skin was all that was left of the giant bear that had killed Bullfrog Charlie the year before. Will felt an involuntary shiver as he recalled shooting the bear. But, he had not done so before it had mauled the old mountain man so badly he didn't survive.

Leaning against the wall to the left of the door, he recognized the travois Bullfrog had fashioned to drag Will to the cabin after he'd fallen into the frozen river last winter. He often thought about how Lone Eagle's father had saved his life then, but how he'd failed to keep the old man alive after the grizzly attack. Will had ridden that travois one other time when last fall he'd been wounded by a grizzly when he'd stepped in to save the

German count's life. Lone Eagle later gave the travois to the Shoshone girl, Butterfly Morning. The fact the travois now leaned against the cabin confirmed in Will's mind that his mixed-blood friend had indeed returned to occupy the cabin.

"Hallo, the cabin!" Will shouted. The horse fidgeted beneath him, startled by the loud challenge.

Will and Luey held their horses steady at the edge of the clearing and waited.

"Hallo, the cabin! Will Braddock here!"

A moment later the cabin door opened, and Lone Eagle Munro emerged. Even at this distance, Will could see the broad smile on his friend's face.

Lone Eagle motioned them toward the cabin. Will dropped his rifle onto the saddle horn and Luey returned his pistol to its holster. They nudged their horses and walked them across the clearing through fetlock-deep snow.

"Welcome, Will Braddock. Why do you bring a soldier with you?"

"This is my friend, Lieutenant Luigi Moretti," Will replied.

Moretti raised a hand. "Greetings, Lone Eagle Munro. I knew your father. It is nice to finally meet you."

"Welcome, Lieutenant. Both of you, welcome. Put your horses in the lean-to stable behind the cabin. There is plenty of room. Only my pony is there. He will welcome the warmth and companionship of your mounts. Then come inside. I'll have Butterfly Morning prepare some food."

"Butterfly Morning is here?" Will asked.

"Yes. We are married. She is with child."

Will grinned broadly. "Well, I'll be. You sure didn't waste time, did you?"

Lone Eagle returned the grin. "No."

A half-hour later, Will and Luey patted their full bellies after gorging on a stew of buffalo hump and wild onions.

Butterfly Morning spoke few words of English, and she mainly remained silent. She smiled each time she looked at Lone Eagle. Twin braids of black hair swung across her shoulders as she went about the task of cleaning up after the meal.

"Oh, I almost forgot," Will said. He rose from a three-legged stool and retrieved his haversack from where he'd hung it on a peg by the door. He dug out the sack of coins and handed it to Lone Eagle.

Lone Eagle tipped the sack open and poured several silver dollars into his palm. "What is this?"

"That's your pay for serving as a scout on Count von Schroeder's hunting trip last fall. I told you General Dodge would send it to Fort Fred Steele, but you never went there to fetch it."

Lone Eagle held his hand out to Butterfly Morning, who stirred the handful of coins with a finger. She faced Will and bowed slightly. "Thank you. Now we buy something for baby."

"The sutler has baby clothes and toys for sale at the fort, miss," Moretti said.

"Oh," Butterfly Morning said. "I think soft blanket best." The Shoshone girl's black eyes sparkled in the light reflected from the logs burning in the fireplace.

A gust of wind slammed against the outside of the cabin and rattled the door. Lone Eagle stepped outside and Will watched him survey the sky. He quickly returned.

"More snow," Lone Eagle said. "It has been a hard winter. Hunting has been slim."

"I can imagine," Will said. "The railroad has had a hard time keeping the trains running. This may even be a worse winter than the one last year."

"At least as bad. The buffalo will be late returning this year, again."

"What are you going to do, Lone Eagle?" Will asked. "You have a family to consider now. You can't fall back on the excuse that all you need to survive you can find by hunting and fishing. Have you given any thought to my suggestion that you become a scout for the Army?"

Lone Eagle sighed. He squatted beside the fireplace and poked at the coals with a stick. "I have thought some about it. But I find it hard to put myself in a position to have to fight my people."

"You are no longer a member of the Cheyenne band, Lone Eagle. You told me last year that Black Wolf forced you to leave. They apparently do not consider you to be part of *their* people."

Lone Eagle glared at Will, then turned and stared into the fire.

"You could really be aiding the Cheyennes, Lone Eagle, if you helped the Army maintain peace between the settlers and the natives." Will moved over to the fireplace and knelt beside his friend. "The Indians cannot win a war in the long run. Oh, sure, they can create panic along the path of the railroad, but the government will never let the Indians stop the westward expansion."

"There you go again, Will, with that Manifest Destiny foolishness. Just because politicians in Washington spout that doctrine, does not make it right. The white man has no right to take these lands away from the tribes."

"It may not be right, to your way of thinking, Lone Eagle," Will said. "But it is going to happen."

"I cannot bring myself to take up arms against my brothers."

"Lone Eagle," Moretti said. "If I may?" He rose and pushed his stool against the wall with a toe. "I think I have a way for you to work for the Army and not have to fight against the Cheyennes."

Lone Eagle stood and looked at the Italian-born lieutenant,

but said nothing. Will rose, also.

Moretti continued. "I need a scout for my small detachment. I only have a dozen men and our assignment is to serve as a bodyguard for General Grenville Dodge until the railroad is completed. This assignment won't last much longer, but I could use your services until it does. The Shoshones have mostly gone to the Wind River reservation . . . perhaps not all bands. The Utes are currently peaceful in Utah, but we do not know if that will last. You could help me, you could help General Dodge, you could help Will Braddock even, by working as my scout. The pay is good. The money will benefit you, your wife, and your new baby."

Lone Eagle looked at Butterfly Morning. She did not hold her husband's gaze, but dropped her head. Lone Eagle turned back to the fire and stood silently for a moment. He looked back at Will and Moretti. "I will think on it."

Moretti extended his hand, which Lone Eagle shook. "That is all I can ask," Moretti said. "I will be at Fort Fred Steele a few more weeks while I await General Dodge's arrival. Let me know your decision as soon as you can."

Lone Eagle nodded.

"That's a good offer, Lone Eagle," Will said. "Think well on it."

Lone Eagle nodded again.

"Now, it's time we head back, Will," Moretti said. He reached to take his hat from a peg.

"I think you will have to stay until morning, Lieutenant," Lone Eagle said. He pointed at the waxed skin that covered one of the two windows that let light into the cabin. Snow had already drifted partway up the windowsill.

CHAPTER 13

Paddy descended from the rear of the passenger coach and stepped onto the platform of the station at Wahsatch. He planned to stay only a day or two, so he hadn't brought any luggage. He looked quickly to his left, up the side of the train, to see if anybody got off who might recognize him. Seeing no familiar face, he slipped around the side of the depot building and hurried up the street, keeping on the boardwalks where they existed. The morning had warmed to well above freezing and the snow that hadn't yet been churned into mud by wagon wheels and horses added melted water to the slush. Gooey muck soon coated his boots.

Mort told him to head to the largest saloon he could find, because that's where most of the tracklayers would hang out at the end of the workday. He saw a half-dozen tents bearing signs proclaiming to be purveyors of liquor, but the place that fit Mort's criteria was the Sweet Adeline. With its false wooden front and raised wooden boardwalk, this establishment looked like it could accommodate a large crowd of workers. He passed through the batwing doors and walked to the bar. The place was empty except for two customers who occupied one of the dozen round tables scattered across the packed-dirt floor.

Paddy slapped a hand on the bar to attract the attention of the bartender. "Aye, and a fine good morning to ye, sir. Is it there will be more customers later?"

"Quite a bit later, lad." The stocky bartender wiped his hands on a grubby apron that had not been white since it left the weaver's loom. "Quitting time around here's at sunset, then the place fills up."

"Railroad workers, to be sure."

"Who else. There ain't nothing else in this godforsaken town except the store keeps and the tracklayers."

Paddy removed his bowler hat and placed it on the bar.

"What'll it be, lad?"

"A beer, if it's fresh, now." Paddy would prefer Irish whiskey, but he couldn't afford it.

"Fresh as you'll find anywhere in Utah." The bartender pulled a glass out from under the bar and filled it from a keg upended on the back bar. He slapped the foam off the top with a spatula and placed the glass in front of Paddy. "That'll be a quarter."

Paddy dropped a quarter on the bar and picked up the beer. He sniffed it. Not bad. Then he slurped a mouth full of foam off the top of the glass. He swiped his tongue around both corners of his mouth. Not bad, at all.

"Aye, and is it that ye draw the same crowd most evenings?" Paddy asked. He tipped the glass and let the warm beer glide into his mouth. He grimaced and squinted one eye when the alcohol touched his aching tooth.

"Same gang every day gravitates to this watering hole."

"They gravitate, ye say?"

"That's what I said. Now, if you'll excuse me, I need to gather some supplies from the back. Can I pour you another beer before I go?"

Paddy shook his head. He finished his beer and left the saloon. The only hotel in Wahsatch sat directly across the street from the UP's depot. He retraced his steps, rented a room, and spent the afternoon napping on the bed.

He must have fallen asleep. Increasing noise from the street woke him. He rolled off the bed and rubbed his eyes. He stepped to the single window of the room and watched the construction workers slog down the muddy road. Across the way, many of them passed through the swinging doors of the Sweet Adeline. Time to go to work.

An hour later, after eating a slice of roast beef and a boiled potato at a café, he headed for the Sweet Adeline. All of the chairs at the card tables were occupied and little open space could be found along the bar. Smoke filled the space between the heads of the men and the ceiling of the room.

"Ah, lad, you're back. Another beer?" The bartender held up an empty glass.

"Aye, and ye're beer ain't too bad. I'll have another, to be sure." Paddy dropped a quarter on the bar and picked up the glass of beer. He turned his back to the bar while he sipped the amber liquid and studied the men at each of the tables.

The noise level precluded Paddy hearing much of the conversation. Most of the men busied themselves playing various games of cards while they sipped their beers and whiskeys. One fellow attracted Paddy's attention at a far table. His voice carried over the span of the room. The Irish accent that punctuated his arguments convinced Paddy this was his best target.

Paddy moved away from the bar and threaded his way between two tables. He took up a position where he could look over the heads of the other men at the table he'd chosen and make eye contact with the loud talker.

"And when, by the grace of God, will the high and mighty owners of the UP be paying us, I ask?" The Irishman slammed his whiskey glass on the table and looked one at a time at the other five men seated with him. "Speaking for meself, I'm mighty close to running out of money. Me mother told me a borrower ye should never be. But I'm close, and that's the truth of it."

"Why don't ye strike, then?" Paddy asked.

All six men at the table turned to glare at whoever had the gumption to intrude on their private conversation. Those directly in front of him craned their necks backward to see Paddy.

"And what be yer interest in our wages, sonny?" the loud talker asked.

"Nay, no interest in yer wages, sir. Just hate to see the railroad stiff the good Irish for their pay, 'tis all."

"He speaks the truth, Brenden." One of the others at the table spoke.

"Aye, and I've been a thinking on that meself." The man identified as Brenden continued to dominate the table's conversation with his loud voice.

"I used to work for the railroad, sure and I did," Paddy said. "I quit when they stopped paying me." Paddy didn't elaborate on the reason for the railroad stopping his pay.

"We'll have to think more on this, Brenden," a third man spoke. "If the railroad gets wind of a strike, they may fire us all. I've family counting on my wages, ye can be sure. Don't want to be losing me job."

The arguments for and against a strike continued late into the evening. The group even made room for Paddy to join them at their table and bought him beers.

Paddy's head ached when two sharp whistles from a nearby locomotive awakened him the next morning. He'd consumed too many beers last night. The men he'd been with had not committed to a strike, but he felt confident he'd stirred the controversy enough that they would continue the debate. If the railroad failed to pay their wages soon, they might take action into their own hands. Enough of them were fed up, he could tell. Mort would surely be pleased with his efforts, Paddy assured himself.

He rolled off the bed and held his head in his hands before attempting to stand. He took a half-dozen steps to the window. From his second-floor vantage point he could see over the top of the depot opposite the hotel. A freight train rolled slowly by on the mainline heading down the steep slope toward Echo City.

Paddy shook the cobwebs from his head and rubbed his eyes. He could hardly believe what he saw. Two familiar faces sat on the rear of the last of a dozen flatcars loaded with ties and rails. "The saints be with me," he said. "Sure, and the luck of the Irish is good today."

Engrossed in a conversation and looking at each other with their legs dangling off the rear of the flatcar, Paddy watched Will Braddock and Homer Garcon drift past.

On a siding parallel to the mainline, and directly opposite the depot platform, sat a string of boxcars. Paddy grinned. That will do the trick. He grabbed his bowler hat, strapped his gun belt on, and hustled down the stairs of the hotel. He'd paid cash for his room the night before, so he didn't need to check out. He tossed the key on the desk, left the hotel, and headed for the switch that connected the siding with the mainline a few yards west of the depot.

Paddy threw the switch, clearing the siding track, and providing access for the boxcars to the mainline. He hurried to the first of the boxcars and climbed the ladder on the end of the car. He twisted the wheel atop the long rod that extended down the rear of the car to the trucks, releasing the brakes on the wheels.

CHAPTER 14

Jenny washed the last of the dishes and stacked them on the shelf above the potbellied stove. The stage for Salt Lake City had departed a quarter of an hour earlier. She wouldn't have to prepare another meal until tomorrow, when the return trip brought passengers from the Mormon capital who intended to board the train at Echo City for their journey eastward.

The weather had turned unseasonably warm for January, and the rapid snowmelt added rivers of mud to the street that passed in front of the Wells Fargo station. She hoped she could find enough of a snowdrift left in the shade along the side of the building in which to bury the iron pot with its leftover stew. There was enough stew left that it would make a meal for her, her brother, and her father later in the day.

The front door of the station opened, and Jenny turned to see Sean Corcoran enter. He carried his left arm in a sling.

"Good morning, Mr. Corcoran," she said.

"Good morning, Jenny. And it is indeed a good morning. That warm sun certainly feels fine after so many days of rain and snow."

"The arm must be doing better if the doctor lets you travel this far from the hospital tent."

"Yes. The shoulder doesn't trouble me quite as much. Doc thinks another couple of weeks and I should be able to start using the arm again."

"What brings you by? Can I help you?"

"The food in that Chinaman's café is so boring, Jenny. I'm sick and tired of the same old fare day in and day out. I thought maybe I could talk you into selling me a meal. Pretend I was a Wells Fargo passenger for a little while." Corcoran grinned. "I'll pay."

"Well, I was going to save this stew for Pa and Duncan, but since you make a good argument for consuming it now, I'll agree. This once, mind you. I'll be in trouble if I try to compete with the Chinaman."

Corcoran lifted a leg over a bench at the table in the center of the room and sat down. "Dollar and a half?" he asked.

"Let's say a dollar this time. It's leftovers after all." Jenny laughed.

"I know it will be good. Bring it on." Corcoran slapped a silver dollar on the table.

"Let me reheat it. Take only a minute." Jenny opened the door of the potbellied stove and stoked the coals to regenerate a flame. She set the iron pot on the top of the stove, lifted the lid, and stirred the contents.

"Smells good," he said.

It made her feel good to see Will's uncle lick his lips. She moved to the table and sat on a bench opposite Corcoran.

"Will not back yet?" she asked.

Corcoran shook his head. "General Jack returned yesterday. He said Will had planned to travel back with him, but Will and Lieutenant Moretti apparently got caught out at Bullfrog Charlie's old cabin during a snowstorm when they went to visit Lone Eagle. General Jack said he couldn't wait for Will. He wanted to hurry back here, what with all the labor unrest and the short timetable to build the Ogden facilities."

"I hope Will is all right. He seems to have a knack for getting himself into tight spots."

"I agree. On the other hand, my young nephew has also

exhibited innovative ways to extract himself from his messes."

"I fussed at him the last time he was here," she said. "Feel kind of guilty about that, now."

"Oh, I wouldn't let something like that be a worry, Jenny. He undoubtedly had it coming. Probably did him good, in fact." Corcoran laughed.

Jenny stood and checked the pot. "This is hot now." She reached above the stove and brought down a bowl into which she ladled a sizable helping of stew. She placed the bowl and a spoon on the table in front of Corcoran.

He wasted no time delving into the food. "My, that is good. Jenny, you're the best cook in Utah."

"Well, I wouldn't know about that, Mr. Corcoran. But thanks for the compliment. And, where are my manners? You'll need a cup of coffee with that, surely."

"That'd be nice."

Jenny filled a mug from the pot she kept on the stove and handed it to Corcoran. "Do you hear anything from General Dodge?"

"Received a telegram from him yesterday, as a matter of fact. Says he's anxious to return, but the negotiations with Huntington in Washington keep dragging out. The CP still won't agree to a meeting place. Guess General Dodge will have to stay back there until something breaks."

Corcoran finished his stew and coffee, lifted a leg over the bench, and stood. "Thanks for the wonderful meal, Jenny. Best cook this side of the Mississippi, I'd say." A broad smile crossed his unshaven face.

"You are prone to exaggeration, Mr. Corcoran." Jenny returned his smile.

CHAPTER 15

"I don't know why we's in such an all fired hurry, Will." Homer pulled up the collar of his coat. "It sure is cold riding on this here flatcar, out in the open, when we could have waited and taken the evening passenger train and been inside with a nice woodburning fire to keep us warm."

"I want to get back and check on Uncle Sean. I missed catching the train out of Fort Fred Steele with General Jack. I don't want to waste any more time returning to Echo City." Will hunched his shoulders to bring the collar of his buckskin jacket higher on his neck.

The two of them sat on the end of the last flatcar in a string of twelve that were loaded with iron rails and freshly hewn ties bound for end of track. Homer's left arm was in a sling to help immobilize his shoulder. He'd remained in Wahsatch to recover from the injuries he'd suffered during the train wreck at the "Zig-Zag" a little over a week ago.

When Will had arrived last evening on the regular passenger run from Wyoming, he'd left that train to look for his friend in order to help him return to Echo City. The passenger train had not waited for Will, so he'd spent the night camped out on a cot in the railroad hospital where Homer was recuperating with his broken collarbone. This morning, Will had recognized Alf Patton readying a freight train for departure, and he'd approached the railroad engineer about hitching a ride to Echo City. Alf had been the engineer who'd been the victim of Paddy O'Hannigan's experiment with nitroglycerin last year, resulting in his locomotive being wrecked at a bridge in the Rattlesnake Hills of Wyoming.

"It's a nice day, Homer. The sun's shining. The snow is melting. This pile of ties behind us breaks the wind, so we can ride in comfort."

"Humph! Ride in comfort? Not my idea of comfort. Besides, my arm don't like being out here in the cold none."

"Oh, stop whining, Homer. We'll be in Echo City in a couple of hours, then you can find a nice potbellied stove to curl up beside."

Homer rubbed his shoulder and stared back up the track behind the train. He leaned forward slowly, and his chin thrust out, as he studied the scene before him.

"Will," Homer said, "that looks mighty strange to me, so it does." He tossed his head upward indicating the direction in which he was looking.

Will followed Homer's gaze, then leaned forward himself. He squinted. "There's no locomotive pulling those boxcars. And there's none behind them either. They're runaways!"

"And they's gaining on us, so they is."

"I have to alert Alf. I don't like the idea of those cars running up our backside."

Will laid his Winchester and haversack on the floor of the flatcar beside Homer. He stood and climbed the pile of ties to the top of the load. Ties were stacked to the sides of the car, leaving no passageway around them. The train wobbled from side to side as it moved down grade toward the "Zig-Zag," which Will estimated to be a dozen miles farther ahead.

This part of the railbed had been laid hurriedly in the Union Pacific's race to move deep into Utah as quickly as possible, and the grade was not level. The flatcar swayed left, then right, and Will had to hold his arms out to the side to balance himself as he made his way along the top of the pile.

When he reached the end of the load of ties, he dropped down onto the bed of the flatcar in preparation for a leap across the space separating the car on which he stood from the next in line. He took a short step backward—that's all the room he had—then stepped forward and jumped as hard as he could. He flew across the open space. His glance down revealed the link and pin coupler connecting the two cars, and below that the ties of the roadbed rapidly flashing by like a dealer riffling a deck of cards.

Will landed with a thud on the next flatcar, his momentum carrying him hard into that car's stack of ties. He grabbed at the wooden ties to steady his balance and wound up with a fistful of splinters. He picked the larger pieces out of his hand and reached up to grab a handhold to assist him in climbing to the top of this load. He wished he had worn his gloves, but they were packed in his haversack.

He surmounted five more cars loaded with ties, then five loaded with iron rails before reaching the locomotive and its tender. He leaned across the space ahead of the leading flatcar and grabbed the rungs of a ladder extending to the top of the water tank, which formed the back end of the tender. When he reached the top of the ladder, he looked into the open cab of the engine. Engineer Patton and his fireman were both watching forward and did not see him. He stumbled over the cordwood stacked on end in the forward half of the tender to reach the cab.

He jumped down onto the floor of the cab. Alf and the fireman whirled in surprise. The fireman reached for a revolver he wore at his side. Will raised his hands. "It's me, Alf," he shouted. The noise from the locomotive's mechanisms, coupled with the roar of the blaze from the firebox, made normal conversation impossible in the cab.

"What are you doing up here?" Alf asked.

"Runaways bearing down on us." Will told the engineer what he and Homer had seen.

"I'll put on more steam . . . try to outrun them. But the 'Zig-Zag' is coming up, and I'll have to stop when we get there. Drop ties on the roadbed and see if we can derail the boxcars."

Will nodded and retraced his steps to the rear of the freight train. The boxcars were now only fifty yards behind.

He fished his gloves out of his haversack and put them on, then laid his rifle and haversack to one side of the car's flat bed and helped Homer to stand. "I'll slide ties off the top of the pile and you kick them onto the tracks. See if we can derail the boxcars. Can you do it, Homer?"

"You drop the ties down here. I'll kick them off the rear."

Will threw one tie after another down to where Homer lodged a foot against the tie and shoved it off the back of the car. Most of the ties bounced onto the roadbed and settled between the rails. The boxcars simply rolled over them.

Every fifth or sixth tie managed to prop itself against a rail, but the wheels of the boxcars crushed them like matchsticks. The boxcars were heavily loaded and the weight of the runaway cars was too much for a wooden tie to affect it.

"This isn't working, Homer." Will stood on the top of the diminishing pile of ties. Sweat ran off his nose.

Homer nodded and heaved a sigh from the exertion.

"We have to disconnect this car and let the boxcars run into it."

"You can't pull that pin out of that coupler, Will. There's too much tension on it."

"I know. I'm going back to tell the engineer to slam on the brakes and give me some slack."

"That's too dangerous," Homer said. "That's how Zeke got

crippled. He became trapped between two cars he was trying to uncouple."

"Well, those boxcars are going to crash into us and derail this whole train. That doesn't give us much choice. I'm going back to talk to Alf about how we're going to do this. While I'm gone, Homer, see if you can move to the rear of the next car."

Ten minutes later Will returned to the rear of the train. Homer had managed to bring Will's rifle and haversack with him and had jumped between the two cars, even with his bad shoulder.

"Good work, Homer. Here's what we're going to do."

Will explained the plan he and Alf had worked out. He levered a chamber into the rifle and handed it to Homer, who stood against the rear of the stack of ties on the car and raised the Winchester above his head so the muzzle would be visible above the pile of wood.

Will climbed down off the deck of the flatcar and straddled the coupler. His feet dangled down either side of the heavy iron connecting rod protruding from the rear of the car.

He took a deep breath and blew it out. Turning, he nodded to Homer. Homer pulled the trigger on the Winchester. A blast of white smoke erupted from the muzzle. Engineer Patton would not be able to hear the rifle shot, but he could see the smoke. Homer levered another round into the chamber.

A loud blast from the whistle signaled Will that the engineer was slamming on the brakes. Each car from the front of the train collided with the one in back of it until the domino-like collapsing motion happened to the final car in the train.

That sudden forward motion of the last car, crashing into the one where Will sat, created a momentary slack in the coupler. When it happened, Will yanked on the pin. It lifted partway out of the coupler, then jammed. Will pulled hard on the pin, twisting it as much as he could. It moved another inch, then another.

On the third twist, Will jerked the pin free from the links in the coupler. The rear car separated from the one Will rode.

Will turned to Homer and nodded. Homer raised the rifle and fired it again. Another puff of white smoke signaled the engineer, who blew his whistle to let Will know he was accelerating again.

Slowly the distance between the freed flatcar and the rest of the train opened. Homer reached down with his good hand and helped Will back up onto the floor of the car. Both Homer and Will leaned back against the pile of ties and watched the boxcars barrel down on the lone flatcar.

CHAPTER 16

Paddy strained to see forward out the window of the passenger coach. He pressed his face against the pane of glass, but the only time he had a clear view of what lay ahead was when the train rolled through a curve. Had it been a summer day, he would have lowered the sash and stuck his head out. Winter still gripped the Utah countryside, however, and the other passengers would throw him off the train if he tried such a thing today.

He'd boarded the regular evening passenger train out of Wahsatch less than an hour ago to make his return trip to Echo City. His headache had diminished as the hours had passed from when he'd awakened. He felt pretty good at the moment. He'd managed last evening to convince the tracklayers to think seriously about striking. That was what Mort Kavanagh had sent him to do. Mort should be pleased with his efforts. Then, the opportunity to loose the string of boxcars onto the mainline to chase after the flatcar on which he'd seen two of his enemies riding provided the crowning point of his day.

Paddy was surprised he hadn't already seen evidence the free-running boxcar string had caught up to the freight train and crushed the rear flatcar. Paddy's train slowed, and he strained for a better view. Something was happening. There—coming into view along his side of the coach—the boxcars lay toppled off the side of the roadbed. A crew of workers busied themselves shifting cargo out of the boxcars and stacking the

90

items alongside the track.

When his coach had rolled past the last of the wreckage, the engine whistle blasted twice, and his train picked up speed. A single flatcar lay upside down in front of the half-dozen boxcars, its load of ties scattered down the slope. Where was the rest of the train Will Braddock and Homer Garcon had been riding?

Two hours later, Paddy entered the back flap-door of the Lucky Dollar Saloon. He nodded to Randy Tremble, who served drinks to a half-dozen customers ranged along the bar. Randy held up an envelope and motioned Paddy to come get it.

"I'm fed up being your personal mailman, O'Hannigan. You never go to the post office yourself. The clerk's tired of holding your letters, so he keeps dumping them on me."

"Well, it's happy I am that ye are so accommodating, Randy, me good man."

"Humph." Randy turned his back.

Paddy only had to glance at the envelope to recognize his younger sister's scrawl. No return address was necessary. She would be pleading again for money for her and their mother. He shook his head and stuffed the envelope, unopened, into a vest pocket.

He trudged across the packed-dirt floor and up onto the wooden one where Mort Kavanagh had his office. He guessed he'd have to send some of the money Mort would pay him back to Brooklyn. He couldn't seem to get ahead.

When he knocked on the door, a loud voice beckoned him to enter.

"Evening, Mort." Paddy removed his bowler hat. He seldom took it off, but his godfather insisted on the old country rule that no hats be worn in the house—meaning his office.

Sally Whitworth sat in one of the two chairs in front of Kavanagh's desk. She wrinkled her nose and frowned when she looked at Paddy.

"Sit down," Kavanagh said, "and tell me when the strike's going to start."

"Well, and sure it is that I don't know."

Kavanagh glared, causing Paddy to fidget as he slid into the chair beside Sally.

"What do you mean, you don't know? Isn't that what you were sent to do?"

"True it is, that was the mission. And to me own way of thinking, I accomplished it."

"And how did you accomplish your mission if they ain't striking?" Kavanagh's voice thundered the question.

Paddy told his boss about his meeting with the Irish tracklayers in the Sweet Adeline saloon, making a point of describing in detail the discussion that extended well into the evening.

A knock on the door interrupted Paddy's story.

"What is it?" Kavanagh shouted.

The door opened and Randy Tremble appeared. He remained in the open door, holding onto the knob as if he didn't plan on staying long.

"Thought you ought to hear the news, boss. The stationmaster stopped in to inform me that shipment of liquor from back east won't be coming."

"What?"

"Seems there was a train wreck back up the line between Wahsatch and the 'Zig-Zag.' All the boxcars were destroyed. The only cargo the UP could salvage was stuff that wasn't breakable."

"What the—" Kavanagh slammed a meaty fist onto the desk.

"Thought you should know right away, boss." Randy stepped back out of the office, pulling the door closed behind him.

"First, no strike! Now, no liquor shipment! What else can go wrong?"

Paddy looked sideways at Sally, who shrugged.

"Get out of here, both of you."

Paddy and Sally left.

"If that strike doesn't take place soon, Paddy O'Hannigan," Sally said, "we're both going to lose our jobs. Mort's counting on the railroad paying the back wages so he can collect on his IOUs. He expected you to do a better job stirring up the workers, you dumb Mick."

Sally lifted her long skirt up from her high-top shoes and stepped down off the wooden floor onto the dirt one. Her hips swayed as she sashayed back into the tented dance hall.

Mort hadn't offered to pay Paddy anything. Now what was he going to do? Where was he going to find money to send to his mother and sister? Where was he going to get money to eat?

CHAPTER 17

On the last day of February 1869, Will, his uncle, and Homer entered Echo City's Wells Fargo home station. The three of them hurried inside and pulled the door closed to keep the chilly breeze from entering the building.

"Good morning, Jenny," Will's uncle said. "Morning, Alistair."

"Good morning, Mr. Corcoran," Jenny said. "Please sit down. Papa and I were ready to have a cup of coffee. Join us."

Will, Homer, and his uncle stepped over a long bench and settled themselves at the main table in the center of the room. Jenny's father sat opposite, his back to the potbellied stove. Jenny's younger brother, Duncan, rocked in a chair beside the door that led to the family's sleeping area.

Jenny gathered a handful of cups from a shelf above the stove and set them on the table. Using a rag to protect her hand from the hot pot, she poured five cups of coffee.

"Homer," she said, "I believe you're the only one who uses sugar."

"Yes, ma'am, I surely does. I likes my coffee sweet."

Jenny set a sugar bowl in front of Homer and took a seat on the bench beside her father.

"Well, Alistair," Will's uncle said, "the UP finally finished laying the tracks through Devil's Gate and will reach Ogden next week. Then what?"

"We were discussing that. It means the end of paid employment for some members of the family. We'll be closing the Echo

94

City station in a few days. I can hang on awhile by helping out in Ogden. Duncan can probably find part-time work as a Wells Fargo telegrapher there . . . but, Jenny probably won't be paid by the company any longer."

Jenny blew her breath across the top of her cup, the steam from it caressing the end of her nose. She shrugged and sipped her coffee.

"Does that mean Wells Fargo won't need a station in Ogden?" Will directed his question across the table to Jenny.

"They already have one," Jenny said. "But Ogden's a regular city. It has hotels and restaurants. They don't serve meals at the Ogden station."

"What about beyond Ogden?" Will asked. He shifted on the bench as he addressed Jenny's father.

"Wells Fargo will continue running stages around the south end of Great Salt Lake until the CP and the UP come closer together," McNabb said. "But, those stations are already staffed. When the two railroads join, everything east and west for Wells Fargo shuts down."

"I'se got an idea," Homer said. He continued to swirl a spoon in his cup, dissolving the heap of sugar with which he'd laced his drink.

Will and the others looked at Homer. "What?" Will asked.

"General Dodge is coming and he asked General Jack if he'd release me from kitchen duty on the work train so's I could be the cook on his special train. My broke shoulder still troubles me some, so I could use some help."

"So?" Will asked.

"I'm thinking, Mr. Corcoran could suggest to General Dodge that Jenny be my assistant cook . . . like Will done two years ago. Jenny's a much better cook than I is. I can cook up a mess of rabbit or deer meat, but that's campfire cooking. Jenny could add lots of more interesting things for General Dodge to serve to his guests."

"Not a bad idea, Homer," Will said. "Assistant cook's pay on the railroad isn't much, I know. But it's better than nothing."

"Jenny," Will's uncle asked, "do you think you could do that?"

Jenny looked at her father, then back at Will's uncle. "I could do it, if Papa would agree."

"I'll agree," McNabb said, "on condition that Homer is always there. I wouldn't want Jenny alone on that train. I trust General Dodge, of course, but he'll have his hands full with his work. He won't have time to look after a girl. I would trust Homer to protect Jenny and keep her from harm from any of the railroad workers."

"That's settled, then," Will's uncle said. "I'll discuss the matter with General Dodge when he arrives."

"Thank you, gentlemen," McNabb said, "for helping solve our immediate problem. What about you, though? What are you going to do after the rails meet?"

Will looked at his uncle, whose mouth tightened when he shook his head. "Hard to say. There's going to be more railroads built, I'm sure. But when, and where, that's the question."

CHAPTER 18

The locomotive drifted past the station platform, the engineer ringing the bell to announce his arrival. The brakes squealed as they were applied to the huge driving wheels. Steam belched from the pistons with a hiss. The couplers rattled and jangled as the half-dozen cars on General Dodge's special train slammed into one another and jolted to a halt.

"There he is," Will said. He pointed to the sole passenger car the engineer had positioned directly opposite the platform.

General Grenville Dodge leaned off the rear platform and waved at the group who had assembled to welcome him to Echo City. Will thought the gray-haired chief engineer of the Union Pacific had aged a little more since he'd last seen him. Dodge's beard no longer contained streaks of black.

Dodge stepped from the car to the platform. "Greetings," he said. "Good to see all of you." He grasped the hand of Will's uncle, Homer, and Will in turn.

"Welcome to end of track, General," Will's uncle said.

Dodge paused in front of Jenny and gave a slight bow and tipped his hat. "Miss Jenny McNabb, as I recall."

"That's right, sir," Jenny said. "I'm pleased you remembered."

"Oh, it's never hard to remember a pretty face."

Will saw a slight blush cross Jenny's cheeks. She fiddled with the ends of the multicolored scarf she wore. She had not replaced her bonnet after giving her old one to her sister last year in Green River, when Elspeth had used it to disguise her appearance and aid in her escape from the wrath of Mort Kavanagh.

"Oh, Sean," Dodge said. "Lieutenant Moretti and his detachment are arriving on the next train. They had to wait for stable cars to bring their horses. I expect they'll be here before sundown. Can you direct him to a place where they can secure their mounts?"

"That I can, sir. Echo City has a decent livery stable, and there is plenty of corral space."

"Good. Will, Lieutenant Moretti tells me it was your convincing arguments that led Lone Eagle Munro to accept a position with the detachment as a scout. He'll be coming with them. Not sure why we need a scout, but the lieutenant insisted."

"Lone Eagle is a good man, sir," Will said. "I'm glad he decided to take the job."

"General Dodge!" A shout from the bay window of the station attracted the attention of everyone on the platform. A man wearing a visor leaned out of the window waving two yellow papers. "Telegrams for you, sir. They just arrived."

"Thank you, Elmo." Dodge went over to the window and took the proffered documents. "Good to see you again, Elmo."

Elmo Nicoletti served as the Union Pacific's stationmaster and chief telegrapher at Echo City. Will had helped Elmo restring a downed telegraph wire the year before in central Wyoming when Ulysses S. Grant traveled west to inspect the progress of railroad construction.

Dodge read through the two telegrams quickly. "Well, this one's not a surprise. It's the official announcement Grant has now been inaugurated as the eighteenth president of the United States. This other one is a surprise, though."

Dodge shook one of the telegrams. "Doc Durant telegraphs that one of Grant's first actions as president was to announce the government is withholding further payments to the railroads, both UP and CP, until they agree upon a meeting place. That certainly complicates the financial situation."

"No pay yet for the men?" Will's uncle asked. "Hopes were high that you might be bringing some money."

"Afraid not. This also means that I won't be staying. Durant is ordering me to return to Washington to enter into negotiations with Collis Huntington about that meeting place."

Huntington was one of the Central Pacific's "Big Four" owners. He worked in the nation's capital lobbying for favorable treatment of the Central Pacific, often to the detriment of the Union Pacific.

"I'm sorry to see you leave so soon, General," Will's uncle said.

"So am I. I'd much prefer to stay out here where at least progress on construction gives a man a good reason for getting up each morning. I'm sick and tired of the constant bickering surrounding all the political posturing that takes place in Washington. I'm glad my term as a representative is over."

Will, Homer, and Jenny stood silently by listening to the conversation between Dodge and Will's uncle.

Dodge turned to Homer. "Did you convince General Jack to release you so you can be my cook?"

"Yas, suh, I did."

"That's good news, at least. Lone Eagle bagged a nice antelope outside Fort Bridger earlier today. They're bringing the carcass along on their train. I want you to fix me a good antelope steak. Haven't had one in months. Makes my mouth water anticipating the taste."

"Suh, if you don't mind," Homer said, "with my busted collarbone, I don't get as much done as I used to. Miss Jenny, here, is available to lend me a hand as my assistant cook. She's much better at cooking than me. I can roast up that antelope, but she can fix some trimmings that'll make this a feast, for sure."

"You're proposing the railroad hire her?" Dodge asked.

"Yas, suh."

Dodge looked at Jenny. "I can agree to that. But, she has to understand that nobody working for the Union Pacific is receiving any cash right now. Are you willing to work on those conditions, Miss McNabb?"

"Yes, sir," Jenny said.

"Good," Dodge said. "All of you join me for dinner this evening in my private car. I'll ask the Casement brothers to join us. This has the makings of a fine evening."

CHAPTER 19

Paddy entered the main room of the Union Pacific's depot in Echo City. "Elmo, you here?" He pounded on a bell on the counter. The stationmaster was nowhere in sight. Paddy would have to find Mort's box without Elmo's help.

Mort had sent Paddy to retrieve a box of poker chips that had arrived the previous day. Nicoletti had dropped the waybill off at the Lucky Dollar to inform Kavanagh his shipment was available for pickup. The UP didn't deliver packages. It was up to the recipient to collect the shipment from the depot.

Paddy headed for the baggage room door that led off the main room. He looked at the waybill. Shouldn't be too hard to find. The number for the shipment was printed on the waybill. He'd check the boxes until he found the matching number. He was growing tired of performing menial tasks for Mort Kavanagh. He kept promising himself that someday he'd find a way to break away from his godfather. He only needed a way to make some money.

Paddy stopped in the doorway and shook his head. Boxes of all sizes filled the baggage room from top to bottom and side to side. Bloody luck. He'd have to climb over and around a lot of packages to find what he was looking for. He left the door propped open to let more light into the dim room. A window facing the platform penetrated one wall of the baggage room, but it didn't allow much light to filter into the large space.

Paddy heard the outside door leading into the main depot

room open. Good, Elmo must be back. He would know right where to find the box. He probably had some system for arranging the items for easy retrieval.

"General, I'm sorry you can't stay longer."

Paddy stopped. That was Sean Corcoran's voice, not Elmo's. Paddy knelt behind a pile of boxes and eased his Colt revolver from its holster.

"I wish I could stay, Sean," General Dodge said, "but this business of Grant withholding money until we reach an agreement with the Central Pacific on where we're going to hook up can't wait. I have to head back east tomorrow."

"At least you'll enjoy an antelope steak before you go, General." That was Will Braddock's voice. "Homer will cook that up really nice."

Paddy shifted his position enough that he could peer between the stacks of boxes to see through the open baggage room door. General Dodge's back faced him, partially blocking his view of Sean Corcoran and Will Braddock. If he had a clear shot, he could blast two of his enemies and put them away. But, there was only one exit out of the baggage room. He might get trapped.

"I'm looking forward to tonight's supper, that's for certain. I'll bet it's been six months since I had an antelope steak. I know Homer can prepare the antelope, and I'm anxious to see what special treats Miss McNabb is going to add to the meal. Her reputation for cooking is well known, but I've not had the pleasure of enjoying it."

"It will be good," Corcoran said. "You can take my word that she's a fantastic cook. She's worth her weight in gold."

Worth her weight in gold. Wait a minute, Paddy thought. Maybe that's the way to lay his hands on a sizable sum. Her father works for Wells Fargo. They handle all those gold shipments. Then there's the Union Pacific. Maybe they haven't paid the workers for a while, but he'd bet there was money to be had from that source, too.

Paddy rubbed the scar on his left cheek. Mother, me dear . . . and little sister, too. Sure, and we're going to come into a small fortune.

All he had to do was kidnap Jenny McNabb.

CHAPTER 20

"Homer," Jenny said, "it doesn't look like anyone's used this kitchen in months."

"I'd say that's about right."

"Where do you suppose General Dodge has been taking his meals?"

"I 'spect he jest ate when the train stopped in some depot town."

Jenny set the box of food she carried onto a counter. She pushed the blue and gold checkered scarf off her head, letting it hang behind her neck and over her shoulders. Her sister, Elspeth, had sent her the scarf and the matching calico dress as a Christmas present from Sacramento. It was the only decent clothing Jenny owned, and this was the first time she'd worn them. She decided she wanted to look her best for serving General Dodge and his guests.

"We'll have to clean this place up before we can cook a decent meal here, Homer."

"Right. I'll have to find some wood for the stove, too. Ain't nothing here to build a fire with. I'll go fetch something off the Casements' work train. They keeps it well supplied with kindling and cordwood."

A long, steady whistle announced the arrival of a train. Dodge's special coach sat positioned on a siding opposite the depot with the mainline passing between the siding and the station building. Sliding into view out the windows of the kitchen,

Jenny watched the 4-4-0 locomotive blowing steam and smoke as it ground to a halt past the depot's platform. A stable car stopped directly opposite Dodge's coach.

While she cleaned the countertops and wiped dust from the pots and pans, she observed a detachment of half a dozen cavalrymen unload their horses from the stable car. She recognized Lieutenant Moretti and Lone Eagle right away. She wiped her hands on her apron and stepped out of the car's single front door onto the small platform.

She lifted her scarf over her head and waved it. "Hello, Luey! Hello, Lone Eagle!"

The two men looked in her direction.

"Jenny McNabb," Luey said. "What are you doing on General Dodge's coach?"

"I'm helping Homer prepare to cook a meal for the general. He told us you were bringing an antelope that Lone Eagle shot. That's what he wants for supper."

Homer joined Jenny on the platform and waved to Luey and Lone Eagle.

"We have it right here in the stable car," Luey said.

Lone Eagle grinned at Jenny and Homer, but said nothing, nor did he raise a hand in greeting.

"Sergeant Winter!" Luey called out.

A soldier with three gold chevrons on his sleeves appeared from behind the stable car. "Sir."

"Move the horses over to that livery stable, then take the men to the work train and see if you can talk them out of some food for the men."

"Sir." Sergeant Winter saluted. "You heard the officer, men. Get your horses over to the stable yonder. Curry, feed, and water them, then we'll go find us something to eat."

A clatter of hooves accented the urgings of the soldiers as they led their mounts off the platform.

"Homer," Luey said. "Lend us a hand with this antelope. He's a big one. We'll hand him down to you."

"Sure thing, Lieutenant." Homer hopped off the platform, crossed the short space separating the two cars, and stood beneath a door leading into the stable car.

A moment later, the sliding door facing Dodge's passenger car opened, and Luey and Lone Eagle appeared directly opposite where Jenny stood on the platform of the coach. Luey and Lone Eagle lowered the gutted, headless carcass of an antelope onto Homer's shoulder. Jenny noticed that Homer swung his good shoulder into position to take the weight of the antelope.

"Whew!" Homer said. "He is heavy, for sure."

"Lone Eagle," Jenny called across the space. "You shot that thing with an arrow?"

A broad grin crossed Lone Eagle's face. He simply nodded.

"Luey, General Dodge wants you and Lone Eagle to join him for supper tonight. He's inviting the Casement brothers. Will and Mr. Corcoran will be here, too. The general wants to have a nice feast. Homer and I are going to work on preparing it."

"Thanks, Jenny. We need to take care of our horses, and I need to make sure the men are fed."

"Will tells me you're going to be a father, Lone Eagle," Jenny said.

"Yes," Lone Eagle said.

"Your wife's name is Butterfly Morning?"

"Yes."

"Where is she?"

"With her people on the Shoshone reservation, north of the Wind River Range. I took her there to be with her mother before I joined Lieutenant Moretti's detachment."

"Well, I hope to meet her someday," Jenny said. "Remember Luey, you and Lone Eagle are to come to supper later."

"Oh, I won't forget. If you're cooking, I wouldn't miss it." Luey shoved the door of the stable car closed.

Jenny stepped back into the coach to clear room on the platform. Homer struggled to climb up the steps bearing the weight of the antelope. He dumped the carcass on the floor of the platform.

Homer blew out his breath. "Whew! Good thing an antelope don't weigh as much as a buffalo or an elk. He's heavy enough as it is."

"Can you carve out the steaks we'll need, while I finish cleaning up the kitchen?"

"Yas, ma'am. I seen a butcher knife in the drawer in there. I'll fetch it."

While Homer worked on taking the carcass apart into usable pieces, Jenny cut up vegetables and worked on a pie crust.

Homer entered the kitchen carrying a pan filled with antelope steaks. "They sure looks good, Miss Jenny."

"That they do. Put the pan right over there and I'll work on the steaks in a minute. We need to get the fire started if I'm going to bake a pie and have everything else ready in time."

"I'll hustle over to the work train and fetch that wood now. When I gets back I'll carve up the rest of that antelope into roasts and such." Homer cocked his head to one side and looked at Jenny. "You be all right here by yourself? I promised your pa not to leave you alone."

"I'll be fine, Homer. Who could possibly want to bother me while I'm working in General Dodge's private car?"

CHAPTER 21

Paddy watched the activity around Dodge's private car from the single window in the baggage room. He'd seen the troop train unload the soldiers and the horses. He'd observed Moretti and Lone Eagle pass an antelope carcass to Homer Garcon. After the troop train pulled away from the station, he had a clear view of the lone passenger car parked on the siding opposite the depot.

Paddy leaned closer to the window when he saw Homer descend from the platform of the coach and cross the tracks heading in the direction of the Casements' work train. Jenny would be alone. He wouldn't have a better opportunity.

He opened the door from the baggage room leading into the main station. Elmo Nicoletti whirled around from a bulletin board where he'd been posting items.

"What are you doing, O'Hannigan?" Elmo asked. "How long you been in there? You're not allowed to go into the baggage room without a railroad official being present."

"Well, now, sure and it is that I don't keep current on railroad regulations. I came to pick up a box for Mort Kavanagh, and seeing as how ye weren't here, I went searching for it meself." Paddy waved the bill of lading at Elmo.

"Only I have the authority to release a package from the baggage room," Elmo said.

"Well, sure as I didn't find it, ye can exercise your authority and find it for me. But I don't have the time to wait right now, don't ye know. I'll return another time. Good day to ye."

Paddy shoved the bill of lading into his vest pocket and left the depot. He headed across the street to the livery stable. He'd heard the orders given to the soldiers to take their horses to the stable. He slipped around the side of the building. No soldiers were to be seen, but several horses bearing the *US* brand milled around in the stable's corral. A couple of these horses would do fine. All he needed were saddles and bridles.

Paddy returned to the front of the livery stable where one of the double doors stood open. He stepped into the shadows and paused. The swishing sounds of a pitchfork tossing hay told him Zeke Thomas worked at a stall toward the rear. Paddy spotted the tool that satisfied his requirements—a manure shovel.

Taking short steps on the balls of his boots only, Paddy slowly approached the last stall in the barn. His stealth, plus the continued swishing and scraping of the pitchfork, covered the noise of his approach. The gate to the last stall stood open. A single horse held its head down browsing through the pile of hay.

Paddy slipped into the stall, the shovel raised shoulder high.

Zeke spun around, holding the pitchfork in front of him. "What the—" he said.

Paddy swung the shovel with all his strength smashing Zeke squarely in the face.

Zeke dropped the pitchfork, collapsed to his knees, uttered a sigh, and toppled forward.

"Sure, and I'll be taking your coat, Zeke." He and the stable hand were about the same size. The nights would be chilly where Paddy was heading, higher into the surrounding mountains. He would need something more than his vest to keep warm.

Paddy stripped Zeke's coat off and also decided to trade hats. He favored a bowler, but the old man's slouch hat would provide him a bit of a disguise as he carried out the next part of his plan. He could always buy a new bowler with all the money he would soon have.

He returned to the corral and selected two mounts, leading them back into the stable by their halter ropes. He saddled and bridled the horses, tying a coil of rope to the straps on the rear of one saddle. Then he led the horses across the street to the depot. He checked the bay window of the station building to be sure Elmo Nicoletti did not sit at the desk where he would have a view of the platform and the tracks.

With the way clear, Paddy led the horses across both the mainline and the siding. Once behind Dodge's special car, he tied them to the side of the coach where the horses would not be visible from the depot. The Army McClellan saddles didn't have horns, so he fastened the reins of one of the horses to an equipment ring riveted to the skirt of the saddle of the other horse.

Paddy climbed up the steps onto the platform where he'd earlier observed Homer carving up the antelope carcass. The animal's gutted remains lay in front of the coach's door. Through the window in the door, he saw Jenny working in the small kitchen. She wore a blue and gold checkered calico dress. A matching scarf lay draped across her shoulders.

He slid his Bowie knife from his boot sheath and opened the door. He quickly crossed the space from the door to the kitchen counter, and before Jenny could react to his surprise entrance he pressed the knife blade against her side.

"What?" Jenny hissed.

She tried to pull away, but Paddy grasped her at the waist and pushed her against the counter. He pressed the knife into her side, feeling her wince when she felt the point of the blade. "Ye best not make any sudden moves or I'll slit yer gut."

"Ow!" Jenny exclaimed. "What are you doing, Paddy?"

"Well, now, sure and it is that ye are going for a ride with me."

"What do you mean, going for a ride? I'm not going anyplace with you."

"Aye, I believe ye are. And, if ye value yer pretty little self, ye'll do exactly as I tell ye."

Jenny squirmed when Paddy pushed the knife point into her side again.

"Sure, and we'll be needing some grub where we're going. Put some of those antelope steaks and some potatoes into that sack, me darlin'."

"I'm not your *darling*!"

"Do it!" He stuck her with the blade once more.

"Ow!" Jenny squirmed, but she dropped the items into the sack.

"Put yer hands flat on the counter in front of ye."

From habit, he stuck the knife blade between his teeth. When his aching tooth bit down on the metal he couldn't suppress a groan. He quickly removed the knife from his mouth and slid it back into the boot sheath. He lifted the scarf off Jenny's shoulders, spun her around, and wrapped the material around her wrists, knotting the ends together.

"Pick up the sack and step out onto the platform with ye."

Jenny grasped the sack with her bound hands. Paddy spun her sideways and pushed her ahead of him, reaching around her to open the door.

Coming across the main track, heading for the siding, Homer approached with an armload of cordwood.

"Well, how convenient. Sure, and I'll be ridding meself of one of me enemies right now."

Paddy forced Jenny down onto her knees in the open doorway and drew his Navy Colt .36-caliber revolver.

"Look out, Homer!" Jenny shouted. "Paddy's got a gun!"

Jenny threw her body against Paddy's legs at the moment he pulled the trigger, and the shot flew wide of Homer. Paddy backhanded her head with the revolver. She toppled onto her side and rolled against the bloody antelope carcass remains.

Homer dropped the firewood he carried and dove behind a stack of ties.

Paddy saw Homer draw his own revolver.

"Sure, and I wouldn't be trying that, nigger!" Paddy cocked his pistol again and held it against Jenny's head. "I'll blow her head off, if ye don't shoot her yerself by accident."

Paddy motioned to Jenny with the pistol. "On yer feet, pick up the sack, and hustle down them steps. Quick, like."

Jenny twisted her head from side to side. Paddy knew she was trying to clear her ringing ears from the knock he'd given her. A cut oozed blood on her cheek where the front sight of the pistol had cut into it.

Jenny struggled to her feet, picking up the potato sack with her tied hands. Paddy shoved her from behind. She stumbled down the steps, lost her balance, and fell to her knees when she reached the bottom. She reached forward to try to break her fall with the sack, but with her hands tied, she pitched forward onto her face. When she looked up, Paddy saw she'd scraped the other cheek on the gravel of the roadbed.

Paddy jerked Jenny back to her feet, gathered up the sack, and shoved her toward the horses. He held his revolver to her side and looked to where Homer couched behind the ties.

"Sure, and ye can see she's still alive, nigger. We'll be leaving now, but I'll send instructions soon on how to get her back. Ye try anything now, and she's dead."

Paddy pushed Jenny against the horse that was tied to the other's saddle. "Lift yer foot and put it in that stirrup."

Paddy dropped the sack onto the ground and guided Jenny's shoe into the stirrup with his free hand.

"Now, lass, reach up and grasp the pommel of the saddle."

Jenny shook her head. Paddy whacked her in the shoulder with the pistol.

"Ow!" She reached for the saddle and did as Paddy ordered.

"Up ye go." He pushed her in the rump and she threw her leg over the saddle. "Sure, and there's no saddle horn for ye to hang on to. Ye'll have to grasp the front."

Paddy retrieved the sack of food, lashed it to the rear of his saddle, and mounted.

"Giddup." He snapped the reins and the two horses trotted up Echo Canyon alongside the railroad tracks. Jenny's horse trailed Paddy's by the length of the reins that fastened her horse to his. He kept his revolver pointed at Jenny until they were a hundred yards away from Dodge's coach before holstering it.

CHAPTER 22

Will turned his head to the side. He'd been watching his uncle and General Dodge talking with the Casement brothers in front of their warehouse. That shot sounded like it came from the depot. Random shots were not unexpected in Hell on Wheels towns, but they usually occurred near one of the saloons.

He stepped around the side of the tent warehouse for a better view of the depot area. He saw Homer running toward him, waving his uninjured arm frantically, a revolver clasped in his hand.

Will hurried back to the front of the warehouse. "Something's happened over by the depot, Uncle Sean," he said. "Homer's coming this way signaling trouble."

The men stopped talking and followed Will back to the side of the warehouse.

Homer ran up, stopping in front of the group while holstering his pistol. "Paddy's kidnapped Jenny!" Homer was panting from his run. He leaned forward, grasping his knees to catch his breath.

"What?" General Dodge said. "How can that be?"

"I don't rightly know, suh," Homer said. "I was fetching firewood for the kitchen stove, and when I came back to the coach, Paddy shot at me. He rode away with Jenny saying he'd send instructions later on how to get her back and for nobody to follow or he'd kill her."

Will took off at a run to the livery stable.

"Where are you going?" Will's uncle yelled.

"I'm going after her. I have to get Buck."

"Hold on," his uncle called.

Will kept running. It only took two minutes for him to reach the livery stable. "Zeke? Hey, Zeke?" He called out to the stable attendant when he ran through the open stable door.

"Over here." Will heard Zeke's weak voice answer from the rear of the stable.

"What happened?" Will asked. He entered the stall and helped Zeke to his feet.

Zeke ran a hand down his face, wiping blood off his lips and nose. "That no-account Paddy O'Hannigan hit me full in the face with a shovel." Zeke held the bridge of his nose. "I think he busted my nose . . . and he took my coat and hat."

"I've got to saddle Buck and go after him," Will said.

"Buck's in the third stall up. I'll help you."

Will and Zeke were saddling Buck when his uncle appeared in the stable door. "What do you think you're doing, Will?" His uncle was breathing heavily. He'd obviously run ahead of the other men to reach the stable.

"I'm going after Paddy."

"That's not a good idea. Homer said Paddy threatened to kill her if anybody followed him."

Will ignored his uncle and tightened the cinch on Buck.

"Homer said Paddy would send instructions later on getting her back," his uncle said.

"Instructions?"

"Paddy evidently plans to demand ransom for Jenny."

"Why?"

"How would I know," his uncle answered. "He wants money."

"Where were the soldiers?" Will asked. "Why wasn't there someone there to protect her?"

"Them soldiers all went to the railroad dining car to eat after they left their horses in the corral," said Zeke. He held a handkerchief to his nose to try to stop the bleeding.

Luey Moretti and Sergeant Winter entered the stable, joining the group at Buck's stall. "What's all the excitement?" Luey asked.

Will's uncle explained what had happened.

"Two of them Army saddles is missing." Zeke pointed to a railing along the inside of the barn where a row of McClellan saddles rested.

"Check the horses, Sergeant," Luey said.

"Sir." Sergeant Winter hurried out of the stable.

Will finished saddling Buck and led the Morgan out of the stall. He raised a foot to insert it into the stirrup, but his uncle grabbed his leg.

"Wait, Will," his uncle said. "Let's think this through before we rush into something that might get Jenny killed."

Will blew out his breath. His pulse raced. He lowered his leg.

Sergeant Winter hurried back into the stable. "Two horses are missing, sir," he reported.

General Dodge, General Jack Casement, Dan Casement, and Homer walked through the stable door.

"Everybody calm down," General Dodge said. "Let's review the situation. We don't want to go off half-cocked and put Miss McNabb's life in more jeopardy than it already is."

CHAPTER 23

Jenny's mount kept dragging back. Bloody horse wanted to return to the corral. Paddy reached down, grabbed the reins from where they were tied to the rear of his saddle, and pulled the horse closer. By keeping a tight grip on the reins, he was able to force the horse to keep pace with his. But, it meant Jenny's horse kept bumping into his leg.

He looked at Jenny, who now rode almost even with him. She fought to keep her balance by holding onto the front of her McClellan saddle with her tied hands.

"You bloody, Irish mick!" That must have been the hundredth time she'd cursed at him since they'd ridden away from Dodge's railcar.

"Ye've sure got a foul mouth for a lady. If it weren't so entertaining listening to ye, I'd gag ye."

A five-mile ride brought them to the mouth of Sawmill Canyon, which led north off Echo Canyon. Paddy had discovered this narrow canyon several days ago while exploring the countryside around Echo City. He'd heard the woodcutters talking about their work there, logging the hills for railroad ties to pave the roadbed as the tracks had crept westward. Having nothing better to do one day, he'd ridden up into the canyon and discovered an abandoned shack that the tie cutters had used. When the woodcutters had moved on to stay ahead of the advancing rails, they had left the cabin with its crude furnishings and some utensils behind. The old shelter would be ideal for what he planned.

Paddy guided the two horses away from the railroad tracks. No train had passed during the hour they had ridden parallel to the rails, so he was pretty certain no one had seen them.

"You're a cussed fool to think you can get away with this, Paddy O'Hannigan," Jenny said.

"Well, sure, and just who is going to be stopping me, I ask ye?"

"They'll come after you. What do you expect out of this, anyway?"

"Why, money, to be sure, and lots of it. I heard Sean Corcoran hisself telling General Dodge that ye were worth yer weight in gold. So I did."

"Humph! That's a figure of speech. You're too dumb to understand that!"

"Sure, and we'll be finding out soon enough. Wells Fargo and the Union Pacific are companies with plenty of money. And, if the luck of the Irish is with me, yer boyfriend, Will Braddock, will be bringing me lots of it."

"He's not my boyfriend."

"Ye could fool me. When he comes, I might have the opportunity to rid meself of him. Then ye wouldn't have to worry about him being yer boyfriend."

They rode in silence for a while as the horses labored to climb the steeper grade in Sawmill Canyon.

"I know you hate Will Braddock because he kept you from stealing Buck, but why do you want to harm Mr. Corcoran and Homer?" asked Jenny.

"Well, do ye see, them two is who started all my grief. I intend to get even, so I do."

"Will has told me about how your father tried to lynch Homer, and why it was necessary for his uncle to defend himself. Your father would still be alive if he hadn't been trying to hang Homer. What did Homer do to deserve such treatment?"

"He and all them blacks was taking jobs away from the Irish, don't ye know. And, why are ye defending the nigger? Ye are a lass of the south. Yer kind fought the war to defend yer right to own slaves."

"My family didn't own slaves. My father fought for states' rights."

"States' rights? Sure, and that's another way of saying fighting for the right to own slaves, in my way of thinking."

Paddy looked sideways at Jenny. She glared back at him.

"So you think Will is going to rescue me? And you intend to kill him?"

"That'd be a side benefit, ye might say. It's the money I'm really after. I intend to use this as my way to shed me godfather."

"Your godfather?"

"Mort Kavanagh."

"Mortimer Kavanagh is your godfather?"

Paddy looked at Jenny, saw her mouth hanging open, and nodded in response to her question.

"Why do you want to get away from him?" she asked.

"He promised me ma to look after me. They be cousins, ye see. But Mort don't look after me as much as he gives me a hard time. He pays me only enough to send a pittance to me ma and sister back in Brooklyn. I need some real money, don't ye know. I want to bring them out west to start a new life. Take them away from that hard labor cleaning other folk's dirty clothes."

Paddy watched Jenny shake her head. "You think you have the right to kidnap me and demand ransom because your godfather doesn't pay you well enough. You're despicable!"

Paddy ignored her and snapped the reins to encourage his

horse to pick up the pace. During the time they had been talking, they had ridden higher up Sawmill Canyon. Patches of snow still clung to the cliffs. The temperature had dropped since they'd turned off Echo Canyon. A shallow stream flowed down the narrow defile. The steep walls of the canyon kept the water from meandering far from the bottom of the deep cut. Adjacent to the creek, the woodcutters had managed to find enough room to carve out a wagon road to facilitate hauling ties down to the railroad.

A half-hour later they reached a fork in the creek where the meager flow of water from two smaller streams joined to form the larger one that raced down Sawmill Canyon. A few yards up the slope, beyond the joining of these two creeks, sat the log cabin that was his destination.

"Sure, and that be yer home for a while, lass." Paddy nodded to the shack. He guided the two horses across one of the branches and reined in before the small cabin.

Paddy dismounted and removed the potato sack and coil of rope from his saddle.

"Aren't you going to help me dismount?" Jenny asked.

"Hold onto the saddle and let yerself down."

Paddy pushed open the door of the cabin and entered. Jenny stepped into the dirt-floored single room behind him. A solid, wooden bed frame was nailed to a side wall. Two chairs sat at a rough, wooden table in the center of the room. A single, bent tin plate and two battered cups rested on the tabletop. An iron skillet, encrusted with the remains of a meal, occupied the center of the hearth where a pile of ashes had been left after the last fire had died out. A battered, tin coffee pot lay on the floor in front of the fireplace.

"What the devil?" Jenny said. "You expect us to stay here?"

"Well, sure, and I plan to stay here. Ye can sleep outside

under a tree, if ye prefer. Ye might get a little cold, don't ye
know."

"Humph!" Jenny responded with a shake of her head.

"Aye, it will be right cozy-like after ye clean this place up."

"Me? Clean this pigsty?"

"Aye, ye got that right. And when it's clean, ye can cook us
something to eat. Sure, and I'll be untying yer hands now, if ye
promise not to run away."

"That's kind of you." Jenny sneered. "Seeing as how I'm to
be your slave, as well as your prisoner, it would be a bit difficult
to clean and cook with my hands tied."

Paddy untied her wrists and hung the colorful scarf on a peg
by the door.

"Before I start my chores, I have to have some privacy."

"Privacy?"

"I have to pee, O'Hannigan!"

"Oh . . . aye . . . sure." Paddy stood aside to let Jenny pass
back out the door.

"No peeking," she said.

Paddy nodded and remained standing in the doorway while
Jenny went behind the cabin.

After several minutes, and Jenny had not returned, Paddy
stepped around the side of the cabin. He could not see her. He
heard a muffled grunt from the slope that stretched upward
behind the shack. He shook his head. Jenny was scrambling up
the hill, falling onto her hands frequently because of the steep-
ness of the denuded ridge. The woodcutters had cut all of the
harvestable timber. All that remained were stumps and saplings.

He had to give her credit. She had chosen the one escape
route on which he could not use a horse for pursuit. Paddy took
off after her. He was soon puffing from the effort to catch up.
He might not have caught her if her dress hadn't tangled in
some underbrush. She was struggling to free her skirt when he

reached her. He backhanded her, hitting her in the mouth and knocking her to her knees. The cut he'd made earlier on her cheek with his pistol barrel reopened and glistened with a seeping of blood. The opposite cheek showed scratches and smudges from where her face had scraped against the ballast gravel when she'd tumbled off the platform of the coach.

He withdrew his Bowie knife and slashed at the bush that had Jenny trapped. A portion of her skirt tore away with the blow, but she was free of the entrapment. Her bare knee showed through a rent in the material and was streaked with blood from when he'd knocked her into the antelope carcass. Paddy grabbed her arm and pulled her back down the slope.

"Paddy, you're hurting me," Jenny cried.

"Ye should of thought of that before ye broke yer promise and ran away."

"I didn't promise anything. I only said I couldn't work with my hands tied."

When he dragged her back to the cabin he pushed her down in front of it. He grabbed one of her feet and jerked off her shoe. He removed the other shoe and walked over to one of the creek branches. He threw one shoe across the stream and deep into the brush on the other side. Then he moved to the other creek branch and threw the second shoe as far as he could across that stream.

He stomped back to the cabin.

Jenny sat on the ground, tears streaming down her cheeks. "Paddy, you can't do this to me. You can't!"

"Inside!" He grabbed her upper arm, hauling her to her feet.

"Ow," she said. "That's hard on my feet."

"Sure, and that's too bad." He pushed her through the open door, back inside the shack.

"But, I haven't gone to the privy, yet."

"Squat in the corner over there. That's yer privy from now on."

"Oh, you miserable, cussed skunk!"

"Whatever. Soon's yer finished with the necessary, straighten this place up."

He kept an eye on Jenny's cleaning work, while he sat on the single bed and scribbled out a note on the reverse of the waybill with the stub of a pencil he'd stolen from the UP depot.

Jenny's long black tresses tumbled down during her exertions, and she pushed the hair back over her shoulders. Paddy saw where her tears streaked through the grime on her face, making rivulets down her cheeks.

"Sure, and I have to be taking this ransom note on the way back to town." He waved the waybill. "But since yer not to be trusted not to run away, I'll be tying ye up."

"What?"

"Sit in that chair."

"I will not!"

Paddy raised his hand in preparation to strike her, but she sat before he could swing.

"You are a danged devil, O'Hannigan," she said.

Paddy shrugged. He used his knife to cut four three-foot lengths off the coil of rope and proceeded to tie her hands and feet to the chair.

"You're not going to leave me like this?"

"Not for long, lass. I be getting hungry and ye'll be fixing us supper soon's I'm back."

Paddy took Jenny's scarf from the peg and rolled the ransom note inside it. He went outside and tied the scarf to a saddle ring on the horse Jenny had been riding. He mounted, grabbed the reins of her horse, and headed down the wagon road to the mouth of Sawmill Canyon.

He paused before riding out of the smaller canyon into Echo

Canyon and surveyed the surrounding area. No trains or workers were visible. He drew Jenny's horse up beside him and looped the reins loosely around the saddle horn atop Jenny's scarf.

"Ye were so anxious to return to the stable earlier, horse, now let's see how fast ye can run there."

Paddy swatted the animal on the rump and watched it gallop off alongside the tracks heading for Echo City.

CHAPTER 24

Jenny let her breath out and told herself she needed to relax. She gave up trying to get out of the ropes with which Paddy had tied her wrists and ankles to the chair. She'd rubbed herself raw in all the places where the rope had chafed against her skin. The bottoms of her feet throbbed. She couldn't see them, but she knew they were cut from walking shoeless around the cabin while Paddy had kept her at the task of cleaning the place. The oozing blood she had felt trickling off the soles of her feet and soaking the bottoms of her stockings when she was first tied to the chair had stopped. She'd been there long enough for those wounds to congeal.

She thought back to the time a year and a half ago when she'd been the prisoner of the Cheyennes. Small Duck had abused her with a rawhide thong around her neck. She could almost feel that strangling feeling, now. At least, the Cheyenne chief's wife had protected her feet with moccasins while she'd forced her to do chores.

How could she possibly be the victim of a second kidnapping? One such terrifying experience was more than most people would ever have to endure. This time she was being held for ransom, not to be used as a slave. Will Braddock had rescued her from the first ordeal. Would he aid her now? Paddy might kill him if he brought the ransom money. She had no way to warn Will of the danger. She felt tears fill her eyes.

The sound of a horse's hooves clopping toward the cabin

jerked her out of her musing. Paddy had returned. She blinked her eyes to clear them of the tears. She didn't want Paddy to see her frustration. How long would her captivity last this time? Where would her father and the others find money to cover whatever ransom amount Paddy demanded?

The door to the one-room cabin opened and Paddy entered.

"Sure, and let's hope it don't take long to raise the money to set ye free."

"You're despicable!" Jenny spat toward him.

"Aye, I've been called worse."

He pulled his Bowie knife from his boot and approached the chair. He ran the tip of the blade down her arm, slicing an opening in the sleeve of the calico dress.

Jenny shivered from the painful contact and pulled her arm back against her body. She glanced at a thin streak of blood where the blade had sliced down the length of her upper arm.

Paddy laughed. "Tickles, don't it?" He glared at her. "And, sure if it won't do more than tickle if ye know what's good for ye."

He waved the knife under her nose, then returned it to its boot scabbard. He stepped behind the chair and set about untying her.

"Now, up ye come." He grabbed her arm and dragged her to a standing position.

"I hate you, you scalawag," Jenny said. "You . . . you . . . rapscallion, you'll get yours someday."

"Sure, and I doubt that lass. But, what I am going to get now is supper. Move yer fanny over there and cook us that antelope steak and some potatoes."

"There's no fire," she said. As much as she didn't want to be forced to build a fire, she realized the temperature would drop as the afternoon wore on and a fire would be welcome. She only had her calico dress—no coat, no shoes, no scarf. It would turn even colder in this mountain cabin tonight.

"Well, sure and build one! There's kindling and firewood right there beside the hearth."

"I don't have any lucifer matches to start a fire, you numskull."

"I'll start the fire with my flint and knife, soon's ye have it stacked and ready."

Jenny set about the task of arranging a pyramid of kindling in the bottom of the fireplace Paddy had made her clean out earlier. Her hands, as well as her dress, were streaked with black from the soot. With the kindling stacked, she drew some larger sticks of wood nearby to be ready to add to the fire once it started to burn. She remembered Will coaching her on how to build a fire when they'd made their escape from her captivity with the Cheyennes. She'd almost smothered that flame when she'd added wood to the fledgling fire too fast.

"Now, step back." Paddy pointed for her to go to the side of the cabin. He withdrew his knife from his boot and a piece of flint from a vest pocket. He knelt and with two quick strikes ignited the kindling. He blew on it, and it burst into flame.

"Get back over here," he said.

Jenny returned to the fire and nurtured it slowly into a suitable cooking fire.

"Sure, and we need water for coffee, darlin'."

"How many times do I have to tell you, I'm not your *darling.*"

Paddy laughed. "Move!"

Jenny picked up the iron skillet and weighed it in her hands. If she were close enough to him, she could whack him over the head with it.

"Don't even think about it, lass."

She laid the skillet back on the hearth and picked up the battered coffee pot. "I don't have any shoes."

"Like I said before, ye should've thought of that before ye ran away. Now, get to the creek with that pot."

Jenny staggered out of the cabin, trying to step from one clump of dry grass to another in order to avoid the rough gravel. She selected the nearest of the two creeks to reduce the steps she'd have to make in her stocking feet.

"Ouch!" She could not avoid the stones that stabbed the bottoms of her feet. No matter where she stepped, it seemed to be on something sharp.

"Hurry it up," Paddy said.

Jenny looked over her shoulder and saw him standing in the open doorway. "If you're in such an all fired hurry, you do it, you cussed, ne'er-do-well."

Paddy chuckled.

At the water's edge she was tempted to sit and dangle her feet in the water to soothe her pain, but then she'd have wet stockings and her feet would be even colder. She filled the pot and limped back to the cabin.

Compared to the rocky banks of the creek, the dirt floor of the cabin almost felt smooth. Her feet were bleeding again, but there was nothing she could do about it. She hobbled over to the fireplace and set the pot next to the fire. She dumped a fistful of coffee grounds into the water. Too bad she didn't have some rat poison to add.

A half-hour later she had cooked two of the antelope steaks and a couple of the potatoes she'd pried into pieces with a stick. Paddy wouldn't let her near his Bowie knife. She wished she'd dropped a knife into the sack on the train.

"Ain't that ready, yet?" Paddy asked.

"It's ready. We don't have any utensils."

"Well, now, we don't need none. I've me knife."

"What about me?"

"Use yer fingers."

Paddy stabbed a steak from the skillet with the tip of his knife, dropping it onto the tin plate, then he added some potato pieces he scraped over the edge of the skillet.

Jenny stood by the fire and watched him sidle to the table where he sat in the farthest chair, keeping the table between himself and her.

He sliced off a chunk of steak with the sharp knife, transferring the meat to his mouth with the point of the blade.

Jenny sneered at the sight of the rotten teeth with which he dragged the food off the knife. She remained beside the fireplace and watched him eat. She ground her teeth together. Her cheeks felt warm, and not from the fire. She imagined flames leaping from the top of her head.

"Ain't ye eating?" Grease ran down his jowls.

"I'm not hungry."

"Ye best eat. Sure, and it's going to be a long, cold night. Ye'll need something inside ye to keep ye warm."

Paddy belched and sat back in the chair. "Now, pour me a cup of coffee, lass."

Humph! *Lass!* He had some gall calling her *lass.* She used her skirt to protect her hands from the hot handle of the pot and poured coffee into one of the tin cups. She carried the cup to the table and slammed it down, splashing dark liquid onto the wooden surface.

As much as she hated to admit it, Paddy was right. She would need energy to see her through the night. She squatted by the fireplace, picked up the remaining antelope steak with her fingers, and bit into the meat. Hmm. The steak had cooked up tender, and she had no difficulty chewing it. She was pleased with herself for having done a nice job of preparing the meat over an open fire. She wondered if General Dodge and his guests were enjoying antelope steaks tonight that Homer would have prepared in the special railcar's elaborate kitchen.

"Yer a right good cook, to me own way of thinking," Paddy said. "Sure, and that hit the spot. If yer not going to finish that steak, darlin', I'll be happy to."

Humph! *Darling!* She'd had enough. She threw the skillet at Paddy. He ducked and the iron utensil clanked against the logs of the wall behind him.

Paddy jumped to his feet, drawing his revolver. "Try that again, lass, and I'll be shooting ye."

"You wouldn't dare. Shoot me and you won't have anything to trade for the ransom."

"Sure, and I wouldn't be killing ye. Jest putting a hole in yer leg."

"I don't believe you, you slovenly pig."

Blam!

A bullet slammed into the floor at her feet, splattering her dress with dirt. Her head ached from the concussive noise. She forced a yawn and a swallow to clear the ringing from her ears. A cloud of white smoke drifted from the end of the barrel of the pistol. The acrid smell of gunpowder ruined the leftover aroma of the antelope steak.

Jenny looked at the hole in the floor, then stared at Paddy.

The sneer on his face wrinkled the scar that ran down his left cheek.

He might shoot her. She'd best be careful around this madman.

Chapter 25

"Gentlemen," General Dodge said, "quiet, please. We can't all talk at once."

Around the large dining table in the center of the railcar, a group of men chattered about how to rescue Jenny McNabb. Dodge sat at the head of the table, while Alistair McNabb sat to his right, his chin resting on the palm of his remaining hand. Sean Corcoran occupied the next seat, staring straight ahead. To Dodge's left sat the two Casement brothers. At the foot of the table Lieutenant Moretti fidgeted with his mustache, twisting the ends to sharp points. Will stood behind the lieutenant, leaning against a sideboard. In one corner of the car, behind Dodge and near the exit door to the rear platform, squatted Lone Eagle.

Homer clinked cooking utensils in the adjacent kitchen where he worked to prepare supper for the gathering.

"I know it has been frustrating," Dodge said. "The wait for something to happen can be more trying than the event itself. I learned that during the war."

Will wanted to speak, but each time something came to his mind he closed his mouth and decided to remain silent. The older men had more experience than he, and they should be able to develop a plan. But so far, nothing had resulted from their deliberations other than to take a wait-and-see attitude. The adrenaline pumping through Will's body kept him on edge.

"Homer?" Dodge called.

The black man appeared in the doorway between the dining room and the kitchen.

"Homer, you said O'Hannigan shouted to you that he would send instructions."

"Yas, suh. That's what he said."

"Well," Dodge said, "I believe the best course of action is to wait for those instructions."

Will leaned away from the sideboard and stepped closer to the table. "General," he said, "with Lone Eagle's help, I can track him."

"As I recall," Dodge said, "Homer also mentioned O'Hannigan's threat to kill Miss McNabb if anyone did that. Is that right, Homer?"

"Yas, suh. He said that."

Will leaned against the sideboard once more. A movement outside the windows of the railcar caught his attention. A riderless horse walked past.

"Look!" Will pointed out the windows. "That's Jenny's scarf tied to the saddle of that horse."

The men seated at the table pushed back and all of them crowded to the row of windows.

"That's one of the horses that was missing from the corral," Moretti said. "See the brand? It's one of our cavalry mounts."

Will was the first one out the front door of the coach. He jumped from the platform to the ground, almost losing his balance when he landed. Regaining his footing, he walked quickly after the horse, careful not to spook the animal into running.

"Whoa, boy. Whoa." Will reached for the bridle, the ends of which were tied together and looped over the horse's neck, but the animal shied away.

"Easy, fellow," Will said. "Easy."

Will increased his pace and lunged for the dangling bridle. He grabbed it this time and held on, pulling the horse's head to one side. Digging his boot heels into the dirt, he brought the horse to a halt.

He patted the horse's neck. "Easy, now." As soon as he had the horse under control, he untied the scarf from the saddle ring. The material flopped open and a piece of paper dropped out. The slight breeze blew the paper under the horse. Will ran around the animal and stepped on the paper with his boot. He reached down and picked up a railroad waybill addressed to Mortimer Kavanagh. He turned it over. Pencil scribbling covered the back of the bill.

A few minutes later, the men gathered again around the dining table in the railcar.

"All right, gentlemen," Dodge said, "let me read this aloud so you can all hear the message." Dodge adjusted his spectacles and held the paper out in front of him.

$5,000 for Jenny McNabb. Paper money only. Braddock brings to Sawmill Canyon midday tomorrow. Only Braddock comes or she dies.

"Sounds like he means business," Dodge said. "From what we know of him, he has nothing to lose if he kills her. Sorry to be so blunt, Alistair."

"Best to speak the truth, General," McNabb said.

"Now, where can we raise that kind of money?" Dodge laid the waybill on the table in front of him.

Alistair McNabb reached over and picked it up. He read the note again, then sighed. "Wells Fargo doesn't keep that kind of cash here," he said. "The company would probably advance me the money, but it would have to come from Salt Lake City. I can't get the money here in time to meet his deadline."

"Union Pacific could also advance the money," Dodge said, "But, like you, I don't have funds in that amount with me, nor does the station manager here have it. There isn't a lot of cash around, since the workers haven't been paid for weeks. I can have money wired from New York, but then I'd have to find a bank someplace to convert the wire to cash."

"I wish we could help," said General Jack Casement, "but Doc Durant hasn't paid our invoices for the last three months, and we're out of cash."

"How about some of the local merchants?" Dodge asked.

"I don't think they have that kind of money, either," Dan Casement said. "Benjamin Abrams has been letting folks rack up credit at his store, so I'm sure he hasn't taken in much cash lately."

Will drove one fist into the palm of his other hand. "There is one man who has that much money. I'd bet on it!"

"Who's that, Will?" asked his uncle.

"Mort Kavanagh."

CHAPTER 26

Jenny shivered uncontrollably. She wore only her calico dress, and it had a tear at knee level and a rip down one sleeve. She'd never been this cold. She lay in front of the cabin's fireplace huddled in a fetal position. With her feet tied together and her hands bound behind her back, Jenny had struggled during the earlier hours of the evening to feed wood onto the fire. When the effort of maneuvering the firewood behind her back became too strenuous and she'd grown too weary, she'd given up trying to keep the fire burning. She must have drifted in and out of sleep, but she wasn't sure.

She studied the fireplace. Only coals remained, and heat no longer emanated from the hearth. Her toes held no feeling. The thin, shredded stockings she wore provided no warmth. Even if she still had her shoes, it was doubtful her feet would be any warmer. She'd rubbed her wrists raw with all the twisting, and although she couldn't see them, she knew blood covered the rope where it cut into her skin.

When the rawhide thongs supporting the bed where Paddy slept squeaked, she turned her head and stared in his direction. He turned over on the cot and opened one eye. The early morning rays of the rising sun filtering through the oilskin covering of the single window scattered patterns of light over the blanket beneath which the Irishman lay. The sunlight hitting his face had awakened him. The shadows created by the scar on his cheek made that wound appear even uglier.

"Aye, and a good morning to ye, lass."

"It is not a good morning." Jenny gritted her teeth to keep them from chattering.

"And why is it ye let the fire go out?" He snickered.

"Humph."

Paddy threw the blanket back and swung his booted feet off the bed. He reached down and picked his hat up from the floor, settling it on his head. He drew the Bowie knife from his boot and sliced a chaw of tobacco off a twist he took from his vest pocket. He lifted the chaw to his lips and slid it off the knife into his mouth with rotten teeth.

"How can you stand to chew that stuff . . . anytime, much less first thing in the morning?" she asked.

"Well, now, if ye had breakfast ready, I wouldn't have to."

"Breakfast? As you can see, I'm in no position to even tend the fire, much less fix breakfast."

Paddy returned the knife to his boot and stood. He walked over to where Jenny lay and pushed her over with a foot. He knelt behind her and untied her hands and feet. "Now, lass, fix us breakfast while I go tend to the horse and me own necessities."

"What about *my* necessities?"

"Use the corner. That was good enough for ye yesterday."

He returned to the bed and dragged the iron skillet from beneath it. He'd secured it there the night before. It was the only weapon of substance Jenny would have had, and he'd removed that from her reach. He dropped the skillet with a clang onto the hearth beside her, then left the cabin.

Jenny fumed as she set about rebuilding the fire. She told herself she wasn't doing it because she had to fix his breakfast, but because she was so cold she needed to get some heat into the shack.

It took a few minutes to coax the remnants of the fire back to life. The freedom to move without being tied created some warmth in her body. She dropped two antelope steaks into the skillet to fry and shoved a couple of potatoes into the coals to roast.

She heard Paddy lead the horse down to one of the creeks, then bring it back to the cabin. He stepped inside. "Where's the coffee?" he demanded.

"There's no water for making coffee, you numskull."

"Then ye will fetch some." He picked up the empty pot, placed it in her hand, and shoved her toward the door.

Oh no. She'd finally begun to get warm. Now it was out into the cold morning air. If she hurried she might not lose too much body heat.

"Ouch." The rocks cut into the soles of her feet, forcing her to slow down. Now the bleeding would start, again.

At the creek's edge she submerged the pot into the swiftly flowing stream. The force of the current tried to jerk the pot out of her hands. She tightened her grip on the handle and tried to keep her hand out of the icy water, but it splashed on her fingers anyway. Goodness that was cold! She almost wished the numbness caused by the tight rope hadn't yet subsided.

Stumbling back into the cabin, she dumped a handful of grounds into the pot and set it in the fire. The steaks were sizzling, and she turned them. Using a couple of sticks, she maneuvered the potatoes around to position their opposite sides against larger coals.

Twenty minutes later, they repeated the scene from the evening before. Paddy ate his breakfast with his knife off a tin plate. He made her take her steak out of the pan with her fingers, then he took the skillet away from her and slid it under the bed.

Jenny gnawed on the antelope steak and picked at a potato. Paddy poured himself a cup of coffee and sat at the table watching her in silence. After she'd drunk her own coffee, he approached the fireplace and jerked her to her feet. Once again he tied her hands, this time in front of her.

"Sure, and we have a wee journey to make now. I sent a note down to Echo City yesterday with instructions for the ransom to be brought to the mouth of the canyon at midday."

Jenny's breathing quickened. Would she be set free today? Maybe this ordeal would soon be over.

"Since we only have the one horse, ye're going to have to step lively to keep up while we head back down the canyon."

"You mean I have to walk?"

"Well, sure it is that I ain't."

"But I don't have any shoes."

"Now, lass, like I told ye, that is something ye should have thought about yesterday when ye ran away."

CHAPTER 27

Will increased his pace to keep up with his uncle, Luey, and half a dozen soldiers who were walking full speed toward the Lucky Dollar Saloon. General Dodge, Alistair McNabb, and the Casement brothers agreed that Mort Kavanagh would have the amount of money required to meet Paddy's ransom demand. Will's uncle volunteered to be the one to confront Kavanagh. General Dodge authorized Lieutenant Moretti to take his detachment to the saloon to ensure order. When they reached the saloon, Lieutenant Moretti sent Sergeant Winter with four troopers, all armed with carbines, around to the rear of the tented structure.

Will's uncle laid a hand on his shoulder. "Maybe you should stay out here, Will."

"Why, Uncle Sean? It was my idea to have Mr. Kavanagh provide the ransom money. Besides, Jenny's my friend. I want to be part of this."

"All right. Stay alert."

Will and his uncle passed through the swinging doors of the saloon. Luey and two other soldiers, their carbines at the ready, followed. All five of them stopped on the raised wooden floor of the false front. Patrons in the tented structure soon noticed the intrusion and turned their attention to the front of the Lucky Dollar. The tinkling piano stopped, and the noise of conversation around the gaming tables quieted.

The back flap of the saloon lifted, and Sergeant Winter and

his four soldiers entered and spread out along the back wall of the tent, their carbines at the ready. The sergeant, who was obviously familiar with the operation of the saloon, pointed at Randy Tremble.

"Barkeep," Sergeant Winter said, "bring that scattergun of yours out from under the bar and place it in sight."

Randy laid a shotgun on the bar in front of him.

"Ease your revolver out of its holster and lay it up there, too," Winters said.

Again, Randy followed the sergeant's orders.

"Now step out here into the main tent, away from the bar," the sergeant added.

The door to Kavanagh's office swung open, and Sally Whitworth stepped out onto the wooden floor. "Why'd you stop playing?" She directed her question across the expanse of the tented area to the piano player, who had swiveled around on the bench. "It's not quitting time."

Sally swung her head around when she realized men stood on the wooden floor nearby. She faced Will and his companions. "What are you doing here, Will? What do you want, Sean Corcoran?"

"We're here to see Kavanagh," Will's uncle said. "We don't want any trouble."

Sally surveyed the soldiers who had spread around the perimeter of the tent, each holding a carbine at the ready. "You need all these men with guns to talk to Mort?" she asked.

"We might," Will's uncle answered. "Now, step aside."

Will followed his uncle through the door into Kavanagh's office. His uncle pulled the door closed behind them.

"Sean Corcoran," Kavanagh said. He sat behind his desk in front of the window that provided light into his office. "Haven't seen you in the Lucky Dollar for ages."

"I prefer to stay away."

"Well, what brings you in this time? How can I help you?"

"Show him the note, Will."

Will approached the desk and handed the waybill to Kavanagh. The heavyset man looked at both sides of the paper, then read the note on the back. Will noticed his eyebrows raise and his eyes widen as he scanned the words.

"Why do you show me this?" Kavanagh asked.

"We have good reason to believe Paddy O'Hannigan works for you," Will answered. "Otherwise, why would he use a waybill made out to you?"

"Are you in on this kidnapping scheme?" Will's uncle asked. He reached across the desk and took the waybill out of Kavanagh's hand.

"I'm a businessman. I run a respectable establishment. I'm not a criminal."

"Do you deny O'Hannigan works for you?" Will's uncle asked.

"He does from time to time. He's my godson."

"Godson?" Will said.

"I'm his mother's cousin. After his father was killed . . . and as I understand the story, that was at your hand, Corcoran . . . I agreed to help Paddy. He does odd jobs for me."

"So, you deny that you are involved in this kidnapping?" Will's uncle asked.

"Absolutely. And I ask again, what do you want from me?"

"You are going to provide the money for the ransom." Will spoke ahead of his uncle. He clenched his fists at the thought that Kavanagh and Paddy were related.

"Ha! Tremble!" Kavanagh shouted. "Get in here and bring your shotgun."

The door to his office opened and Luey appeared.

"You might want to take a look around, Mr. Kavanagh," Luey said. He stepped out of the doorway to provide the saloon owner a clear view of the interior of the Lucky Dollar.

"What's going on here?" Kavanagh asked. "You have no right to enter my saloon with a gang of armed soldiers."

"We thought you might need a little encouragement," Will's uncle said. "You are the only person in Echo City who has the amount of cash on hand to meet O'Hannigan's ransom demand. We only have a few hours left to take the money to Sawmill Canyon to save Jenny McNabb's life."

"That's of no concern to me. Her father works for Wells Fargo. They have a lot more money than I do."

"True, but not here in Echo City," Will's uncle said.

"And what are you going to do if I refuse?"

Luey had stepped into the office after Kavanagh had seen what faced him in the saloon. "I will declare martial law and shut this place down," Luey said.

"You can't do that. This is the Territory of Utah. You have no authority here. This is Mormon country."

"I believe," Luey said, "that Brigham Young would be delighted for me to shut down one of the temptations that plagues the Mormon community."

Will watched Kavanagh's jaw clench. He saw the saloon keeper's fingers curl into fists on the top of his desk.

"And how will I get my money back?" Kavanagh asked.

"Hard to say," Will's uncle answered. "Alistair McNabb might pay you back for saving his daughter, but it would take some time, he's not wealthy. You could petition the Union Pacific and Wells Fargo, but they have no real interest since this is a family matter, not a company one."

"Make up your mind," Luey said. "The railroad will pay their workers sooner or later. Then you can make plenty of money. But not if this place is shut down."

CHAPTER 28

Will, Lone Eagle, and Lieutenant Moretti approached the mouth of Sawmill Canyon. General Jack had shown them the location on a map. They'd ridden away from General Dodge's coach a little over an hour ago, moving at a trot alongside the Union Pacific's tracks, up Echo Canyon.

All three men reined in. Lone Eagle dismounted, bent low, and studied the ground.

Lone Eagle swung back into his saddle. He rode a standard cavalry horse, instead of his pony. Will still found it strange to see his friend dressed in buckskin trousers and moccasins, and wearing a plain, blue cavalryman's blouse. His mixed-blood friend wore no hat, his hair pulled back into a single braid secured around his head with a red band.

"Two horses went up this road not long ago." Lone Eagle pointed to the northwest, up the length of the narrow canyon leading away from the railroad tracks.

"That has to be Paddy's and Jenny's horses," Will said. "I'll go on alone from here."

"I don't like the idea of you riding into that canyon by yourself, Will," Luey said. "I should have brought the detachment to provide you an escort. At least, I will go with you."

"No, Luey. I know Paddy O'Hannigan, and you don't. He will kill Jenny in a minute, if he sees you beside me. You and Lone Eagle stay back."

"What's to keep him from shooting you?" Luey asked. "He

can kill you, grab the money, and kill Jenny, too."

"That's a chance I'll have to take. We agreed that you and Lone Eagle would stay far enough behind me that he could see you, but not be threatened by you. He'll know that if he harms me or Jenny, you will pursue him."

"All right," Luey said, "but I don't like the plan."

Will flicked his reins. "Let's go, Buck." He headed up the woodcutter's road, holding his Winchester in one hand. Looking back, he saw Luey and Lone Eagle following a hundred yards behind him.

Blam!

A bullet slammed into the dirt of the road in front of Buck. Will pulled back on the reins and halted.

"Far enough, Braddock!"

Paddy's warning came from someplace above. Will scanned the slopes on both sides of the canyon.

"Sure, and I told ye to come alone."

Will followed the sound of Paddy's voice and spotted him halfway up the slope on the opposite side of the creek that flowed beside the road. "I am here alone," Will said.

"Then why are them two behind ye?"

"They will stay back as long as Jenny is safe, and as long as you don't kill me."

"Ye see that boulder ten yards ahead of ye?"

Will spotted a large rock outcrop that forced the stream to bend around it. "Yes."

"Ye have the money in them saddlebags on yer horse?"

"Yes."

"Dismount," Paddy called, "and put the saddlebags on that rock. Ye understand?"

Will stayed mounted, looking up the slope at Paddy. "Not until I see Jenny. Where is she?"

He watched Paddy drag Jenny upright beside him. Her hair

hung loosely around her shoulders, her dress was torn in places, and streaks of dried blood were visible on her cheeks.

"You all right, Jenny?" Will called.

She nodded her head.

"Speak to me, Jenny," Will said.

"Sure, and she won't be doing that, Braddock. I told her I'd shoot ye if she uttered so much as a single word."

"Is that right, Jenny?"

She nodded again.

"Well, now," Paddy said, "leave yer rifle and yer gun belt with yer horse. Walk slowly to that rock and lay the bags on top."

Will dismounted, dropping Buck's reins to the ground. He shoved the rifle between the girth strap and the sweat pad of the saddle and unbuckled his gun belt, laying it across the saddle seat. He untied the saddlebags from the Morgan's rump and lifted them.

"Make sure them two stay back," Paddy pointed his pistol down the road to where Luey and Lone Eagle were visible.

"They'll stay there, as long as you don't shoot Jenny or me."

"Well, then, get a move on."

Will looked up the slope from time to time, while surveying the creek bed and the wagon road as he approached the rock. Paddy must have his horse secured nearby. He wasn't sure what he could do if he located the horse. If he tried to run it off, he'd antagonize Paddy to do something to Jenny, or himself.

Will placed the saddlebags on top of the boulder and stepped back. "There, O'Hannigan, is your money. Now, let Jenny go."

"Sure, and ye think I'd let her go before I have the money? Get back to yer horse and I'll bring her down."

Will gritted his teeth, but he had no choice. He turned and walked back to Buck.

Chapter 29

Jenny winced when Paddy's grip on her arm tightened. He jammed his revolver hard into her side. She felt a tear gather in each eye. They blurred her vision.

"Sure, and ye ain't home free, yet, lass. If ye try anything, I'll shoot ye fer sure. I'll have plenty of time to grab the money and hightail it before Braddock can reach ye. Understand?"

Jenny looked up at Paddy and blinked the tears away. The gaps in his rotten teeth expelled foul breath into her face. The sneer on his lips wrinkled the scar on his cheek.

"Yes." She nodded.

Paddy poked her with the pistol. "I told ye no talking. Right?"

She nodded again.

Paddy dragged her out from their hiding place and down the steep slope. Each step brought excruciating pain to her feet. She unintentionally pulled back on Paddy's grasp because she couldn't keep up with his pace.

"Come along, lass. We've no time to waste now."

Paddy grabbed her arm tighter. His hand bore more strength than his scrawny build implied. Her arm would be bruised, for sure.

Halfway down the slope she stubbed her toe on a large rock and collapsed. She exhaled sharply when her knees hit the ground. Paddy lost his grip on her arm, but he quickly grabbed her by the hair.

"Up!" he commanded.

He yanked hard on her hair, hurting her scalp. The flow of her tears increased. When she looked down the slope, she saw Will take a hesitant step forward from Buck.

"Ye stay back, Braddock. Don't come no closer." Paddy pulled upward on Jenny's hair, dragging her back to her feet.

"You, danged devil." Jenny hissed the curse in a low voice.

Paddy whacked her on the shoulder with his revolver. "I said no talking."

Jenny ground her teeth together and fumed silently. She forced herself to take careful steps down the hill. Rocks and pebbles scooted loose beneath her bloody feet. Her thigh muscles burned from the effort she had to make to keep from sliding out of control down the steep slope. Every other step she did slip, and her feet slid downward across the top of the rocky surface. She curled her toes in an attempt to grasp the ground to keep her balance.

The level surface near the creek finally brought relief. Her thigh muscles quivered and shook from the intensive tension they'd borne. The few patches of dry grass and clumps of dead weeds along the bank provided a soothing cushion for the soles of her feet.

Paddy dragged her into the fast-moving waters of the creek.

"Oh." She couldn't contain the exclamation. The cold water jolted her. The cuts in her feet stung.

The narrow creek necessitated only a dozen steps to cross it, and then Paddy dragged her up the other bank and over to the rock where Will had placed the saddlebags.

Paddy shoved her against the back of the rock, releasing her hair. She reached up with one hand to massage her scalp, and with the other she reached forward and placed her hand on the surface of the rock, glad to hold on to something that stabilized her shaking legs.

Paddy pinned her body against the rock with his own and

gathered up the saddlebags. He unbuckled each pocket in the bag and checked the contents. Then Jenny felt him step back.

"Here she be, Braddock. Sure, and ye stay right where ye are until I'm gone around that cliff bank yonder." Out of the corner of her eye, Jenny saw Paddy point behind him with his pistol.

"I hate you, Paddy O'Hannigan," Jenny said. "You'll get yours someday."

"I said no talking!"

He raised his revolver and she watched it descend on her skull.

She wasn't sure how long she'd been unconscious, but she smiled when she recognized the voice speaking to her.

"Jenny," Will said. "Wake up, Jenny."

"Will." She looked into brown eyes that bored into her and saw a smile form on his lips. She liked it when she could make him smile.

"Jenny," he said, "I'm sorry, Jenny."

"Sorry? What for? You saved me . . . again." She grinned, but squinted from the pain in her head.

"But I didn't keep Paddy from hurting you."

"I'm still alive. That's the important thing." She sighed. The ache in the back of her skull did not diminish.

"I think it's time we go, Will." Jenny looked to the side and identified Lieutenant Moretti as having spoken.

Luey and Lone Eagle stood a couple of paces away, holding the reins of their horses.

"Can you stand?" Will asked.

Jenny nodded. "If you help me up."

Will put his hands under her elbows and lifted her. She leaned into him. It felt good when he wrapped his arms around her.

"We weren't thinking," Will said. "We should have brought a

horse for you. You'll have to ride double with me. If that's all right?"

That sounded much better to Jenny than having to ride her own horse. "I'll manage."

"Where are your shoes?" Will asked. "Can you walk?"

"Paddy threw my shoes away to keep me from escaping. My feet hurt. They're cut and bleeding. I don't think I can take another step."

Will slipped an arm beneath her knees and scooped her up. "I'll have to lift you onto Buck, then."

Jenny laid her head on Will's shoulder and smiled. "I like that plan."

CHAPTER 30

Paddy adjusted the saddlebags on his shoulder and approached the back entrance to the Lucky Dollar Saloon. He could feel the grin on his face—felt the muscles in his cheeks pulling the corners of his mouth upward—felt the scar on his cheek wrinkle. He'd returned to say goodbye to Mort Kavanagh. How long had he dreamed of this day of freeing himself from the domination of his godfather? He patted the saddlebags. Now, he had the wherewithal to do it.

He'd spent an uncomfortable night hiding in the hills above Echo City after collecting the ransom money for Jenny McNabb. He had to wait until Kavanagh arrived to work in the morning. A half-mile short of reaching Hell on Wheels, he abandoned the Army-branded horse and walked the rest of the way to the town. No need to attract undue attention to himself.

Lifting the rear flap to the saloon, he entered. "Sure, and a fine morning to ye, Randy, me good man."

Randy Tremble looked back at him with an open mouth, but said nothing. What was wrong with Randy? Paddy expected to receive the usual caustic remark in return to his greeting.

He walked across the dirt floor of the saloon, heading for Kavanagh's office in the corner of the elevated wooden floor in the false front of the Lucky Dollar. He looked back over his shoulder at the long bar after he stepped up in front of the office door. Tremble still stared at him with no change in his expression.

Paddy rapped once on the door and pushed it open without waiting for an invitation to enter. Kavanagh sat in his office chair behind the wooden desk. Sally Whitworth perched on the edge of the desk, displaying a polished, high-buttoned shoe beneath the short skirt of her red dress with each swing of her leg.

"Top of the morning to ye, Mort," Paddy said. He purposely did not remove the old slouch hat he'd taken from Zeke Thomas. It felt good to defy his godfather's admonition about wearing a hat in his office. Paddy didn't wait to be asked to sit down—he simply dropped into an unoccupied chair and flopped his saddlebags onto Kavanagh's desktop in front of him.

Neither Mort nor Sally spoke. Paddy looked from one to the other. That's not normal. They would usually both be accusing him of something. He drew his Bowie knife from his boot top and pulled a plug of tobacco from his vest pocket. While he sliced a chaw off the plug and transferred it to his mouth, no one said a word.

"Sure, and I've come to say goodbye, Mort." Paddy slipped the knife back into his boot.

Mort nodded slightly and raised his eyebrows. "Goodbye?" he said.

"Aye, 'tis something I've been hankering to do for a long time. Now, ye see, I've come into some funds that will permit me to bring me mother and sister out west and start a new life for meself."

"I see," Kavanagh said.

Sally, who normally would have pulled as far away from him as she could, claiming his breath was too foul for her liking, slid off the desk and sat in the chair next to him. She still did not speak, but she leaned closer to him.

"Well, and, sure it is I seem to be surprising ye both," Paddy said.

151

"You could say that." Kavanagh nodded. "Sally, my dear, why don't you ask Randy to join us? Tell him to bring something appropriate to the occasion."

"Of course, Mort." Sally pushed up from her chair, brushing her hands down across the front of her dress. The color of the dress matched her long tresses, which caressed her bare shoulders.

Paddy felt his smile broaden again as he watched Sally sashay away. He had enough money he could treat the beautiful redhead in the way she expected. Now, she would show him some respect.

After Sally left the office, Kavanagh opened a desk drawer and brought out a cigar. He kept his eyes on Paddy while he rolled the tobacco between his fingers and thumb. Raising the cigar to his nose, he inhaled the crisp aroma released by caressing the rolled leaves. With a guillotine cutter, he clipped off an end and dropped it into the spittoon. He struck a lucifer match across the top of the desk and held the flame to the cigar. He dragged his breath in deeply, coaxing the end of the cigar to a bright, orange glow, and blew a smoke ring at Paddy.

"Tell me, Paddy," Kavanagh said, "how is it you acquired this treasure that allows you to depart my employ?"

While he'd ridden the back way down out of the rugged country surrounding Sawmill Canyon, Paddy had mulled over the story he would need to tell.

"Well, now, don't ye see, Mort, I've been up to Wahsatch the past couple of days, and I had a fantastic streak of luck at the faro tables."

"At the faro tables," Kavanagh said. "And how is it that the railroad workers had enough cash on them to enable you to become independently wealthy? Has the railroad paid their wages, and I haven't heard about it?"

"Nay, it weren't railroad workers. T'were land speculators,

what were on their way to Ogden. Wealthy, they were, to be sure."

"Land speculators? Well, I guess I should thank you for putting a stop to my competition. It's enough that I have to battle the railroad in acquiring land, much less have a bunch of speculators in the mix."

The office door opened and Sally entered carrying a tray on which rested a bottle and a single glass. Paddy noticed that Randy Tremble approached the door, but did not enter.

"Ah," said Kavanagh, "thanks for bringing my special rye, darlin'."

Sally set the tray on the desk, then stepped over to the side wall. Why didn't she sit down? Why was there only one glass? He'd expected Kavanagh to offer him a toast in farewell.

Kavanagh placed his cigar in an ashtray, then poured himself a shot from the bottle. He raised the glass in a salute to Paddy and downed the liquor in one gulp. He slammed the glass onto the desk and reached into the desk drawer he'd left open after he'd pulled out the cigar. He brought out a revolver, pointed it across the desk at Paddy, and cocked it.

"What the—" Paddy said. He looked from Mort to Sally, then to Randy, who stood in the doorway. Randy raised a shotgun he'd concealed behind his hip and cocked both barrels, which he aimed at Paddy.

Kavanagh dragged the saddlebags across the desktop out of Paddy's reach. "That's some story you concocted about winning all that money gambling."

"Sure, and that's how I got it, Mort. And that be the truth. 'Tis my money, for certain, it is."

"No, Paddy, it's my money. Where do you think the cash came from to pay the ransom for Miss McNabb?"

Paddy felt his eyes widen and his mouth drop open. What was Mort saying?

"The Army threatened to declare martial law and shut down the Lucky Dollar if I didn't advance them the five thousand dollars for the ransom. Since the workers haven't been paid in months, it happened I was the only person around who had enough cash on hand to meet your demand."

Mort had provided the money? He couldn't believe what he was hearing. Paddy looked again at Sally, then Randy, then back to Mort. Surely, this was a bad dream.

"You are right about one thing, Paddy O'Hannigan," Kavanagh said.

"Sure, and what's that, Mort?"

"We're saying goodbye. You're fired. You're lucky I don't blow your head off. Now take your mangy butt out of my sight . . . for good. I don't ever want to see you again. Don't expect me to honor my obligations to be your godfather, either."

"Mort . . . I." What was happening? This was not the way Paddy had planned things. How had he gotten himself into this mess?

Paddy looked at Sally. Her smirk expressed how pleased she was with Kavanagh's actions.

Paddy kept his eyes on Kavanagh's revolver as he rose from the chair, then he turned and walked toward the open door. Randy stepped back, but kept the shotgun pointed at him.

"Randy," said Kavanagh, "see that he exits through the rear. I don't want trash like him seen going out the front entrance."

Randy nodded and motioned with the shotgun toward the back of the tent area. Paddy walked across the dirt floor and lifted the canvas flap rear door. He looked back. Mort stood outside his office on the wooden floor, the revolver still in his hand. Sally lounged in the open door, leaning against the jamb. The sneer on her face was visible from across the room.

Randy waved the shotgun at him. Paddy spat his tobacco

wad onto the dirt floor at Randy's feet and left the Lucky Dollar.

Behind the saloon, the alley stretched empty in both directions. No one was visible. He stood alone. How had things come to this pass? What was he to do now? He hadn't even transferred some of the ransom money from the saddlebags to his pockets.

CHAPTER 31

Jenny and Will stood on the boardwalk in front of the Wells Fargo station. She clung to Will's arm as they observed her father giving final instructions to Franz Iversen, the station's stockman.

Franz looked down at his boss from his horse. He held lead ropes to a string of five other horses that trailed behind him down the street in front of the station. Duncan, Jenny's younger brother, sat mounted on a horse behind Franz's string, leading five other horses. Jenny's father had received orders to send the two six-horse teams to Salt Lake City and close the Echo City station.

"Franz," Jenny's father said, "after you turn these horses over to the stationmaster in Salt Lake City, you and Duncan catch a ride on the coach to Ogden. It might be tomorrow before you can hitch a ride, so use the money I gave you to find yourselves a hotel room for the night. We'll expect to see you in Ogden no later than tomorrow evening."

"Sure thing, Mr. McNabb," Franz said.

"Duncan," Jenny's father said, "you listen to Franz. You haven't been over the Wasatch Range yet. It'll be a long, hard ride, but I have confidence you can do it."

"Yes, Pa."

"All right, Franz, on your way."

"Giddup," Franz flicked the reins of his horse and headed north down the main street toward Weber where they would turn west to cross the mountains into the Mormon's capital city.

"Good luck, Duncan." Jenny grinned up at her ten-year-old brother as he rode past her. "Don't fall off."

Duncan shook his head, but grinned. "I'm not going to fall off." He kicked his heels into his horse's flanks and led his string down the road behind Franz.

Jenny, Will, and her father watched until the horses passed beyond the end of Echo City.

"Papa," Jenny said. "If you don't mind, I'd like to go over to Abrams General Store to see if he has a dress and a bonnet. I washed and patched this dress, but I'd like to have something nicer to wear for the festivities in Ogden. Will says he'll walk over with me."

"Go right ahead. I'll finish packing up the office records. Everything else is already over at the depot for loading on the train. Meet me there in an hour."

"Yes, Papa."

"You're going to Ogden too, Will?" Jenny's father asked.

"Yes, sir. My uncle, Homer, and I are headed there to help Mr. Reed with the construction of the new yards."

"That was quite some gesture on the part of Brigham Young to donate all that bottom land to the railroad for the yards. I expect some of those farmers weren't too happy about being forced to sell their parcels though."

"Uncle Sean says Mr. Young wanted to control the situation and not let the land speculators, like Mortimer Kavanagh, mess things up."

"That makes sense."

"Come on, Will." Jenny shifted her reticule to her right hand, linked her left with Will's right arm, and the two of them stepped off the boardwalk into the dirt road.

"Those moccasins feel better than regular shoes?" Will asked.

"My feet are so sore. I'm not sure when I'll be able to put on regular shoes again." Jenny glanced down at her moccasins. "I'm glad I kept these."

Jenny held onto Will's arm as they maneuvered diagonally across the street, weaving their way through the freight wagons rumbling down the road. Echo City remained a busy railroad town, but Ogden would replace it soon as the Union Pacific's main facility in Utah. Echo City would continue to serve as the staging point for the helper engines needed to pull trains up the steep grade into Wyoming.

The bell above the door of Abrams General Store tinkled when Will opened it for Jenny. She let go of Will's arm and stepped up onto the wooden floor of the tent store.

"Good morning, Miss McNabb." Benjamin Abrams greeted her from behind a counter. He wiped his hands on his apron. "What can I do for you, today?"

"I need a new dress, Mr. Abrams," Jenny said. "I hope you have something to replace this." She held up one arm and brushed a hand down the sleeve to show the storekeeper where she'd sown the ripped material together. She raised a knee to reveal the patch in her skirt.

"I'm so sorry about the ordeal you had to go through, Miss McNabb. I heard tell Paddy O'Hannigan had to give the ransom money back to Mortimer Kavanagh."

Jenny's mouth dropped open and she looked from Abrams to Will, then back to Abrams. "What? Where did you hear that?"

Will stepped farther into the store and moved up beside Jenny. "I hadn't heard about that, either," he said.

"Randy Tremble was over to the Chinaman's café this morning blabbing to everybody about it while he ate breakfast. Seems O'Hannigan came to say goodbye to Kavanagh, not knowing he was the one who'd provided the ransom money. Kavanagh took back the money and fired the rascal."

Jenny grinned and watched a broad smile light up Will's face. "Well," she said, "maybe there is some justice."

Abrams had one calico dress Jenny's size.

She held out the orange and green checked dress with its matching bonnet and studied it. "Not my first choice in color," she said, "but it will do."

She went into the store's back room to change clothes, then returned carrying her ruined dress. "Mr. Abrams, do you have a pair of scissors?"

The shopkeeper reached beneath the counter and handed her a pair.

She snipped off the buttons, dropped them into her reticule, and returned the scissors. "I'll send the buttons to my sister in Sacramento. She can use them on a new dress. You may cut up this old one for rags, if you wish, Mr. Abrams." She handed the ruined dress to the storekeeper.

"Thank you," he said. "I will."

A half-hour later, Will helped Jenny climb the rear steps of the last coach as they boarded the train bound from Echo City to Ogden. Her father, Sean Corcoran, and Homer Garcon were already seated on wooden bench seats near the center of the car.

Hobart Johnson served as conductor on the train and stopped to check their tickets and passes after the train departed the station. "Nice to have all you folks on board for this run into Ogden. We have two full coaches in this train headed for the big celebration. The engine *Black Hawk* steamed into Ogden yesterday, making it the first Union Pacific locomotive to reach there. Since it was a Sunday though, the city fathers insisted everybody wait until today for the official welcoming of the UP. I understand they're expecting quite a crowd."

"Oh, what fun," Jenny said.

The train rolled along at a good clip for about eight miles

alongside the meandering Weber River, then slowed and stopped.

Conductor Johnson came back into the rear coach. "A special treat today, folks," he said. "The engineer has agreed to stop for a few minutes to allow you all to see two interesting landmarks. We will be here at the first feature about ten minutes . . . long enough for you to disembark if you choose. The lone, tall pine tree you see yonder on the left side of the tracks is the Thousand Mile Tree. Of course, you can all read the sign attached to the tree attesting to that fact. This marks the exact spot where the Union Pacific's rails are one thousand miles from Omaha."

Some passengers left the coach, but Jenny decided to remain on board. "Don't you want to get off, Will?" she asked.

"Don't need to. I passed through here before. I saw the tree right after they put the sign on it."

Ten minutes later, the train eased down the tracks a couple of miles and stopped again.

Conductor Johnson returned to the rear coach. "This is the second feature, folks. I'll ask you to stay on board this time. There's no good place to stand alongside the tracks. We'll only stop here a couple of minutes. Out the windows on the left side of the train you can see the Devil's Slide. Sorry, ladies, that's what it's called. Geologists tell us the Devil's Slide is two parallel limestone strata, which originally formed as part of an old sea bed. They were tilted vertically by the forces of nature and exposed to view through erosion. The two strata are twenty feet apart and extend up the mountainside over two hundred feet."

Jenny marveled at the spectacular rock formation through the windows of the coach. "It really does resemble a children's slide," she said.

"Now folks," said Conductor Johnson, "I'm going to ask you to take your seats and remain seated until after we cross the trestle at Devil's Gate. It's pretty rickety, and the car will sway as we pass over the bridge. I wouldn't want anyone knocked off their feet and hurt."

The locomotive whistle blew, and the train lurched back into motion. It was only a matter of minutes until the train slowed to a crawl. Jenny felt the instability transmitted from the rails through the cars' trucks and into the body of the carriage itself.

She grabbed hold of Will's arm. "Are we going to be all right? I don't like this."

"I don't care for it, either," Will said. "This trestle was erected in a hurry to get the tracks through this gorge and on down the Weber River and into Ogden. Someday, it will have to be replaced."

Less than an hour after crossing the Devil's Gate trestle, the train exited Weber Canyon and approached Ogden. Conductor Johnson once again entered the coach. He paused in the door after closing it behind him and withdrew his pocket watch from a vest pocket. "Let the record show," he said, "that the first Union Pacific train bearing passengers entered Ogden at two-thirty in the afternoon of March eighth, in the year of our Lord one-thousand, eight-hundred, and sixty-nine."

A cheer from the passengers greeted Johnson's announcement.

Jenny, sitting at the window seat, pulled the sash down and leaned her head outside. "Oh, look, Will. There are hundreds of people . . . all dressed in their finest. They're spread out all along the tracks. How exciting!"

Jenny leaned across Will and pointed to the opposite windows. "Why, they're on both sides of the tracks. Just look at the crowd. They've come for a grand celebration."

Boom! Boom! Boom!

"I haven't heard artillery fire like that since the war," Jenny's father said. He sat in the seat in front of her. "Looks like they've brought out the local militia to fire a twenty-one gun salute for our arrival."

A band struck up a tune Jenny thought she'd heard before. She giggled as she watched the smoke from the cannon fire wrap itself around the festively costumed bandsmen. "What's that song they're playing, Will?"

"The Star-Spangled Banner."

"Oh, yes." She remembered now that the song had become a favorite of the Yankees during the recent war.

Hobart Johnson passed back down the aisle.

"Can we get out and join the crowd, Mr. Johnson?" Jenny asked.

"In a minute," he answered. "We're not quite to the end of track. The crowd has spilled over onto the rails, and the engineer is having trouble pressing through them."

The train crawled slowly ahead. The locomotive's whistle blasted two quick notes, followed quickly by two more, then yet another two.

"The engineer's trying to signal the people the train's moving forward," Will said, "but, they're not paying any attention. Reminds me of the buffalo blocking the tracks in Nebraska."

Sean Corcoran leaned forward from behind Jenny and Will and laid a hand on their seat back. "These folks have never seen a train before, so they don't know to stay clear."

A long, steady blast emitted from the engine's whistle and the train lurched to a halt. Jenny happened to look toward the front of the train when the engine blew excess steam from the cylinders. The spectators closest to the locomotive pushed back against those behind them to escape the engulfing white vapor. Black soot shot into the air from the smokestack and drifted down onto the crowd.

Shouts from the gathered throng intensified. *Move! Move! Get away!*

Jenny watched mothers grab the hands of frightened children

and run from the locomotive and its cloud of steam and rain of ash. Whole families dashed into the swampy ground that lay a few rods away on either side of the gravel roadbed. Children fell. Mothers and fathers helped them up, their dressy clothes covered in mud.

"Oh, those poor people," Jenny said. "Their day is ruined. They aren't afraid of the warlike firing of cannon, but they panic at the peaceful sounds of a locomotive."

CHAPTER 32

Two weeks after entering Ogden, the Union Pacific pushed its rails twenty-five miles farther north up the eastern shore of the Great Salt Lake and swung west another six miles along the northern end of the lake to reach the new town of Corinne. On March 23, 1869, Corinne, advertising itself as the *Gentile Capital* of Utah, became the final major location for Hell on Wheels. Smaller versions of the sinful town would follow the UP all the way to Promontory Summit.

Will Braddock, his uncle, and Homer, entered Abrams General Store, which the Jewish merchant had relocated to Corinne along with all the other Hell on Wheels merchants.

"Good afternoon, gents," Benjamin Abrams said.

"Afternoon, Ben," Will's uncle responded. "I need a dozen cigars. You have my brand?"

"I do." Abrams took a wooden box from within a glass-topped case and pushed it across the top. "What can I get for you two?"

"Nothing for me," Homer said.

"I only have a nickel," Will said. "Guess I'll spend it on some jawbreakers."

Will looked at Homer and grinned when his friend wrinkled his nose in disgust at the sloppy candy.

"Here you go," Abrams said. He lifted a glass container from a shelf behind him and set it on the counter. "The price has gone up to two cents each, Will."

"I can only afford two, then."

Abrams took the lid off the jar. "I'll tell you what. I'll sell you three for five cents. How's that? Or, I'll give you a penny change."

Will smiled broadly. "I'll take the jawbreakers. A penny won't do me much good." He selected his three jawbreakers while his uncle finished counting out his dozen cigars.

"How much for the cigars, Ben?" Will's uncle asked.

"They've gone up a bit, too. They're fifteen cents each now. So, your total comes to one dollar and eighty cents."

Will's uncle dropped two silver dollars on the countertop and Abrams gave him his change.

"Now, gents," Abrams said. "You've been good customers these past two years. I'd like to treat you to a drink at the Lucky Dollar Saloon."

"Ben," Will's uncle said, "I've avoided that place ever since Julesburg."

"I know, Sean, but it's the best place here. I'd really like to buy you each a drink. Surely you can give me that pleasure . . . once."

Will's uncle looked at him, then at Homer. "All right . . . once."

Abrams hung a closed sign on his front door and locked it behind everybody. They all headed across the dusty street to the false-fronted Lucky Dollar.

"Ben?" Will's uncle asked. "Are you planning on staying in Corinne after the railroads join?"

"I think so, Sean."

"But, this is called a gentile town."

"Sean, I believe a Jew like me stands a better chance of being accepted in a gentile town than in a Mormon one. I've thought about heading on west, but Sacramento and San Francisco already have plenty of merchants. If Corinne succeeds in becoming the railroad's main economic center in Utah, as some folks are saying, I think I'll do better here than elsewhere."

"I wouldn't count on Corinne supplanting Ogden as the UP's rail center," Will's uncle said.

Abrams pushed through the swinging doors of the saloon and led the three others across the dozen wooden planks and down onto the dirt of the main floor.

Will had been inside the Lucky Dollar only once before, and that was when he'd demanded that Mortimer Kavanagh provide the ransom money for Jenny McNabb. He surveyed the tent-covered area, half expecting to see Paddy O'Hannigan. He'd heard the stories that Kavanagh had fired Paddy, but he wasn't sure he really believed them. His search did not reveal the Irish thug. Railroad workers occupied most of the tables, as well as the long bar.

Toward the rear of the tent, Sally Whitworth sat on the edge of a bench beside a piano player. She unfolded a sheet of music and spread it across the front of the upright, then spun around on the bench to face the center of the tent. She nodded and smiled when she saw Will and his three companions settling into chairs at a nearby table.

"Welcome, gentlemen," she said. "I was about to sing for the boys."

The piano player pounded an opening chord and the conversation in the saloon subsided. The drinkers and card players turned their attention to the pretty redhead who treated them to a kick of her high-button shoes, revealing the petticoats beneath her skirt. A roar of approval arose from the crowd as the piano player finished a run through the tune's refrain. The men quieted, and Sally sang.

> *When the blackbird in the spring,*
> *On the willow tree,*
> *Sat and rocked, I heard him sing,*
> *Singing Aura Lea.*

Aura Lea, Aura Lea,
Maid with golden hair;
Sunshine came along with thee,
And swallows in the air.

"I haven't heard that sung so prettily since the end of the war," Will's uncle said.

"I thought you didn't like Miss Whitworth," Abrams said.

"Her singing the song well doesn't have anything to do with whether or not I like her."

Abrams raised a hand and motioned for one of the serving ladies to approach the table.

"What'll it be, boys?" she asked.

"Rye whiskey for me," Abrams said.

"The same," Will's uncle said.

Homer rocked back and forth for a moment, obviously pondering his choice. "I reckon I'll have a beer."

"And for you?" The server looked at Will.

"Try the sarsaparilla, Will," Abrams said. "It's the best in the country. I import it for Mort Kavanagh all the way from Philadelphia."

Will nodded. "Sarsaparilla, please."

A few moments later the girl returned with the drinks. When she'd finished serving them, Abrams held out a five dollar bill. A hand reached over Abram's shoulder and pushed the offered money down.

"Drinks are on the house."

Will turned at the sound of the familiar voice, as did the other three at the table. Mort Kavanagh stood behind Benjamin Abrams.

Kavanagh pulled a chair over from an adjoining table. "If you don't mind, I'll join you." He held up a finger as a signal to the girl who had served the table.

The young lady hurried to the bar and soon returned with

another glass of rye whiskey, which she placed in front of Kavanagh.

"I've been meaning to ask you a question, Corcoran," Kavanagh said.

"What's that?"

"Tracklayers from both companies are out there on Promontory Summit, grading past each other. Doesn't sound economical to me. When and where are the two railroads going to meet up, anyway?"

"I'm not the man with that kind of information. Perhaps you should ask Sam Reed."

"I did. Sam doesn't know, either. He says Dodge is back in Washington City, negotiating the meeting place with Harrington."

"That's what I've been told," Will's uncle said. "I agree with you it's a waste for both companies to grade past one another, especially since the Treasury Department already handed over the bonds to the Central Pacific to cover the costs of grading into Ogden."

"I'd guess it's Doc Durant's doing," Kavanagh said.

"Likely as not. He's determined to milk every dime out of the construction of the road."

"Is that why he doesn't pay the workers their wages?"

"I couldn't say."

"Well," Kavanagh said, "I'll be glad when the workers do get paid. I have a lot of IOUs outstanding."

"I'm sure the workers are anxious to get their money, too. There's a lot of unrest among them. Hard to tell what they might do if they aren't paid soon."

Kavanagh took a final sip from his drink and pushed back his chair. "Gentlemen, it's been a pleasure. Now if you'll excuse me, I have work to do."

Will's uncle lifted his glass. "Thank you for the drink, Mr.

Kavanagh."

Kavanagh nodded, stood, and walked back toward his office.

Will took the final sip from his bottle of sarsaparilla and smacked his lips. He hadn't had a sarsaparilla since he'd left Burlington, Iowa, two years ago. "You were right, Mr. Abrams. That's the best I've had."

"Good. I thought you'd like it."

Sally finished her song and the tent fell silent. The words to the sad song that'd been popular around the campfires during the war had placed a dampening edge on the usually boisterous crowd.

Will watched her rise from the bench and whisper something in the piano player's ear. The player nodded and riffled his fingers down the keyboard before striking up a lively polka. The bright tune reinvigorated the customers and the noise level escalated.

Sally walked across the center of the tent, which was kept free of tables and had a small wooden floor to permit dancing. When she reached the table where Will and his companions sat, she stopped behind Homer and looked across at Will's uncle.

"Sean Corcoran," she said, "would you care to dance this polka with me?"

"No, I would not."

"Aw, that's a shame. As I recall, you're a very good dancer."

His uncle did not reply. Will remembered Benjamin Abrams telling him that Sally Whitworth had tried to get her hooks into his uncle before, and he had avoided her.

Sally shifted her gaze to Will. "How about you, Mr. Braddock? Will you dance with me?"

"I don't dance."

"Now you've used that excuse before. Surely, in all the time you've been out west, hasn't that cute Miss McNabb taught you how to dance?"

"No, ma'am."

"And I asked you before not to call me ma'am, didn't I?"

"Yes, ma'am . . . I mean, Sally."

"Well, you ask Miss McNabb to teach you dancing. She has her eyes set on you, I know. She's not going to let you get by forever without knowing how to dance. She'll have her way with you, mark my word." Sally turned away from the table and sashayed back toward the piano.

Will's face turned warm. With his head slightly bowed, he looked at each of his companions with raised eyelids. Broad smiles greeted him. Will felt his blush increase.

CHAPTER 33

"Uncle Sean." Will called through the open entrance to General Jack Casement's warehouse tent. "Mr. Reed is here to see you."

Will and Homer had been waiting outside the warehouse for Will's uncle to finish going over some measurements with General Jack that were marked on a large map laid out on a trestle table. The two men had been reviewing the grading the Union Pacific had performed from Corinne westward across the swampy flats bordering the north shore of the Great Salt Lake and up the sharp ridge that climbed onto Promontory Summit.

"In here, Sam," Will's uncle called.

Will stepped out of the opening to allow Sam Reed to pass through, then he and Homer followed. Will noticed Reed's sallow cheeks reflecting the stress he bore as the UP's construction superintendent. His wavy hair, full beard, and mustache showed more gray each day.

"Sam," said Will's uncle, "you don't look well."

"I'm tired, Sean. I can't keep up with all the changes Doc Durant and Silas Seymour keep making."

"Tell me about it," General Jack said. "We've wound up with the steepest grade and more sharp curves than anyplace else on the entire route."

"It's too bad General Dodge isn't here," Will's uncle said. "He has the knack for keeping Durant and Seymour from making stupid decisions."

"General Dodge is finally on his way here, gentlemen," Reed said. "I've received a telegram from him informing me he's reached an agreement with Collis Huntington resolving where the lines are to join."

Will's uncle nodded. "That sounds good."

Reed unfolded a yellow sheet and handed it to General Jack. "You read it, Jack."

Casement took the telegram and read it aloud.

DODGE TO REED. STOP. REACHED AGREEMENT WITH HUNTINGTON YESTERDAY AND CONGRESS APPROVED. STOP. ROADS TO JOIN AT PROMONTORY SUMMIT. STOP. CENTRAL PACIFIC WILL BUY OUR LINE FROM THERE TO OGDEN. STOP. CEASE GRADING BEYOND PROMONTORY. STOP. PLAN TO COME WEST SOON. STOP.

"All right," Will's uncle said, "that means the official terminus will become Ogden. Hardly seems fair since we've laid track well beyond there, and the CP isn't any place near Ogden."

"It's probably the best Dodge could do," Reed said. "Huntington had already finagled the bonds out of the Treasury Department for the mileage into Ogden. The grading we've been doing across Utah and into Nevada is not going to be paid for."

"What do we do now?" Will's uncle asked.

"Stop grading, of course," said Reed, "and concentrate on laying the rails to Promontory Summit. We want the UP to be the first there with a locomotive. Can't let the CP beat us on that. Can you do this, General Jack?"

"We'll give it our best shot." Casement slapped his ever-present riding crop against his calf-high boot.

Will's uncle rolled up the large map and handed it to Reed. "Won't be needing this, since we've reached the end of the line. Won't be any more changes to record."

"I'll include your map with the rest of the files I'm preparing to send back to Omaha. But you're not done, yet."

Will noticed his uncle raise his eyebrows.

"I want you to go to the CP's camp," Reed said. "You know their managers better than anyone because you met them during the trip you made to California last year."

Will's uncle nodded.

"Coordinate with them on the actual meeting point. Where, when, how . . . all the details. Promontory Summit is a broad plateau. We need to nail down the place for the ceremonies that will commemorate the completion of the Pacific Railroad."

"All right, Sam," Will's uncle said.

"I'll be anxious to read your report when you return," Reed said.

An hour later, Will led Buck and two riding horses up a ramp into a boxcar that had been coupled to the end of one of Casement's supply trains, which was loaded with precut bents, sills, posts, and other components for the wooden trestle being constructed over a wide gap in the route to Promontory Summit.

Will tethered the three animals to a rope he'd strung across the front of the car. He left them saddled because the train ride would not last long.

Homer dragged on the halter rope of a reluctant Ruby, urging her up the ramp. The mule, bearing a loaded packsaddle, tried to resist joining the three horses in the closed-in space. Homer tugged hard to encourage the stubborn animal to climb up the ramp. He tied Ruby next to Buck, and she settled down once she found herself standing next to the familiar Morgan.

Will and Homer would travel with Will's uncle by rail to the end of track, then head farther west on horseback to find the Central Pacific's construction camp. The three of them climbed aboard the boxcar and waited in the open doorway for the train to start.

General Jack stood below them on the roadbed looking up into the car. "Sean, I can't take you any farther than the *big cut*. We're still erecting the trestle across it. But that huge gap is the last major obstacle between here and the summit."

"We appreciate you getting us that far. Saves time in the saddle."

"Stay alert, Sean. The CP is filling the wide gap adjacent to our bridge with dirt, and the competition between their boys and ours is nasty sometimes."

"Who's going to win the race across the gap?" Will's uncle asked.

"With the agreement between Dodge and Harrington to stop grading past each other, I suppose we will in the short run. It's four hundred feet across that gap, and it takes less time to build a timber trestle than it does to fill the gap with dirt one wagonload at a time. In the long run though, we'll probably shift the tracks to the fill. It'll provide a more stable surface, allowing faster speeds than we can achieve over a wooden trestle."

Twenty miles from Corinne the supply train stopped at the end of track. A gang of workers promptly set to work unloading the bridge components. Will, his uncle, and Homer led the horses out of the boxcar and alongside the rails to a point where they could look across the deep gap. Out ahead of them, builders worked to span that gap with dozens of bents extending eighty-five feet down from the highest point on the bridge at its center.

"That's almost as big as the Dale Creek Bridge," Will said.

"And twice as rickety," Will's uncle said. "General Jack's right. The UP shouldn't use it any longer than it has to. I hate to admit it, but that fill the CP's putting in over there is much better."

"I expected to see Chinese workers on the fill, Uncle Sean." Will could see dozens of Caucasians hauling wagonloads of dirt to the end of the steep fill that rose as high from the base of the gap as the bents on the trestle did.

"Leland Stanford hired Mormons from Brigham Young to do their grading work in Utah, like we did. The Chinese still lay the rails, but they're a long way from here. We'll see them tomorrow. Let's mount. We have forty miles of riding from here to where we'll find CP's end of track. Once we pass Promontory Summit we'll ride on our graded surface, since we won't be laying tracks on it. That'll make for faster traveling."

"We can't make forty miles before sundown, Uncle Sean," Will said.

"I know. That's why I asked Homer to bring some grub along. You do have it, don't you, Homer?"

"Yas, suh, I'se got plenty enough packed on Ruby. I also brung the tent. I figure it'll turn mighty cold tonight."

"Good," Will's uncle said. "Let's go."

Will's uncle mounted, pulled the reins over the neck of his horse, and headed down the slope away from the trestle. Will and Homer fell in behind. They would have to ease their way down one side of the gap, cross it, then climb the other side before reaching level ground.

CHAPTER 34

After spending a chilly night near Spring Bay on the far north shore of the Great Salt Lake, Will, his uncle, and Homer continued riding westward. The land stretched away in an unbroken, barren plain on both sides of the UP's graded route. The CP's right-of-way paralleled the UP's, occasionally crossing it. Will and his companions found the riding easy down the center of the UP's grade. Since the Union Pacific would not be using it to lay tracks, the fact that their horses' hooves dug holes in the surface did not matter. Out of courtesy, they avoided riding on the CP's grade, which their competitor would use to lay its tracks. About twenty miles from where they had started earlier that morning, they spotted clouds of dust ahead of them.

"I think we're almost there," Will's uncle said. "That dust has to be at the CP's railhead."

An hour later, the three horsemen approached the CP's end of track. Spread out on either side of the tracks were clusters of white tents. A crew of gandy dancers wrestled iron rails off horse-drawn wagons that raced forward from flatcars being pushed ahead of two diamond-stacked locomotives. Will knew the shape of the stack indicated the CP still burned wood in their steam engines. The UP had switched to coal. Most of the UP locomotives now bore straight stacks, it no longer being necessary to trap burning wood cinders in a diamond-shaped chimney.

"Chung Huang!" Will reined in and yelled when he spotted

the Chinese youth he had met the summer before at the sum-mit of the Sierra Nevada Mountains in California.

Will waved when his friend looked in his direction. Chung Huang held a bucket in one hand from which he took two iron spikes at a time and dropped them atop each tie he passed.

"Back to work, ye no-account Celestial!" The snap of a whip accompanied the shouted command.

Chung Huang's woven, straw hat jarred askew when he jerked his head in response to the cracking whip. He quickly straight-ened the hat and bent his head to concentrate on his job of dropping spikes, keeping pace with the Irish work crew who laid down the iron rails in a steady procession.

Will glared at Kevin McNamara, the same supervisor who had disciplined Chung Huang last year for dropping his buckets of tea into the snow. It had been Will's fault that the accident occurred, but the Irishman had lashed his whip across Chung Huang's shoulders, nonetheless.

McNamara returned Will's stare and snapped his whip again.

"Come on, Buck." Will clucked at his horse and caught up to his uncle and Homer.

"You'll have to visit with your friend after *tools down* is sounded tonight," Will's uncle said. "You don't want to create trouble for him."

"I know. Chung Huang said he wanted to become a track-layer, and he's been successful achieving that position. I won't mess it up for him." Will looked back over his shoulder for another glimpse of the tracklaying crew, then urged the Morgan to keep up with the other two.

The three rode alongside the construction train, which resembled the one used by the UP. The locomotives pushed the cars loaded with rails and ties from the rear. Idling on the tracks a few yards behind the construction train, Will identified another train he knew belonged to James Strobridge, the Central

Pacific's construction superintendent. He remembered this train from his visit to Truckee, California, the preceding summer. Hanna Strobridge's converted boxcar occupied the last position in this train, as it had in Truckee. Flowers bloomed in windows she had cut into the sides of the boxcar. A canary twittered from a cage suspended above a narrow balcony that stretched along one side of the car.

"Well, goodness, gracious, look who's here." Hanna Strobridge, who'd been feeding seed to the bird, leaned over the balcony's railing and looked down at Will and his companions.

"Hello, Mrs. Strobridge." Will's uncle tipped his wide-brimmed hat. "Where might we find your husband this time of day?"

"I would imagine you would find him in the next train back." She pointed down the tracks to where yet another locomotive emitted smoke from its stack and steam from its cylinders. "That's Crocker's train. Stro will most likely be huddled up with Charley and Monty in the last car."

"Thanks," Will's uncle said.

"You going to be in our neighborhood for a spell?" she asked.

"Don't know rightly. It depends on how our conversation goes with Stro and the other CP folks."

"Would you join us for supper this evening?"

"That's kind of you, Mrs. Strobridge. It depends on whether Mr. Crocker will permit us to stay that long." Will's uncle chuckled.

Hanna Strobridge laughed. "Charley may be a bit gruff, but he's not inhospitable. I'll invite him, too. That way you can't refuse. When you see Stro, tell him I've extended the invitation."

"Very well. And, thank you." He tipped his hat again, and shaking his reins guided the horse down the length of Crocker's train toward a passenger car coupled at the rear.

When they reached the last car of the train, his uncle dismounted and handed his reins to Will. "I'll see if anybody's home."

Before his uncle could mount the steps at the rear of the passenger car, the door opened and James Strobridge stepped onto the platform. "Well, this is a surprise. Sean Corcoran and Will Braddock . . . welcome."

"Stro," his uncle said, "it's nice to see you again. Sam Reed sent us on behalf of General Dodge to talk about arranging a meeting place for completing the Pacific Railroad."

"Come on in. Crocker and Montague will have to discuss that with you, not me."

"Homer and I will wait here, Uncle Sean."

"Fine. Maybe Stro can recommend a place for us to pitch our tent for the evening." Will's uncle looked back up to Strobridge on the platform.

"Sure." He pointed to a row of tents stretched out several yards from the tracks. "That's our supervisors' campsite yonder. Pitch your tent at the far end."

"Homer," Will's uncle said, "you two set up camp while I tend to business here."

"Yas, suh. Come on, Will."

An hour later, Will's uncle rode up to the tent he and Homer had pitched at the location Strobridge had pointed out. Will stopped tightening the front guy rope on the wall tent as his uncle slid from the saddle. The despondent look on his uncle's face told Will the meeting had not gone well. Will took the reins from his uncle. "I'll unsaddle him for you," he said.

"Thanks."

Will stood holding the horse without moving and looked at his uncle. Finally, he raised his eyebrows in an unspoken question.

His uncle shook his head. "Crocker refuses to talk about a

meeting place."

Homer emerged from the tent and joined them. "He say why, Mr. Corcoran?"

"Seems Stanford is coming to Ogden in a few days to discuss the matter with Seymour."

"Uh-oh," Homer said.

"Leland Stanford, the president of the Central Pacific?" asked Will.

"The one and only Leland Stanford, former governor of California. The same one who's been negotiating with Brigham Young and beating us to the punch in contracting with some of the best track graders."

"General Dodge won't like this," Will said.

"You can bet on that. It's discouraging, to say the least. If I hadn't already accepted Hanna Strobridge's invitation to supper, I'd say we'd strike camp and head back now. As it is, we'll leave at first light tomorrow."

"Uncle Sean, if you don't mind, and if you think it would not be rude to Mrs. Strobridge, I'd prefer to not join you for supper."

"Why's that? You enjoyed the supper we had with the Strobridges in Truckee last year."

"I know, but I want to find Chung Huang and talk with him. If we're leaving in the morning, I won't have another chance."

"All right. I'll explain to Hanna. Going to be an interesting evening if she did invite Crocker."

"I'se gonna fry up a couple of steaks for Will and me, then," Homer said. "After we eat, I can start packing up for our return ride."

Will's uncle nodded. It was understood by all three that Hanna Strobridge's invitation did not include the black man.

After he and Homer had eaten, and his uncle had departed for his supper with the Strobridges, Will went in search of

Chung Huang. He inquired about the location of the tracklayers' campsite and soon found his Chinese friend.

Will and Chung Huang walked east from the end of track on the CP's graded route. Their footprints would not damage the surface like hoofprints. They brought each other up-to-date on what had transpired since they'd last been together.

"So, you say Mr. Crocker intends to put on a special show on how fast your team can lay track?"

Chung Huang nodded, the rim of his straw hat bobbing in front of his face. "Cholly Clocka has big plan for how we do it. I overhear him discuss with Mr. McNamara."

"You think the CP can really lay more track in a day than the UP?"

"I sure. We good at tracklaying. Even One-eye Bossy Man say that now."

Will grinned at the Chinese's name for Strobridge, who'd lost an eye in a blasting accident five years earlier.

The two youths stopped and turned to look back at the construction camp.

"I going to miss this," said Chung Huang. "It be fun. Hard work, but fun."

"What will you do when it's over?"

"I go to China."

"China!"

"I want to see the country of my ancestors. I want to tell them I worked on great American railroad. China will build railroads, too. I can help."

"China. That's a far-off place. I'll never see China."

"Why not? Come with me. Together we build great railroad in China." He laughed. "What will you do when Pacific Railroad finished?"

Will shook his head. "Don't know. At one time . . . long ago . . . I thought I'd make a lot of money working on the railroad.

Then I'd return to Iowa and buy the family farm back. But . . .
I didn't make a lot of money. Besides, I might be arrested if I
go back. Judge Sampson may still want to make me a blacksmith
apprentice. I don't want that."

"You think about coming to China with me."

Will smiled. That was a possibility he hadn't considered
before.

CHAPTER 35

"Welcome to Ogden, folks." Jenny held the Wells Fargo station door open and greeted a half-dozen passengers who had arrived earlier from Corinne on the train. "The stage to Salt Lake City will depart in an hour."

Four male passengers and one female stepped single file into the interior of the station. A final man leaned down to pass through the open door, but he bumped his top hat against the upper sill of the doorway, knocking the hat off.

Jenny grabbed the hat before it hit the floor and returned it to the passenger.

"Thank you, young lady," he said. The bearded, middle-aged man stood up straighter and his eyes widened when he looked into Jenny's face. "Oh my, I know you. You're Jenny McNabb."

"Why, Governor Stanford. I'm flattered that you remember me."

"I'll never forget that meal you prepared in Green River last December. Collis Huntington and his wife had ridden with me on the UP as far as the tracks then extended from Omaha. We were on our way back to Sacramento and boarded the stagecoach in Green River for the journey on to Salt Lake City. The Huntingtons and I marveled at how you could prepare such a wonderful supper in that out-of-the-way place. Are you going to be serving a meal today? I would certainly enjoy it."

"Yes, sir. Wells Fargo does not provide food service in Ogden. There are many fine restaurants available here."

"So, if you're not cooking, what do you do for Wells Fargo?"

"I help my father with the teams and the ticketing of passengers."

"Wells Fargo will soon be out of the cross-country stage business . . . with the railroads about to join up. What are you going to do after that?"

"I don't know. I've been thinking I might join my sister in Sacramento. She's opened a millinery shop there."

"Hmm. So you're not essential to the operation of the Ogden station, then?"

"Well," Jenny answered, "I guess if you put it that way, no. My father and brother could handle the teams and the passengers without me."

"Great! I have an idea."

Stanford smiled at her, but did not continue. To encourage him to speak, Jenny cocked her head slightly to the side and raised her eyebrows.

"I need a cook," Stanford said. "A chef, actually. I had a Chinaman on board my train who prepared decent meals, but he jumped ship so to speak when we reached the tracklaying crew and joined up with them. I'm looking for someone with the talent to create special dishes. When it comes time for the celebration to commemorate the completion of the Pacific Railroad, I plan to bring a special train from California with several guests. I want to feed them well. You could do the job. How about it . . . do you want the position?"

Jenny's father had finished hitching the teams to the coach and had entered the station in time to catch the tail end of her conversation with Stanford. "What's this about a position?" he asked.

"Ah, Mr. McNabb," Stanford said, "I'm offering your daughter a way to get to Sacramento faster than she might otherwise have thought possible. Of course, the job would require a brief return trip to Utah before she could permanently reside in California."

"Tell me more," Jenny's father said.

Stanford and Jenny recounted their conversation for the benefit of her father. He nodded when they had finished.

"Well, I agree she's a good cook," her father said, "and she has plenty of spunk, as well as the ability to look after herself. Still, she's not yet fifteen years old, and I would need assurances that she would be looked after and protected from any riffraff that might be encountered on the journey."

"Oh, I quite agree. You need not worry about that. She will be protected from any sort of trouble. In Sacramento, she will have the company of my wife. Whom, incidentally, I call Jennie." Stanford smiled at Jenny and bobbed his head. "Everybody else, however, calls her Jane, or Mrs. Stanford, as the case may be."

"Well, Governor," Jenny's father said, "I'll leave the decision up to her."

"Miss McNabb," Stanford asked, "what do you say?"

Jenny looked at her father, who closed his eyelids, smiled, and nodded. She felt a broad smile cross her lips. "Yes . . . yes, Governor Stanford, I'd be honored to be your chef."

"Excellent! I have to make a quick trip down to Salt Lake City to confer with Brigham Young. After that I will return to Ogden to discuss some business with 'Colonel' Seymour. Probably be a couple of days before I'm ready to head back to California. Can you be ready by then?"

"Yes, Governor, I'll get ready." She whirled around and headed for the back room where the family members slept. She had to pack her little trunk.

"Not so fast, young lady," Jenny's father said.

She stopped and turned back to face her father and Governor Stanford.

"There will be time to pack later. Right now, you still work for Wells Fargo, and we have a coachload of passengers to ticket."

"Oh. Of course, Papa." She felt her face flush, but she smiled anyway.

Her father and Governor Stanford laughed.

CHAPTER 36

Will stood on the platform of the Corinne depot with his uncle, Jacob Blickensderfer, and Samuel Reed. Reed had received a telegram from Dodge alerting him to the fact that Leland Stanford should be arriving from Ogden on the train.

"I don't like doing this," Sam Reed said.

"You don't have any choice, Sam," Will's uncle said.

"General Dodge makes it pretty clear in his telegram," Blickensderfer said, "that he expects you to put an end to this mischief right now."

Reed shook the yellow sheet of paper in his clinched fist. "Why didn't he send a telegram to the Central Pacific's headquarters in Sacramento? Let them take care of it."

"He probably doesn't want Stanford blabbing about his agreement with Seymour all along the route," Will's uncle said. "It might be harder to kill the deal after everybody working on the CP hears word about the agreement. That could put General Dodge in an untenable position."

"I agree, Sam," Blickensderfer said. "Best to end this thing sooner than later."

Reed sighed deeply. He looked at the yellow telegram once more. "All right. I suppose this is the best way. I wish I wasn't the one that had to confront Governor Stanford."

A long wail on an engine whistle signaled the arrival of the train from Ogden. The locomotive drifted past the platform, steam hissing from the driving cylinders, and a black cloud belching from the smokestack. The engineer clanged the bell a half-dozen times, and the wheels of the engine screeched on the iron rails as he brought the train to a halt with the single passenger coach aligned precisely in front of the station's waiting room.

Will had been watching the windows of the passenger coach as it slid past. He gave a start when he saw a black-haired girl wave at him from one of the raised windows.

"Jenny? Jenny McNabb. What are you doing on the train? Where are you going?"

"If we're going to be stopped at the station for a few minutes," she said, "I'll come out and tell you about it."

Will glanced at his uncle and the other two men who were waiting for Stanford. "There'll be time," his uncle said.

As soon as the train stopped, the stationmaster climbed aboard the coach. He quickly returned, followed by a medium-set man with a graying beard and mustache. Governor Leland Stanford touched the brim of his top hat as he descended from the rear of the coach and stepped onto the station platform.

"Gentlemen," Stanford said, "I don't believe I have the privilege of your acquaintance, but the stationmaster tells me it's imperative that you speak with me."

"Governor Stanford, I'm Samuel Reed, the UP's construction engineer. This is Jacob Blickensderfer, my assistant, and Sean Corcoran, my associate and advisor."

While Reed made the introductions, Will helped Jenny step from the rear of the coach onto the platform. "Jenny, I want to hear your answer to my questions, but if you don't mind I want to eavesdrop on this conversation first." He nodded his head toward the four men who stood a couple of paces away.

"All right." Jenny stepped closer to Will and slipped her hand into his.

"Sir," Reed said, "I have received a telegram from General

Grenville Dodge that he wants me to share with you." Reed handed the wrinkled, yellow sheet of paper to Stanford.

Stanford scanned the paper, a scowl darkening his face as he read.

"What's the meaning of this?" Stanford shouted and slammed a fist against the yellow paper. "I met with 'Colonel' Seymour yesterday in Ogden. I told him that I found the Union Pacific's tracks and trestle between here and Promontory Summit inferior in quality. Seymour agreed with me and said he would wire Dodge, recommending the Union Pacific accept the Central Pacific's line."

"As you can read in his telegram," Reed said, "General Dodge refuses to accept Seymour's recommendation."

" 'Colonel' Seymour told me he represents Doc Durant, your vice president and general manager. Isn't Durant senior to Dodge?"

"In operations," Reed said, "that's true. But in construction of the line, General Dodge is the Union Pacific's chief engineer and he has been given full authority by the government to decide what line is best. I'm afraid General Dodge's decision is the UP's final answer on this matter."

"Well I never! What do you propose I do now, Mr. Reed?"

"General Dodge sent this wire from Council Bluffs earlier today. He's on his way out here and should arrive in a few days. You can wait and discuss it with him. But, I wouldn't count on him changing his mind."

"Humph! I don't have time to wait around here for Dodge. I have to return to Sacramento and assemble my guests for the return trip to Promontory Summit for the ceremony linking the roads."

Stanford handed the telegram back to Reed and stalked back to the rear of the train. He passed Jenny and Will as he did so. He paused before mounting the steps into the coach. "You coming, Miss McNabb?"

"Yes, Governor. I'll be right there, as soon as I say goodbye to my friend."

Stanford disappeared into the rear of the coach. Will blew out his breath. "Wow! He has a temper."

"From what I heard them discussing, can you blame him?" Jenny asked.

"I suppose not. It's just that *'Colonel'* Seymour keeps making decisions that nobody on the UP likes, except probably Mr. Durant."

The engineer sounded two blasts on the whistle. The conductor stepped to the rear of the coach and shouted. "All aboard!"

"I have to hurry, Will. I'm going to Sacramento with Governor Stanford. He's hired me to be his chef on the special train he's bringing back with his guests to attend the ceremony he mentioned. I'll be able to see Elspeth while I'm in Sacramento, and maybe I can make a decision about whether I want to work in her millinery shop after Wells Fargo shuts down cross-country operations."

"I see. I'm glad you have the opportunity to be the governor's chef. And, it's also nice you'll have the chance to consider what you will do with your future."

"What about you, Will? Have you decided what you want to do after this is all over?"

"No."

CHAPTER 37

Governor Stanford's special coach glided to a stop in front of the Sacramento station. Out the left windows Jenny had a view of the waterfront business section of California's capital city spread along the east bank of the Sacramento River. From the right-hand windows she saw dozens of paddle wheelers, barges, and sailing vessels plying the river or tied to the extensive docks.

"We're here, Miss McNabb," Governor Stanford said.

Stanford helped Jenny descend from the rear platform of the coach.

"Thank you, Governor."

The two of them walked through a covered passageway separating the passenger depot from the freight warehouse.

"Miss McNabb, are you sure you want to go to your sister's store rather than come home with me? Mrs. Stanford and I have plenty of room, and you are welcome to stay with us."

"No thank you, Governor. I can see my sister's millinery shop from here. It's right there on Front Street." Jenny pointed across a wide street separating the station from a row of business buildings facing her. She had identified the street from a sign visible on the corner.

"McNabb's Fineries?"

"Yes, sir. That's what she named her store. I am most anxious to see her. She wrote that she resides in an apartment above the store. I'm sure she will find room for me while I'm in Sacramento."

"Well, all right. You can take the rest of today off, but I must insist you start work tomorrow. We need to prepare to make the journey back to Utah in a few days. You don't have much time to make out your menus and place your orders for provisions."

"I've already been making notes on my menus, Governor. It won't take long to finish."

"Good. Tomorrow you report to my office. If you'll look to the left you can see the sign for the Central Pacific Railroad Company over there on K Street. It's the white building right next to the yellow one that says Huntington & Hopkins Hardware. That's the business owned by two of my partners."

"Yes, I see it. Tomorrow, then. About nine o'clock?"

"Nine o'clock will be fine. Run along now. I'll have your trunk sent over to your sister's place."

"Thank you, again, Governor."

Jenny settled her traveling bonnet on her head, gathered up her reticule, and crossed the station's wooden platform. Other departing passengers, who had joined the train at various stops along the route from Utah, jostled her as they vied to signal hacks and carriages jamming the wide cobblestone expanse of Front Street.

"Miss! You need a ride to a hotel?" A driver perched on the seat of a hack shouted the question at her.

"No, thank you, I'll walk."

She slipped between two parked omnibuses and headed to a row of white-painted, brick buildings stretching between I and J streets. Each of the structures abutting one another down the length of Front Street sported a covered portico above its boardwalk. In the evenings, residents who occupied the upper-floor apartments obviously enjoyed the rocking chairs Jenny could see on the porticos. Her sister's store contained such a porch. Jenny thought it would make a pleasant place for her and her sister to reminisce about their past.

McNabb's Fineries rose only two stories and sat squeezed between much larger, three-story structures. Jenny stepped from the cobblestones up onto the store's boardwalk, crossed over it, and opened the glass-paned door. A bell tinkled. She entered the dimmer interior and saw that her sister was engaged in conversation with a customer.

"I'll be with you in a minute, ma'am," Elspeth said.

When she realized her sister hadn't recognized her, Jenny whirled around and pulled her bonnet down around her ears. She grinned as she kept her back toward her sister and pretended to be engrossed in studying a hat displayed in the window.

"I shall call for the hat on Tuesday," the customer said.

"It will be ready, Mrs. Forsythe. You can count on it."

"Good day, Miss McNabb"

"Good day, Mrs. Forsythe."

The tinkling sound accompanied the customer opening and closing the door behind her.

"And now, ma'am," Elspeth said. "What can I do for you?"

Jenny turned slowly around and raised her head. She smiled broadly.

"Well, I declare," Elspeth said. "Look who the cat dragged in."

Elspeth held her arms wide and Jenny cuddled into her warm embrace.

"Hello, Elspeth. I'm impressed with your shop."

"And I'm impressed with your appearance. If you'd shown up wearing your manure-stained coveralls, I'd have recognized you sooner."

Both sisters dissolved into laughter.

"How's business, sister?" Jenny asked.

"It's not easy, what with the new competition. You alerted me awhile back about Madame Angelique Baudelaire coming to town. She opened her millinery over on the corner of K and 2nd Streets. It's a much larger place than mine, and her French accent seems to appeal to the local residents more than my southern drawl. Plus, she has two assistants to help her. I do everything here myself."

"I knew she'd be trouble. I didn't like her when she said you wouldn't know anything about artistic design. Look at that hat in the window. It's gorgeous. Did you design it?"

"I did. And made it myself."

"Well, I'm sure business will improve once you can afford to hire some help."

"Perhaps you're right. I do hope so. But I'm remiss. What are you doing in Sacramento? The newspapers haven't reported the shutdown of Wells Fargo's stage business yet, or did I miss something?"

"No. It's only a matter of days, though. Then, Papa will be out of work."

"How is Papa? And Duncan?"

"They are well. They'll be coming on to California in a short while, I imagine. Although, Papa hasn't said what he plans to do. He's very quiet about the future. It's so uncertain for all of us now that the railroads are joining."

"The railroads joining isn't a bad thing," Elspeth said. "New residents arrive here every day, and when the railroad provides unbroken transport from the east, hundreds more will travel to California. But, we were sidetracked talking about Papa. You haven't answered my question about why you're here."

Jenny explained about her position as a special chef for Governor Stanford. "That job will end almost as soon as it begins," she said. "Then, like Papa, and so many others who have lived off the railroad construction, I'll be looking for something to do myself."

"Can you sew?"

"A little . . . and I'm a fast learner."

"Then perhaps your earlier observation that I could use a helper is the solution to both our problems. You can work here. Do you have any money saved?"

"Some."

"If you care to invest it, I'll make you a partner . . . a minor partner, of course." Elspeth laughed. "But at least you won't be only a worker. You interested?"

Jenny grinned broadly and hugged her sister. "Yes, Elspeth. I had hoped you would offer me a place. I accept. It will be perfect."

The door to the shop opened again with a tinkling sound. A burly man entered carrying Jenny's small trunk on his shoulder.

"Ye be Miss Jenny McNabb?" His Irish accent easily identified his origin.

"Yes."

"The gov'nor said to bring this over to ye. Where do ye want it?"

"Set it down there," Elspeth said. She reached into a pocket of the work apron she wore and handing the man a dime.

"Thank ye, ma'am." He tipped his hat and left.

"It's time to close up shop for the day," said Elspeth. She locked the glass door and turned the sign hanging on it so CLOSED faced out. "You grab one handle and I'll take the other. Let's take your trunk upstairs. And since you're the much better cook, you can prepare supper."

Jenny whacked her sister on the shoulder. They grinned at one another.

CHAPTER 38

"There's General Dodge's private coach." Will pointed at a single passenger car attached to the rear of a short freight train approaching the Corinne depot.

"And a welcome sight it is, too," Will's uncle said. The two of them, along with Sam Reed and Jack Casement, stood on the station's platform to welcome the Union Pacific's chief engineer back from his extended stay in the nation's capital.

Two short chirps of the whistle signaled the locomotive was preparing to stop. The bell clanged a half-dozen times, and the engine slipped past the platform, its driving wheels screeching as they ceased rolling on the iron rails, its cylinders spraying the loading dock with warm steam, and its smokestack belching a black cloud. The only other cars in the train, two boxcars, rolled by, followed by Dodge's passenger coach, which stopped directly in front of the depot building.

Standing on the rear platform of the coach, Dodge tipped his hat to the group who awaited his arrival. "Gentlemen," he called out. "Nice to see you all."

Conductor Hobart Johnson dropped off the rear platform and placed a stool beneath the lower step of the car's exit stairs.

Dodge alighted from the coach. "Thank you, Conductor Johnson," he said.

"My pleasure, General Dodge."

Dodge exchanged handshakes with each of the men who greeted him on the platform.

"General Dodge," Reed said, "if you would like to step inside, Lars Frederiksen, the new stationmaster and telegrapher here in Corinne, has put a fresh pot of coffee on the stove."

A few minutes later, Frederiksen served Dodge a mug of steaming coffee, then poured one for each of the others in turn.

"Nice to meet you, Lars," Dodge said. "Good coffee."

"Thank you, sir," Frederiksen said.

After each man had received his coffee, Reed handed a yellow sheet of paper to Dodge. "General, this telegram arrived this morning from Durant."

Dodge took the paper and scanned it. He frowned when he looked up. "All of you aware of the contents?" He looked around at the gathering.

"Only Lars and I have seen it," Reed said.

Dodge handed the telegram back to Reed. "You best read it to them."

ACCEPT BET OF TEN THOUSAND DOLLARS THAT CP CAN LAY TEN MILES OF TRACK IN ONE DAY. STOP. DODGE AND SEYMOUR WILL WITNESS ATTEMPT AND CLAIM THE BET FROM YOU. STOP. NAME THE DAY. STOP. DURANT.

"Any of you aware of this before?" Dodge asked.

Each man shook his head except for Will, who lowered his chin slightly, breathed in deeply, and exhaled. He raised his head to face Dodge. "I was, sir."

"You?" Will's uncle said. "When? How? Why didn't you say anything?"

"I didn't think it was possible. I thought it was an idle boast."

"How did you learn about it?" his uncle asked.

Will told them about his conversation with Chung Huang when he'd accompanied his uncle to visit the Central Pacific's construction camp over a week ago.

"Do you think they can do it, General Jack?" Dodge asked.

"It's possible. We've been receiving reports that their Chinese tracklayers are improving every day."

"Can we beat them?" Dodge asked.

Jack Casement shook his head. "It's not whether we could beat them, General. The problem is, we have less than ten miles of track to lay before we reach the meeting point at Promontory Summit."

"Oh, my," Dodge said. "That Charley Crocker is one sly fellow. He waited until he knew we wouldn't have the chance to best him before he made the bet."

The group stood silently, sipping coffee for a minute.

"Does Seymour know about this?" Dodge asked.

"I believe he should, General," Reed said. "The message was addressed to Crocker, Seymour, and you. I'd bet Seymour has already received his copy in Ogden."

From the table at the window overlooking the platform, the telegraph key clattered to life.

Frederiksen stepped over to the table and tapped out his call sign. In a moment the key chattered a few more clicks, then Frederiksen signed off. He scribbled the message on a sheet of yellow paper and hurried back to rejoin the group. "The date's been set, sir." He handed the telegram to Dodge.

Dodge read the telegram. "Tomorrow! Crocker's set the date for tomorrow, April twenty-seventh."

A collective sigh escaped the lips of all of the men.

"Sam," Dodge said, "bring Seymour up here on the next train from Ogden. Gentlemen, we all have a trip to make this afternoon. Don't want to be late for collecting Durant's bet from Crocker."

"This should be interesting," General Jack said. "I wonder if they can do it."

"Gather your gear together, fellows," Reed said. "We'll pick up a wagon and team from General Jack's camp at end of track, but we also need horses to ride from our end of track to theirs. Can you get five saddle horses on board the general's train, Will?"

"Yes, sir."

"We'll need six," Dodge said. "Braddock's going with us. He'll want to see if his Chinese friends can actually lay ten miles of track in a day."

"I'm sorry, General." Will spoke almost in a whisper. "I should have said something earlier."

Dodge shook his head and smiled. "Let's make this interesting, shall we, Mr. Braddock? I'll wager you this month's pay that the Central Pacific can't do it."

Will's mouth dropped open. "That means I have to bet against the Union Pacific, sir."

CHAPTER 39

In addition to the saddle horses, Will had loaded Ruby onto the boxcar before General Dodge's train departed Corinne. Will's uncle suggested they take along shelter and the ability to prepare meals. Homer joined the group, and in addition to cooking and eating implements, Homer packed two Army wall tents. The shelters turned out to be welcomed by Dodge's party, since they wound up camping at the Central Pacific's construction site for two nights.

Dodge's party rode the train to the end of track on the Union Pacific line, where they mounted their horses for the fifteen-mile journey to where the ten-mile tracklaying feat was to occur on April 27.

"Colonel" Seymour refused to ride horseback, so Homer borrowed a wagon from the UP's tracklaying crew and hitched Ruby and Seymour's horse to the tailgate. He had to help Seymour climb up beside him on the front seat of the wagon.

They had not ridden far when Dodge pulled his horse over beside Will. "I see you still have Buck. He looks to be in good shape."

"Yes, sir," Will said. "Buck's a fine horse. I'm lucky to have him. I have General Rawlins and you to thank for that, sir."

"Did you hear that General Rawlins is now President Grant's new Secretary of War?"

"No, sir."

"Poor man still suffers from consumption. I hope the

tuberculosis doesn't kill him before he has a chance to prove himself. The Army is lucky to have Rawlins at its head."

When Dodge's party reached their destination, Charles Crocker met them and apologized for an unexpected delay. A locomotive hauling one of the trains loaded with the rails and ties needed for the performance had derailed. Crocker announced he would reschedule the project for Wednesday, April 28.

Homer procured food from the CP's stores and prepared an evening meal for Dodge and his fellow travelers. The group sat around a campfire after eating and talked until late.

At sunrise on Wednesday, Will stood beside Homer in front of one of their two tents. Dodge, Reed, and Will's uncle conversed with Crocker and Strobridge alongside the CP's construction train about twenty yards away.

Homer laughed, his gravelly voice trailing off to an extended rumble.

"What's so funny, Homer?" asked Will.

" 'Colonel' Seymour." Homer pointed to where Durant's consulting engineer stood slightly away from the rest of the party, holding an umbrella above his head. "He was so comical on the ride from Promontory to here. I was reminded of them Pawnee scouts' poking fun at him when he paraded around under his umbrella at the founding of Cheyenne."

Will chuckled. "You're right. But this time, at least, he rode in the wagon. You didn't have to load all that gear he drags around onto his horse, like I did on the ride from Julesburg to Cheyenne. Whew! I had to wrestle that mountain of stuff on and off his horse twice a day back then."

The snap of a whip caused Will to look to the side. Approaching the gathering of railroad managers, Kevin McNamara flicked his whip a couple more times. "Top of the morning to ye, Mr. Crocker," he said. "And to ye, Mr. Strobridge. George Coley and his crew are ready, if ye are."

Strobridge flipped open his pocket watch. "It's seven o'clock. A good time to start."

McNamara spun around and cracked his whip as he returned to where nine Irish workers waited beside a flatcar at the rear of the construction train. "Ye heard the man!" he shouted. "Hop to it. Ye gandy dancers pay attention to George Coley's instructions. Ten miles . . . that's all ye've got to do."

Will had saddled the horses and now led them forward for his uncle and the other Union Pacific observers. Seymour had to ride a horse because Homer would stay behind to load the wagon with the tents and supplies.

"How many work trains have you assembled, Stro?" Will's uncle asked.

"Five trains of sixteen cars each are lined up from here to the west. Each train consists of sixteen flatcars loaded with enough rails and materials to build two miles of track."

"Now, gentlemen," Crocker said, "let's all follow along and watch a record being set for tracklaying."

A swarm of Chinese workers clambered onto the flatcars of the first train and commenced throwing rails and other materials over the side.

Strobridge had been looking at his watch while this took place. "Eight minutes flat to empty that train."

The first train reversed and left the scene, soon to be replaced by the next loaded train. While this exchange of trains took place, two dozen Chinese workers lifted half a dozen small handcars onto the track and transferred sixteen iron rails from the ground onto each handcar. They also loaded each car with a keg of spikes, a keg of bolts, and a bundle of fishplates—enough material to install the sixteen rails. While the handcar loading occurred, workers hitched two horses, each with a rider, to the handcar.

The horses pulled the handcar at a fast pace to the end of track, where the eight Irish gandy dancers, four on either side of the car, lifted each six-hundred-pound rail with tongs, walked it forward, and dropped it into place. An Irish supervisor with a wooden track gauge measured the distance between the thirty-foot rails to ensure they were exactly four feet, eight and one half inches apart. Meanwhile, on top of the handcar, a gang of six Chinese used picks to break open the kegs of spikes and bolts and cut the bindings on the fishplates. Another Chinese crew of six stepped in to distribute the bolts and fishplates alongside the rails, while the spikes were allowed to drop through the bottomless handcart directly onto the ties.

Will spotted Chung Huang in one of the crews engaged in distributing the spikes along the ties. Each thirty-foot rail lay on a total of twelve ties supporting it. After a spike had been dropped on either side of each rail on top of each tie, forty-eight new men with sledgehammers filed into position along that length of track. Twelve men on either side of each of the two rails hammered the same spike into place on each side of each rail on each tie. Then that crew of forty-eight shifted to the next thirty-foot section that had been placed by the gandy dancers, where they repeated the spike-driving process. There were so many workers clambering over each thirty-foot section of track that Will had trouble counting them.

Other crews swept in to place the fishplates into position, threading the bolts through predrilled holes to connect a length of rail to the preceding one. Following them, an additional crew swept in with picks and shovels to raise the end of each tie and distribute enough ballast beneath it to ensure it was level.

After the ballasting crew had completed its job, an Irishman whom Will thought resembled a preacher more than a railroad worker sighted along each rail and motioned members of another team to adjust the level of the track using shovels and tamping bars.

This breakneck speed continued all morning except when the tracks had to make a curve. Even this work was accomplished with what Will could tell was a record-setting pace. A crew of Irishmen supported a thirty-foot length of iron rail on wooden ties set near each end of the rail, then proceeded to beat the rail into the desired arc with sledgehammers.

A bell signaled a halt for the midday meal at one-thirty. The hundreds of Chinese drifted away to their individual gang shelters for their repast.

Will stayed close to his uncle and General Dodge as they trailed along with Crocker and Strobridge, who circulated among the work crews offering their congratulations. The eight Irish gandy dancers and their foreman were devouring their food when Crocker approached their table.

"Great work, men," Crocker said. "You've laid six miles of track already! You've earned a rest. I'll bring the next crew in for the afternoon shift."

"No! No!" The objection was voiced by all of the Irishmen simultaneously.

"Mr. Crocker," foreman George Coley said, "these men have voted and want to return for the afternoon work themselves."

"But aren't you tired?" Crocker asked.

"No! No!"

Crocker reached under the brim of his hat and scratched his head. "You sure? We don't want to fail to make the ten miles."

"They'll make it, Mr. Crocker," Coley said. "I've been working with this gang for a long time. They can do it."

Homer had packed Ruby and the wagon during the morning and had brought them forward. He had a meal ready for the Union Pacific observers at the same time the Central Pacific workers had broken for their midday one.

"I figured they's no use making you gents go backward to

find your meal," Homer said. "When I seen they's making right good progress laying track, I figured I'd best be moving the camp."

"Good thinking, Homer," Will's uncle said. "They are going fast. Will, your bet with General Dodge is looking safer by the hour."

"It seems so." He hated to see the Central Pacific set the tracklaying record, although he did wish his Chinese friend well in the attempt. But, he also hated the thought of losing a month's pay. General Dodge had really put him in a spot.

Crocker decided to let the morning crews continue working, and after the meal break the same Irishmen and Chinese returned to laying track.

At seven o'clock in the evening, Charles Crocker called a halt to the work. He looked at Strobridge and smiled. "I believe we've done it, Stro."

"Ten miles and fifty-six feet, Charley," Strobridge said.

"Now," Crocker said, "I'll have to pay all the men the four days' pay I promised."

"An expensive day's work to be sure," Strobridge said, "but we set the record, and that included slowing down to bend the rails for the curves. If the roadway had been straight all the way, I'll bet we could have laid fifteen miles."

"General Dodge," Crocker said. "I've decided to call this place Camp Victory. What do you think of our accomplishment?"

"I offer my congratulations. It certainly proved to me that the Chinaman is a good worker. There's only one problem."

"What's that?" Crocker asked.

"How do you talk to them? I can't understand a word they say."

Later, after Homer had fed the members of the Union Pacific party their evening meal, Will slipped away to find his friend.

"Congratulations, Chung Huang." Will extended a hand.

The Chinese youth grasped Will's hand and squeezed it. "Thank you," he said. "I surprised to have strength left to squeeze so hard." A broad grin creased his lips.

"I understand you earned four days' pay." Will didn't mention that he'd earned a month's pay off his bet with Dodge.

"It will help pay passage to China, where I can tell them I know how to build railroad fast."

After saying goodnight to Chung Huang, Will returned to the Union Pacific's tents.

The next morning on the ride back to the Union Pacific's end of track, General Dodge swung his horse up beside Will and Buck. "Well, Mr. Braddock, the CP laid their ten miles of track in one day. You won our bet."

"Yes, sir. I guess so."

"You'll have to collect later though. The railroad still hasn't paid the workers what they're owed. And now, Doc Durant has to pay Crocker ten thousand dollars. Be interesting to see where he plans to find the money to meet all his obligations."

CHAPTER 40

"Miss McNabb," Governor Stanford asked, "do you have all the provisions on board?"

"Yes, Governor."

"Good. Our guests should be arriving any minute now. I want to depart the station promptly at six. Do you have refreshments ready to serve?"

"Yes, sir. I've prepared an assortment of canapés, and we have champagne chilling on ice."

"You made canapés? What time did you arrive here this morning?"

"Five o'clock."

"Very good, young lady. I'm pleased that you are prompt. And speaking of prompt, here they come."

A conductor wearing a blue jacket and short-billed cap led a group of twenty people, all men except for one woman, out of the waiting room of the Sacramento depot. They filed down the platform past the locomotive *Antelope* and its tender, and a specially constructed subsistence car that resembled a short version of a baggage car, before reaching the Director's passenger coach.

"Conductor Dennison is in charge of the train today, Miss McNabb. You met him when you first came on board?"

"Yes, sir. He helped me store the provisions in the ice chests in the subsistence car."

"Do we have some chickens?" the governor asked.

"Yes, sir, a dozen laying hens in cages in the subsistence car."

"Good. We'll have fresh eggs for breakfast."

Stanford stepped onto the rear platform, lifted his top hat, and waved it at the approaching passengers. "Welcome. I am pleased you can all join me in this momentous occasion. Come on aboard."

Jenny stood in the background where she could hear Governor Stanford greet the arrivals by name as they mounted the steps of the platform and entered the coach.

"Governor Safford," Stanford said. "Congratulations on your appointment by President Grant to be the new governor of the Arizona Territory. On behalf of the Central Pacific Railroad, I thank you for the special spike you are providing. We will pick it up on our way through Reno."

"Thank you for inviting me, Governor," Safford said. "Actually, J. W. Haines had the spike made with a gold head and silver shaft." He pointed to the man behind him.

Stanford welcomed Haines, one of the three federal commissioners of inspection of the Central Pacific Railroad, as well as his two associates, Frederick A. Tritle, who was also a candidate for governor of Nevada, and W. G. Sherman, the brother of General William T. Sherman.

Jenny continued to watch as other guests filed into the coach and greeted Stanford.

"Judge Sanderson, welcome." Stanford shook hands with the judge. "I trust the Supreme Court of California can still function during your brief absence, Silas?"

"I'm sure they will do fine, Leland." The judge nodded at Jenny as he moved toward a cushioned seat in the rear of the coach.

Jenny shook herself away from the fascination of seeing so many dignitaries and scurried back to the tiny kitchen. She pulled the cork from a champagne bottle, placed it on a tray with a dozen crystal glasses, and returned to the seating area where she offered the bubbly drink to each of the arriving passengers.

"Mr. Hart." Jenny heard Stanford greet the last boarder. "I expect you to document this entire occasion with splendid photographs."

"I shall do my best, Governor."

Jenny knew Alfred Hart by reputation. He served as the Central Pacific's official photographer. She wondered if he knew Andrew Russell, the Union Pacific's photographer whom she had met last year at Green River.

"Governor," Conductor Dennison said, "everyone is present. The *Antelope* is ready to get under way with your permission, sir. We will follow the regular six o'clock eastbound train."

"Have we taken the necessary precautions to alert others that we will be passing today?"

"Yes, Governor. The *Jupiter*, pulling the regular, carries the green flag on her boiler to signal to everyone that a special is following close behind."

"Very well," Stanford said. "Let us depart."

As the train worked its way up the slope out of Sacramento and into the High Sierras, Jenny served her canapés, along with more champagne. The passengers closed the windows one by one as the warm air of the riverfront city turned cooler with the climb of the train into the forested mountains.

On particularly sharp curves, Jenny caught glimpses from the windows of the Director's coach of the regular train leading the way up the steep grade. Every ten miles or so, both trains stopped at a water tank and refueling station. The regular train gradually pulled farther ahead of the special as each engine took its turn at the resupply of wood and water. By the time they passed beyond Summit Tunnel and headed through the snowshed-covered tracks and intervening tunnels leading down the eastern side of the Sierra Nevada Mountains toward Truckee, she could no longer see the regular train.

Jenny busied herself preparing the noonday meal for the guests. When she had everything ready to serve, Conductor Dennison invited the passengers to gather in the dining area. Jenny served Governor Stanford first, and he smiled and nodded his appreciation.

The passengers completed their midday repast and returned to the coach seats while the train paused at the Truckee station taking on water and wood.

Dr. Harvey Harkness, editor and publisher of the *Sacramento Press,* and Stanford's personal physician, announced he planned to ride on the cowcatcher down the Truckee Canyon and enjoy the beauty of the river and the surrounding hills covered with pine and fir trees.

"What are you going to do if there's a cow on the tracks, Harvey?" Judge Sanderson teased. "Aren't you going to be cold?"

"No, Mr. Dennison has given me a buffalo robe." Dr. Harkness wrapped the heavy, furry robe around his shoulders with a flourish and exited the coach.

Jenny cleared away the dishes and washed them in preparation for the evening meal service. She secured the china and glassware in cupboards equipped with retaining rails that prevented items from falling—similar to what would be found on a ship.

She finished the cleanup task and wiped her hands on her apron. She looked forward to sitting for a time before she had to start her chores again.

Wham! Bang! Bang!

The deafening noise ricocheted down the side of the coach. Shouts and cries from the seating area added to the clamor.

Jenny grabbed the edge of the kitchen counter to keep from

being thrown off her feet. She slid to the floor anyway. Several pans clattered from the stove and landed beside her. She was fortunate to have stored the breakable items before the accident.

The train slammed to a stop. Jenny's head banged the cabinet behind her.

She'd managed to climb back to her feet when Stanford and Dennison rushed past and exited the car onto the platform separating the coach from the subsistence car. Jenny saw the conductor surveying the right side of the train.

"What's wrong, Mr. Dennison?" Stanford asked.

"It's a huge log, Governor. It's lying in the ditch behind us, but when it slammed down the side of the coach it tore the steps loose on this side."

Conductor Dennison squeezed past Stanford to reach the other side of the platform. "We'll descend on this side. We need to check the engine to see what damage was done to it."

Dennison jumped to reach the roadbed from the bottom step. He reached up to help Stanford make the leap down, struggling to keep his balance when the weight of the CP's president fell against him.

Jenny watched the two men hurry up the side of the baggage car toward the locomotive. She stepped onto the platform and leaned as far out as she could to see up the tracks. Dr. Harkness, who'd been riding on the cowcatcher, climbed up out of the ditch, brushing dirt and twigs from his clothes.

In a few minutes, Stanford, Dennison, and Harkness hustled back into the coach. Jenny followed them into the seating area so she could hear what had happened.

"Folks," Stanford said, "I apologize for this. I hope none of you were injured." The governor looked from one passenger to another to ensure they were all right.

Dr. Harkness continued to brush dust and debris from his clothing.

"Harvey," Stanford said, "I trust you are not seriously hurt."

"No," Harkness answered. "Just shaken up. I jumped when that log hurtled down the slope onto the tracks. The buffalo robe cushioned my landing. This is going to make a terrific story for my newspaper." He laughed.

"We let the regular train travel too far ahead of us," Stanford said, "and the Chinese woodcutters upslope either didn't see the green flag or ignored it. They should never have loosed that log from above if they'd known we were coming along. We'll get to the bottom of this matter later, but for now we need a new locomotive. The engineer says the *Antelope* can drag us into Reno, but it's damaged too badly to pull us all the way to Utah."

"What do you plan to do, Governor?" Judge Sanderson asked.

"The fireman's shinnying up a telegraph pole to make a connection for our key. Mr. Ryan, my personal secretary, has prepared a telegraph message to send down the line to stop the regular train. We'll take their engine onward from Reno or Wadsworth . . . wherever we can stop it. What locomotive did you say they have, Mr. Dennison?"

The conductor stepped farther into the seating area. "Number sixty. The *Jupiter.*"

Chapter 41

Paddy had gradually worked his way east from Echo City after Mort Kavanagh had fired him. He'd walked or hitched rides on Mormon farmers' wagons moving along the Union Pacific's right-of-way. He begged or stole food from the Mormon settlers wherever he could. On rare occasions, he performed chores in exchange for a meal.

When he'd reached Wahsatch a month ago, he sold his Bowie knife to a tracklayer for enough money to join in a card game. He played a reasonably good hand of poker, and after a few days he'd doubled his funds.

One evening, after tracking down the saloon frequented by the worker who'd bought his knife, Paddy laid low in a nearby alleyway. When the fellow staggered out drunk, Paddy enticed him into the dim space between two buildings and brained him with the butt of his revolver. After retrieving his knife, he stuck it into the man's rib cage. No need leaving a witness behind who could identify him. Not only had he gotten the Bowie knife back, but a search of his victim revealed a pocketful of coins that added to Paddy's growing stash of cash.

Now, two months after departing Echo City, he reached the railroad town of Piedmont, Wyoming. Similar to Echo City, Piedmont served as a staging area for helper locomotives required to pull trains westbound up the steep grade to Evanston and across Aspen Divide before the tracks dove down into Echo Canyon.

In Piedmont, the Union Pacific had an extensive array of sidetracks, as well as a roundhouse and turntable for servicing the helper engines. However, what impressed Paddy the most about the town were the hordes of workers who lounged about on the rickety boardwalks or staggered in and out of the four saloons. They were woodcutters and tracklayers who'd been laid off now that the railroad construction neared completion.

Two men slugged it out in the center of the street in front of Muldoon's Saloon. Paddy slipped up behind a ring of spectators who egged the fighters on.

"Sure, and why be they fighting?" Paddy asked the man in front of him.

"Don't rightly know. Just blowing off steam, I expect. Men have lots of time on their hands these days. No work. No pay. No future."

Paddy left the circle of men and entered Muldoon's. He stopped after passing through the swinging doors and surveyed the smoke-filled room. Men lined the bar shoulder to shoulder—most of them drinking draught beer instead of the more expensive whiskey.

All of the half-dozen tables were occupied. In the far corner he spotted a familiar face at a table with an empty chair. He worked his way through the crowd toward that table.

"And a fine good evening to ye, Brenden MacBride." Paddy placed his hands on the back of the unoccupied chair. "Might I be joining ye?"

MacBride studied Paddy from across the table. "Ye look familiar, ye do, but the name escapes me."

"O'Hannigan. Paddy O'Hannigan. We met in Wahsatch a few months back."

"Aye. Sure, and we did. Sit, iffen ye have money."

Paddy joined the group of seven other players and placed a short stack of silver dollars in front of him. He nodded at Collin

Fitzgerald and Liam Gallagher, two of MacBride's henchmen he recalled from an earlier meeting in Wahsatch. MacBride shuffled the cards and dealt. Between hands the card players groused about not having been paid for months.

After an hour of play, Paddy had only a handful of coins left—none of them silver dollars. MacBride had most of the money in front of him. One by one, the other six players had declared they were broke and quit.

MacBride tapped the table with the deck of cards. "One more hand, O'Hannigan?"

Paddy had determined MacBride to be a better player than any of the others at the table, including himself. If MacBride were to draw good cards and raise the stakes too high, Paddy could lose the rest of his money. "Sure, and I think not, MacBride. No hard feelings?"

MacBride laughed and dropped the deck of cards onto the table. "No hard feelings, O'Hannigan. Maybe another night."

"If these men are all going broke," Paddy said, "and there's no plan afoot by the railroad to pay them, why do they stay here? Why is it they haven't all up and left town?"

"Interesting ye should ask. Thinking back on the first time ye and I met, I recollect ye advocating a strike. Am I right?"

"Aye."

"Well, with the work ending, there be nothing to strike about. But, I got to thinking there might be a variation on what ye proposed. Come on down to the depot tomorrow. Something exciting is going to be happening in the morning."

The next morning, Paddy spent some of his remaining money on breakfast at one of the cafés. He sopped up the undercooked eggs with a crust of bread. Steam rose from the cup of coffee he held in front of him. At least it was hot, if not as strong as he liked. Looking over the rim of the cup, out the front window of the café, he watched men drift down the street and gather along the UP's mainline on the far side of the depot.

Several of the workers set about dismantling a stack of ties and piling them across the main track. In a matter of minutes, the pile stood shoulder high. The tracklayers and woodcutters were planning on stopping a train. Why?

Paddy swigged the rest of his coffee, placed the cup on the table along with a half dollar to pay for the meal, and pushed back his chair. He adjusted the Navy Colt revolver on his hip and departed the café. This must be the excitement MacBride had alluded to last night. He didn't want to miss it. He walked across the road and approached the depot building.

MacBride stood on the depot's platform observing the men building the barrier of railroad ties. "That be enough," he bellowed. "That'll stop any locomotive. Now get yer guns, fellas, and take up position along both sides of the tracks."

Paddy climbed the short steps at the end of the platform and slipped down the front of the building, selecting a spot behind MacBride. Collin Fitzgerald and Liam Gallagher stood on either side of the Irish foreman. At least three hundred men, some armed with rifles and others brandishing axe handles, flooded the rail yard stretching in front of the depot. No locomotives moved in or out of the nearby roundhouse. No regular railroad employees could be seen.

The wail of a long whistle penetrated the rumble of grumbling from the crowd of workers.

"Here she comes, boys!" MacBride shouted. "No killing! Won't do us no good if we kill the fatted calf. Ye men make sure nobody leaves the train, lessen I say so."

A locomotive pulled two Pullman hotel cars and a baggage car past the depot, gliding to stop where it could position the last car, a Pullman palace coach, directly in front of the station's platform. The engineer leaned out the cab's left-hand window, shook a fist, and shouted back at MacBride. "Move them ties off the rails! Don't you know this is a special train with Doc Durant on board?"

Fitzgerald and Gallagher raised their pistols and pointed them at the engineer.

"We know who's aboard," MacBride said. "Now if ye rest easy a bit, ye'll be on yer way again."

MacBride motioned with a sideways wave of his hand to a dozen workers who'd remained next to the pile of ties. "Take 'em away, lads."

The men made short work of clearing the ties from the track. Paddy kept his back pressed against the wall of the depot and watched a man step between the Pullman palace car and the baggage car ahead of it. The man used a hammer to knock the pin out of the link and pin coupler, then signaled MacBride by lifting the pin.

"Now, engineer," MacBride said, "move on. Yer passengers are anxious to reach their destination. All except Doc Durant and Mr. Duff, of course." He laughed.

"You can't—" The engineer stammered his objection but stopped when Fitzgerald and Gallagher cocked their pistols. The engineer grabbed the Johnson bar and shoved it forward. The locomotive belched a cloud of black smoke, the pistons hissed a burst of steam, and the engine inched forward. In less than five minutes the train disappeared up the track toward Evanston.

Paddy watched a half-dozen armed workers escort two men off the rear platform of the Pullman car. Paddy recognized the slender, stooped man as Doc Durant, the Union Pacific's vice president and general manager. Durant stopped in front of MacBride on the platform and raised his head. He stared at the Irish foreman with dark, piercing eyes from beneath a low-crowned, brown hat. He jammed his hands into the pockets of his black velvet coat.

"What's the meaning of this?" Durant demanded. "I'm supposed to be at Promontory Summit on Saturday for the ceremonies celebrating the joining of the railroads."

"Sure, and ye might still make it, iffen ye do as yer told," MacBride replied. "This being only Thursday." MacBride laughed again.

"What do you want?" Durant asked.

"Well now, me and the boys want to be paid, don't ye know. We reckon two hundred thousand dollars would do it."

"What! Two hundred thousand dollars? We don't have that kind of money with us."

"Sure, and I don't doubt ye one bit. But ye see, we have a telegraph operator standing by so ye can send whatever message is required to wherever to get the money here fast."

CHAPTER 42

Will sat beside Homer on a seat in General Dodge's special coach. They'd departed Ogden a half-hour ago, in a steady drizzle of rain, bound for Echo City. Will's uncle stood next to the Union Pacific's chief engineer going over a drawing spread out on the coach's dining table.

A middle-aged man with white hair and fluffy, white burnsides extending down his cheeks and well below the jawline sat at the head of the dining table observing the conversation between Dodge and Will's uncle. Unlike Union General Burnside, for whom the side whiskers were named, the man didn't have a mustache. His upper lip and chin were cleanshaven. Dodge had introduced him to Will as Sidney Dillon, a director of the Union Pacific Railroad and the head of Crédit Mobilier, the UP's construction company. Dillon had come west to participate in the ceremony marking the completion of the transcontinental railroad.

"Sean," Dodge said to Will's uncle, "I think we can enlarge the yard along here to accommodate more locomotives. After the Pacific Railroad is completed, I anticipate greatly increased freight and passenger traffic. That means more trains, and more trains means we need additional helper engines to haul them up the grade through Echo Canyon and over the top at Aspen Divide. I know you no longer have the members of your survey inspection team together, but I'm hoping you can do this."

"I can use Will and Homer to serve as chainmen on this job.

It won't be complicated."

Dodge looked across the table to where Will and Homer sat. "I suppose they'll expect pay increases for this work." He chuckled.

"That would be nice," Will's uncle said, "but I believe they'd appreciate receiving their back wages."

"You're right. But enough of that. It will be resolved sooner or later. In the meantime, let's concentrate on making this improvement."

"Expanding Echo City's railyard is just one of the improvements needed," Will's uncle said.

"How's that?"

"We're coming up on one of the weak points in the line, General. The trestle at Devil's Gate is so flimsy it can't stand frequent, heavy traffic. I'm particularly worried about this rain continuing and creating flash flooding out of the mountains. That trestle could be washed away."

"You're right about that, of course. I noticed significant swaying on that trestle when I headed into Ogden the other day. I'll make a note to address that issue as soon as we complete the joining up with the CP. For now, the bridge builders have their hands full trying to finish the trestle across the big gap so we can move trains up to Promontory Summit."

When Dodge's train reached the Echo City depot several minutes later, Elmo Nicoletti, the stationmaster, waited for the chief engineer on the platform. He held an umbrella above his head with one hand and frantically waved a yellow telegram sheet in the other.

Dodge alighted from his car, pulled his collar up to fend off some of the rain, and reached for the paper. "What's all the fuss about, Elmo? If you stand out here to deliver a telegram to me, it's going to be so soaking wet I won't be able to read it."

"You're not going to like this one from Piedmont, General

Dodge," Nicoletti said.

"Let's move in out of the rain." Dodge took the telegram from Nicoletti, who held the door open for all of the group to enter the depot.

Dodge shook the water off his hat, then unfolded the sheet and read the message. Will clearly saw Dodge's mouth drop open and his eyes widen.

"I was afraid something like this might happen," Dodge said. "I'm just glad it happened to Durant and not me."

Dodge handed the telegram to Sidney Dillon, who quickly scanned it, then passed it on to Will's uncle. "What are we going to do, Grenville?" Dillon asked.

"Send a couple of our own telegrams, Sidney. Come on, Elmo. I've need of your services."

Nicoletti went behind the ticket counter and handed Dodge a pad of blank telegram forms and a pencil. While the chief engineer scribbled his message, Will's uncle described to Will and Homer the contents of the Piedmont telegram demanding the ransom payment.

"Elmo, this first message goes to the commanding officer at Fort Bridger. I want him to bring a company of infantry up to Piedmont right away and put a stop to this nonsense."

"Yes, sir." Nicoletti took Dodge's message and returned to his desk where he busied himself tapping out the words on his key. After a couple of minutes, he looked back over his shoulder. "Done, General."

Dodge finished writing on a second page, tore it off the pad, and handed it to Dillon. "Sidney, we need to send this one to New York for Oliver Ames. The UP's president has to transfer two hundred thousand dollars out here right away. These workers are demanding more money than I have access to locally. Do you agree?"

"I agree, Grenville," Dillon said. "We need to get the money before the unrest spreads."

"Good," Dodge said. "Now, everybody must keep this quiet. If word gets out to the other workers, they may decide to take similar action. You gentlemen must hold knowledge of this to yourselves." He looked at Will, his uncle, and Homer.

"Of course, sir," Will's uncle said. He glanced at Will and Homer, who each nodded.

Dodge took the telegram back from Dillon and passed it over the counter to Nicoletti.

"There's coffee on the stove there, General," Nicoletti said. "You folks help yourselves while I send this second message on its way."

Will went to the potbellied stove in the corner of the waiting room and filled mugs for Dodge, Dillon, and his uncle. He served them where they sat on waiting room benches, then offered one to Homer, who shook his head.

"No, thanks," Homer said. "I likes mine sweet, and he ain't got no sugar."

Will poured a fourth mug for himself, then took a seat on a bench.

"Second message is gone, sir." Nicoletti called out from his desk, but he remained beside the telegraph key. "I can't understand why I haven't had an acknowledgment from Fort Bridger. There's been plenty of time for that message to have reached there."

Nicoletti's telegraph key clattered to life. Will stood and looked over the counter to watch the man copy the message onto a form.

Nicoletti stepped out from behind the counter and handed the message to Dodge. "We have acknowledgment of receipt from Mr. Ames's office in New York, sir. But I still haven't heard anything from Fort Bridger."

CHAPTER 43

Paddy stayed in the shadows, leaning against the side of the Piedmont depot, watching as MacBride motioned for his henchmen to take Doc Durant and John Duff into the waiting room. Paddy reached over and held the door open for everybody. He followed the group inside and found a perch atop a pile of cargo boxes stacked against one wall.

"Brenden MacBride," the stationmaster said. "You better make good on your promise. I'm going to have to disappear as soon as this is all over. I won't have a job with the UP any more."

"Stop fussing, me good man. I keep me promises. As soon as we lay hands on that two hundred thousand, ye'll be paid."

MacBride dictated a telegraph message that he wanted Durant to send to the Union Pacific's headquarters in New York directing that two hundred thousand dollars be provided as soon as possible.

"You'll never get away with this, you thugs!" Durant paced the floor while the stationmaster, who doubled as the telegrapher, finished tapping out the message about the ransom.

"Sit yerself down, Doc," MacBride said. "We may be here a wee bit."

"I would prefer to return to my coach."

"In good time. For now, ye stay right here . . . 'til we hear word about the money."

Durant collapsed on a bench next to Duff and ran his hands

back through his graying hair, then caressed the sides of his straggly goatee. His shoulders slumped.

Whatever the outcome of this escapade, Paddy had to give MacBride credit for his nerve.

The telegraph line stammered to life. MacBride left Durant's side and stepped to the counter. The telegrapher rose from his desk and handed a yellow sheet to the Irish foreman. "You want me to pass this one through?"

MacBride read the telegram, leaned over the counter, and grabbed the telegrapher by the collar. "Well now, what do ye think? General Dodge wants this message sent on to Fort Bridger so soldiers can interfere with what we're doing. Use yer head, man! No, I do not want this message passed on. Hand me a pad. I'll send a message back."

MacBride licked the end of the pencil the telegrapher gave him and scratched out a short message on the yellow paper.

"How does this sound, Doc?" MacBride read the words he'd written. "Sending soldiers will get Durant killed."

A sneer crossed MacBride's lips when Durant looked at him without responding.

MacBride handed his message to the telegrapher. "Send it to General Dodge in Echo City . . . seeing as how Doc Durant has no objection."

After the short message had been tapped out by the telegrapher, the depot's waiting room turned quiet, except for the ticking of a large wall clock.

A couple of minutes later, the telegraph rattled again. The telegrapher brought another yellow page to MacBride.

"Of course this one goes through. Hop to it man." MacBride handed the sheet back to the telegrapher who returned to his desk and tapped out the message.

"That one's also from General Dodge, but it be addressed to Oliver Ames in New York agreeing to the transfer of funds. Now we're getting somewhere."

"Can I return to my coach?" Durant asked. "I have a terrible headache."

"Not yet. Sure, and ye may have a bigger headache iffen we don't get a positive reply soon."

"This is robbery, you know," Durant said.

"Robbery? Now, how do ye think that? We're only asking to be paid what we're owed. We ain't asking for nothing that don't belong to us."

"The Union Pacific is short of funds," Durant said, "what with President Grant refusing to issue any more bonds until the railroads join. You would have better luck holding up the CP's train coming out of Sacramento. Word is Governor Stanford's bringing golden spikes to Promontory to drive into the last tie to commemorate the completion of the Pacific Railroad."

Paddy's head jerked up. Golden spikes? He'd heard how rich the Big Four owners of the Central Pacific would become from building their part of the railroad. Were they that rich they could throw money away in the form of golden spikes? Paddy wasn't going to receive anything out of the ransom being demanded here by the tie cutters and tracklayers. He was no longer an employee of the railroad. The UP didn't owe him any back wages. But golden spikes—now there's something that could make him rich. If he could lay his hands on those spikes before the ceremony, the Central Pacific would have to pay him a handsome ransom to get them back.

The telegraph jumped to life, and a minute later the telegrapher handed MacBride the message. After reading it, he handed it to Durant.

Durant read the telegram and handed it back to MacBride. "Fifty thousand," Durant said. "There's not two hundred thousand dollars available. So . . . that's all for now. But, you have my word you'll have the rest later if you let me get on my way, now. That's the condition the company demands for paying the fifty thousand."

"Fifty thousand as a down payment!" MacBride crumpled the telegram and threw it over the counter at the telegrapher. "Send back an answer that the fifty thousand better be here by tomorrow. Then, and only then, will we let Doc Durant go."

Paddy saw Durant's shoulders slump farther.

"At least let me return to my coach. My headache is killing me."

MacBride grabbed Durant by the arm and pulled him off the bench. "Come on," he said. "We'll all relax on yer plush upholstery 'til morning. I'll bet ye've even got good whiskey on board."

Paddy jumped off the cargo box and opened the door again for MacBride, who led the way as his two associates dragged Durant and Duff out of the depot.

MacBride called back over his shoulder to Paddy. "Join us, O'Hannigan. Not sure why I'm inviting ye. Maybe I like yer gumption. Aye, that must be it. Come have a stiff drink with me."

Paddy followed the group across the platform and into the Pullman palace car. His mind churned over how he could proceed to Promontory Summit and find the Central Pacific train carrying Governor Stanford and the golden spikes.

CHAPTER 44

Will had helped his uncle and Homer finish the surveying of the railyard at Echo City in the rain, then the three of them caught a supply train headed to Ogden. General Dodge and Sidney Dillon had departed in Dodge's special train the evening before, after word arrived over the telegraph that the ransom for Doc Durant had been arranged.

The heavy rains that were falling in Weber Canyon dissipated as the work train approached the flatter land around Ogden.

"Hey!" Will said. "There's Jenny." He waved to her from the window of the passenger car as it eased into the Ogden station. "I thought she was with Governor Stanford. What's she doing here?"

"There's your answer," Will's uncle said. "That's Governor Stanford coming out of the depot with Sam Reed. But how did Stanford get here? The tracks aren't connected yet."

After the conductor opened the rear door of their car, Will and his two companions stepped down onto the station's platform. Will hurried over to Jenny.

"I'm surprised to see you," he said. "What brings you to Ogden?"

"When we heard the kidnapping of Doc Durant would delay the ceremonies, Sam Reed brought the governor and some of his guests to Ogden on a work train. They're here to see the sights. I'm here to buy provisions. We're running out of food because of the extended stay."

Will studied a pile of cartons and boxes surrounding Jenny. "All this?"

"I'm feeding two dozen people three meals a day, Will. But, I'm not sure how I'm going to haul all of this to Governor Stanford's train. I hate to ask his visitors to lug groceries."

Jenny cocked her head to the side, causing strands of her black hair to escape from beneath her bonnet and shimmer on her shoulders. She straightened her head, tucked her hair back under the bonnet, raised her eyebrows, and smiled at him.

"Me?" Will gazed mesmerized into her unblinking blue eyes.

"I assume you're going to Promontory for the ceremony. If you're not busy here, perhaps you could go a little early and lend me a hand?"

Will felt a flush creep up his face. When she smiled at him, like she was doing now, he didn't know how to respond.

"I . . . ah—" he stammered. He blew out his breath. "How did you get all these packages here?"

"Father and Duncan helped me, but they have to stay here to run the Wells Fargo station. I could really use your help, Will."

"Let me ask Uncle Sean if he'll be needing me."

Will went over to his uncle who stood talking with Sam Reed and Governor Stanford. Homer remained silently beside Jenny. Will waited until his uncle completed his conversation and Reed and Stanford moved away.

"Excuse me, Uncle Sean," Will said. "May I speak to you a minute?"

"Certainly."

"Are you going to be needing me before the ceremony on Monday?"

"No, General Dodge said we've done all he had for us to do. Why?"

"You remember Jenny is cooking for Governor Stanford and his guests. She's in Ogden to buy food, and she's asked me to help her take it back to the governor's train."

Will's uncle studied the pile of cartons where Jenny stood. "That's a lot of boxes."

"Yes, sir."

"I don't suppose the governor or any of those dignitaries are going to volunteer to tote them. All right. Take Homer along. He has a strong back."

Will returned to Jenny and Homer. "Homer, you want to join us and carry some boxes?"

"Sure thing. I'se happy to help Miss Jenny."

"Oh, wonderful," said Jenny. "Homer, you can help me with the cooking, too." She smiled at the black man and wiggled her eyebrows.

"Yes, ma'am. I reckon I can do that."

Will and Homer loaded Jenny's supplies onto the work train preparing to return to Promontory. After the dignitaries had boarded and taken their places on the wooden benches, Jenny introduced Will and Homer to Governor Stanford.

"Pleasure to meet Miss McNabb's friends," the governor said. "Thank you for helping."

"You're welcome, Governor," Will said. "Sir, when we pass through Corinne, if you wouldn't mind, I'd like to bring my horse and Homer's mule on board. We'll be needing them at Promontory."

"We'll be making a refueling stop in Corinne, I suppose. Getting your mounts on board won't delay us. Is one of the cars in this train a stable car?"

"No, sir," Will said. "We'll load them onto one of the regular boxcars. That'll be fine for the short trip up to Promontory."

A couple of hours later, the work train stopped at the Union Pacific's end of track a hundred yards short of Promontory Summit. In addition to the UP's construction tents scattered alongside the tracks, several false-fronted structures had been erected at the site since Will had last been here.

Sitting on the Central Pacific's mainline, across the open space to the west, Will saw what had to be Governor Stanford's train. The locomotive named *Jupiter* had its steam up in readiness to depart. Parked on a siding beside Stanford's special, Will recognized Strobridge's work train. Stretching down the CP's tracks, on either side of the two trains, another tent camp provided living quarters for the Central Pacific's Chinese and Irish laborers.

General Jack Casement approached, tapping his riding crop against his boot. He greeted the Central Pacific dignitaries as they alighted from the workers' coach. "Governor Stanford," he said, "I hope the ride into Ogden and back was satisfactory."

"It was, General. Thank you for arranging it. Now, if we could borrow a wagon again to take us the short distance to my train."

"Certainly. I'll send one right over."

General Jack took a step away, paused, and looked back. "Will Braddock, what are you doing with the Central Pacific folks?"

"Helping Jenny McNabb. She has boxes of groceries to take to Governor Stanford's train. The wagon will certainly help."

General Jack laughed and walked away waving his crop in the air. "It'll be here shortly."

A few minutes later, Will and Homer stacked Jenny's boxes of provisions down the center of the wagon bed. Then, Will and Homer helped the members of Governor Stanford's party climb into the wagon where they found seats atop the boxes or on the wagon's sideboards.

Governor Stanford stood at the rear of the wagon with Jenny, Will, and Homer.

"I've decided to take our train back to Monument, Jenny,"

Stanford said. "It's thirty miles to the west. There's a nice view of the Great Salt Lake from there. I want to have a picnic along the shore for my guests tomorrow. It will be more pleasant than sitting around this barren place." He waved a hand to take in the ramshackle structures forming the beginnings of a station town at Promontory Summit.

"Governor," Jenny said. "I'd like to have Will and Homer come with me. Homer's a great cook, and he can help me prepare a first-rate picnic."

"That sounds fine, Jenny. And Will Braddock? What will he do?" Stanford smiled.

"Oh, I have something in mind for him." Jenny grinned.

"But we have Buck and Ruby to take care of," Will said.

"I don't have any way for you to take your mounts on my train," Stanford said. "But, James Strobridge will be taking his work train to Camp Victory later this evening to pick up more workers to bring them here for the celebration. You can probably put your animals on his train. It's only a two mile ride from Camp Victory to Monument."

"Great!" Jenny said. "That's settled."

Will lifted Jenny onto the tailgate, where she sat with her feet dangling off the rear. "Thank you. I'll see you both in the morning, then?"

Will nodded. "I guess so."

The governor climbed onto the wagon's front seat beside the driver. "Let's go," he said.

The driver snapped the reins and the wagon moved away. Will watched for a couple of minutes and waved one final time to Jenny before returning to the boxcar to unload Buck and Ruby.

What did she mean she had something he could do?

CHAPTER 45

Paddy sat by the aisle next to Brenden MacBride on the last wooden bench seat in the coach. Collin Fitzgerald and Liam Gallagher sat opposite on a rear-facing seat. Rain drummed on the roof and streaked down the windows. Keeping the windows closed because of the downpour intensified the humidity in the car from the passengers' breaths, clouding the inside of the panes and making it even more difficult to see out.

The fifty-thousand-dollar down payment of the ransom money had been received at Piedmont earlier that morning, and MacBride had divided the amount among the workers who'd helped with the kidnapping. MacBride then decided to stay close to Durant in hopes of keeping pressure on him for the rest of the men's back pay. Doc Durant's Pullman palace car was reconnected to the train, which had been brought back to Piedmont from Evanston, where the engineer had held his train awaiting instructions from the Union Pacific.

Paddy grabbed this opportunity to transport himself closer to Promontory Summit and the golden spikes. Claiming he worked for Mort Kavanagh, Paddy said he could arrange special prices for whiskey for MacBride at the Lucky Dollar Saloon in Corinne. MacBride, his henchmen, and Paddy had transferred to seats in one of the regular coaches and left Durant and John Duff alone in the comfort of the doctor's special car.

After a brief refueling stop in Echo City a half-hour earlier, the train had proceeded at a moderate speed toward Ogden.

Now it slowed. Paddy heard a long blast from the engine's whistle, and the train glided to a stop.

The door to the front platform of the coach opened, and a broad-shouldered man wearing a poncho stepped inside. Water poured from his gutta-percha rain gear and the brim of his hat, puddling on the floor of the car. He quickly surveyed the passengers.

"Folks," he said, "my name's Grady Shaughnessy. I have some good news and some bad news. The bad news is that the trestle here at Devil's Gate is partially washed out. It's not safe to take a heavy locomotive across."

A collective groan escaped the passengers. Paddy glanced sideways at MacBride who shook his head and sighed, expressing his frustration.

"Ordinarily," Shaughnessy continued, "the UP would back this train up to Echo City and ask you folks to rest there until repairs could be finished on the bridge. However, as you know, Dr. Durant and Mr. Duff are on this train, and they're already late getting to Promontory Summit for the celebration originally planned for today. I assume many of you are also heading there. So . . . here's the good news. We're going to push the passenger cars by hand across the bridge one at a time and couple them to another locomotive on the other side. Engine No. 119 is standing by over there to take you the rest of the way."

"That the best ye can do, Grady?" MacBride stood and called over the grumbling conversation of the other passengers.

"Morning, Brenden," Shaughnessy said. "I thought you fellows in Piedmont had been paid your ransom money and would be celebrating. What are you doing on this train?"

"Going to Promontory, that's what."

"That looks like Paddy O'Hannigan sitting beside you . . . if I'm not mistaken."

"Yer not. He be going with us as far as Corinne." MacBride sat down.

"I'd keep my hands on my wallet, if I were you," Shaughnessy said. "The UP fired that sorry rascal two years ago for stealing from the company."

Shaughnessy removed his hat and shook more water from it. "Now, folks, this train is going to back up about a mile to a siding where this locomotive will swap ends with the cars and push you back to the trestle. When you return, I want everybody to get off. You can leave your bags on board, but you passengers have to help push the cars one by one over the bridge."

"What?" "How?" "Why?" Questions flew at Shaughnessy from several passengers at once.

"Sorry, you'll have to get wet folks, but that's the way it's going to be." Shaughnessy put his hat on and left the front of the coach.

Paddy didn't plan to wait around for this foolishness to play itself out. He needed to head to Promontory Summit now.

"Sure, and I'm going to take a piss, MacBride," Paddy said. "Can't wait 'til we reach a siding." Because he sat on the aisle in the last row, he only had to spin off the seat to grab the door handle and leave the coach.

He jumped from the platform steps. When he hit the wet ballast alongside the track, his feet slipped out from under him, and he wound up sliding into the ditch on his butt. The blow of his feet striking the ground aggravated the bullet wounds in his leg. He rubbed the sore area, mentally cursing Will Braddock. Before he could stand back on his feet, the rain soaked him thoroughly. Mud coated his bruised and scratched hands where he'd used them to brake his slide. He winced from the pain when he wiped them on his vest. His bowler hat had stayed on his head, but it did little to keep his eyes free of water.

He stayed in the ditch below the tracks and headed toward

the front of the train. He'd only taken a couple of steps when the engine whistle sounded two short blasts, and the train lurched rearward.

"O'Hannigan, ye better get back on board, we're leaving."

MacBride leaned off the rear platform of the coach motioning to him. Paddy kept moving up past the cars toward the trestle abutment, which he could see ahead. The train moved farther away down the tracks behind him.

When he reached the abutment, he looked down into the raging waters of a tributary creek that flowed into Weber River. The trestle allowed the tracks to pass from a narrow ledge the UP had blasted into the canyon's wall on one side of the creek across to a ledge that continued on the other side. A crew of bridge builders worked below in the rain wrestling heavy timbers down the side to where several bents in the structure had been broken by the force of the flood waters.

Paddy swiped a hand across his face to clear his eyes of water. Staring through sheets of rain, he surveyed the wooden trestle, which stretched almost a hundred yards ahead of him. He would have to walk across.

He stepped from the last tie embedded in solid ground onto the first tie that lay across the trestle. If he slipped off one of the trestle ties, his foot would descend into open space. He knew he had to take his time and ensure he had a firm grip on the next slippery tie before shifting his weight from his back foot to his front. The rushing water pounding against the trestle's bents anchored in the stream bed shook the flimsy bridge beneath him.

It took ten minutes to thread his way the length of the Devil's Gate bridge. He blew out his breath when he reached the abutment at the other end. Only now, he realized how soaked his clothing had become. When he took a normal step along the right-of-way after leaving the bridge behind, his groin chaffed from the wet material that grabbed at his crotch.

Now, how was he going to get on to Ogden? Ahead of him, Engine No. 119 idled on the mainline. He could force the engineer to take him to Ogden, but that would attract too much attention. Grady Shaughnessy had announced No. 119 had been selected to take Durant to Promontory Summit. If this locomotive unexpectedly departed the scene, Shaughnessy would notify the officials in Ogden, and Paddy would be stopped. He had to find another way.

He spotted a handcar parked on a tiny perpendicular siding a few paces in front of No. 119. That's what he needed. It was downhill all the way to Ogden. It would take no effort once he had the car rolling. First, he had to move it onto the tracks. It was too heavy for him to lift alone.

Paddy approached the cab of the engine and shouted. "Hey, engineer!"

A man leaned out of the cab window and looked down at him. "Yes?"

Paddy recognized engineer Sam Bradford from when he'd been employed by the UP. "Sure, Sam, and I need ye and yer fireman to help me get that handcar onto the tracks." He pointed toward the siding.

"Why?"

"Well now, Grady Shaughnessy sent me to take the handcar down to Ogden with word ye'll be coming right along with Doc Durant's train. Don't ye see?"

"Why doesn't he send somebody up a telegraph pole and send a message?"

"Don't ask me. I'm just a worker, and I takes me orders. If ye want to argue with Shaughnessy, be my guest."

"All right. Come on, Cyrus. We've got to get wet to help this skinny runt."

CHAPTER 46

Jenny arranged the canapés on a platter. She planned to serve them to Governor Stanford's guests as their first course in the elaborate picnic he'd requested her to prepare. She opened the door to the oven and peeked at the loaves of bread baking on the top rack. The crusts of the loaves glowed a light golden brown, indicating they would be ready soon. Reaching into the bottom rack, she used a workman's glove to lift the lid on the pan where a dozen roasting plovers emitted enticing aromas. Some of the men in Stanford's party had shot a flock of plover along the shore this morning and had asked her to prepare them for their picnic instead of chicken. She inhaled the delicious smell, returned the lid, and closed the oven door.

The sound of hooves drew her attention once more to the two windows that allowed light into the kitchen of the Director's coach. She had checked repeatedly since sunup, but had seen no sign of Will and Homer. Now, they finally approached. She wiped her hands on her apron and stepped out of the kitchen. She crossed the narrow hall in front of the water closet and went out onto the front platform of the car.

Will on Buck and Homer on Ruby reined in at the foot of the platform's steps.

"What took you so long?" She looked down at the two with her hands on her hips.

"We've been riding," Will answered.

"Riding? From where? Promontory Summit?"

"No, Jenny. Mr. Strobridge didn't bring his work train to Victory until this morning. We waited overnight at Promontory. I didn't want to ride thirty miles in the dark. Not to mention it rained all night at Promontory. How about here?"

"A few sprinkles last evening, but none this morning. Governor Stanford has already taken his guests down to the lake."

Jenny pointed behind her to where a point of land extended a short distance out into the lake from its northern shore. A small rocky hill rose out of the water to a height of about fifty feet at the end of a slender spit of stony land connecting it to the point. Without the spit, the hill would have been an island, forming the only interesting feature along the otherwise barren lakeshore. The water of the lake lapped against the shore from a southerly breeze that wasn't strong enough to create whitecaps.

"Well, we're here, now," Will said. "What do you want us to do?"

Jenny grinned at the tone Will used to phrase his question. He obviously would rather be someplace else and had no idea what she had in mind for him.

"Homer's going to help with the cooking. You, Mr. Braddock, are going to help me wait tables."

"Wait tables!"

"You heard me. Tie Buck and Ruby to the subsistence car." She indicated the car coupled in front of the Director's car. "You can stack your saddles inside on the floor of the car."

Will led Buck over to the car and leaned forward to peer inside. A cackling sound emitted from the interior. He looked back at Jenny. "There's chickens in cages in there," he said.

"I gather the eggs each morning," said Jenny. "And I wring the necks of a couple of hens from time to time to prepare a meal."

Will and Homer slid from their saddles.

"Now," Jenny said. "Be careful where you put your saddles in the car. Don't ding that polished, laurel wood tie lying in front of the cages."

"Laurel wood tie?" Will asked.

"Yes, Governor Stanford is going to drive the golden spikes into it at the celebration. Then he'll take everything back to Sacramento and put them in some museum, I guess. Be careful you don't knock those fancy boxes off the shelf above the cages."

"What?"

"There are four cigar-like boxes lined up on that shelf. Each one contains a gold or silver spike. They're worth a lot of money. Be careful."

"All right." Will gathered up Buck's reins.

"Come in here when you're finished," she said.

Jenny reached to open the coach's door, then stopped. "Oh look. Here comes the wagon train." She pointed to the east. "Mr. Hart climbed up that hill over there early this morning when we saw them approaching. He's up there now, so he can take a photograph of the old-style train rolling past the new-style one."

"Who's Mr. Hart?" Will asked.

"Alfred Hart is the official photographer for the Central Pacific . . . like Andrew Russell is for the UP."

"We passed those wagons about a half-mile back," Will said. "Remind you of anything, Jenny?"

"Yes, it brings back memories. This has to be one of the last cross-country wagon trains anyone will see. Poor folks. They have a month more to go before they reach California. They should take those wagons back to Ogden, sell them, and ride the train. They could be in Sacramento in two days."

"I doubt they'd receive enough for their wagons to pay the fares for themselves and the freight charges for their belongings," Will said.

239

A few minutes later, Will and Homer entered the Director's car. "We can't all three fit into this tiny kitchen," Will said.

"*We* don't have to," Jenny said.

"Huh?"

"Homer and I will work in the kitchen. You are going to stand right there in front of the water closet while I hand trays to you."

"Trays? Aw, Jenny."

"Now, Will, you promised."

"Humph!"

"First, though. Homer I want you to go to the subsistence car and gather up some potatoes and onions. The sacks are on the floor opposite the chicken cages. Also, bring some lettuce, tomatoes, and radishes you'll find in one of the ice chests."

"Ice chests?" Homer said. "You gots chicken coops and ice chests?"

"Yes, Governor Stanford had the subsistence car built special for trips with the Director's car. It's equipped with ice chests for storing wines and fresh food."

"Where do you find ice out here in the desert?" Will asked.

"California imports ice from Alaska. Our ice has been on board for three days now, and it's melting fast. But, it should last through the ceremonies tomorrow and probably partway back to Sacramento."

"All right, Miss Jenny," Homer said. "I'll go fetch them vegetables. What you want done with them?"

"Fry up the potatoes and onions. They're to accompany the plovers you'll find roasting in the pan on the bottom shelf in the oven. Then make a tossed salad and be sure to keep an eye on the bread. I don't want it to burn."

"Yas, ma'am." Homer excused himself and left the Director's car.

"Now, Mr. Braddock." Jenny placed her hands on her hips.

"What?" Will shuffled his feet.

"You can't be a server wearing a buckskin coat and carrying a rifle."

Will glanced at the Yellow Boy he held in his left hand. He ran his other hand down the front of his fringed jacket.

"Hang your coat on the back of the door in the water closet and stash the rifle in here." She opened a door of one of the kitchen's cabinets. "And the pistol, too."

"My revolver?"

"These are civilized people traveling with the governor. You won't see any of them wearing pistols. What kind of impression would you make if you served them wearing one?"

"I'm not a server." Will stood straighter and pulled his shoulders back.

Jenny narrowed her eyes and concentrated her stare on Will's face. She felt her smile slowly crease her lips when she saw him wither under her gaze.

He shed his weapons and his hunting coat and stored them where she directed. "What if somebody comes in here and steals my guns?" he asked.

"Not to worry." She pulled a key out of her apron pocket, locked the cabinet door, and dropped the key back in the apron. "I lock my reticule in there with my revolver . . . along with what little money I have."

Will sighed. Jenny knew she'd won that argument.

"Now," she said, "put on this waiter's jacket and help me take the dishes and utensils down to where the conductor has erected the tent-fly. Then we'll return and pick up the food."

Will slipped his arms into the white waiter's jacket and struggled to pull the front together over his chest. "It's too tight. I can't wear this."

"Don't button it."

"Humph!"

"Here, take this tray of plates and glasses." Jenny handed a large wooden tray to Will. She giggled while listening to his continued grumbling.

"I haven't gone anyplace for two years without my Colt," he muttered. "I feel naked."

CHAPTER 47

Paddy had abandoned the handcar at the approach to the railyard in Ogden where he'd slipped onto a work train shuffling final construction materials up to Promontory Summit. The steady rain had kept workers away from the tracks, making it easy for him to climb into a boxcar. At the summit, he'd hidden out overnight in a tent with Collin Sullivan, the tracklaying gang leader who had helped him escape a pursuing Will Braddock in January along the banks of the Weber River. From Sullivan, Paddy learned Governor Stanford had withdrawn his train to Monument. He also learned the Central Pacific's James Strobridge made frequent runs with his work train between Promontory and Victory, which according to Sullivan was only two miles from Monument.

Early the next morning, Paddy had snuck onto Strobridge's work train. After reaching Victory, he'd located a picket line strung behind a row of tents occupied by CP supervisors. He almost got caught after he'd untied the horse he'd chosen to steal, and he had to ride away without a saddle. He'd ridden only a half mile beyond Victory when he overtook a wagon train. Rather than ride bareback all the way to Monument, he'd offered to give the last driver in line a quarter to let him ride in the wagon. The driver shrugged, looked at his wife beside him, and accepted the money. Paddy had tied the stolen horse to the tailgate and climbed into the back of the canvas-covered wagon. He'd ridden in the wagon only a short distance when Will Braddock and Homer Garcon rode past. He had been tempted to draw his Colt .32-caliber revolver and shoot them on the spot. But that would have given his hiding place away, and he first had to lay hands on those golden spikes. Then, he could worry about carrying out his vendetta.

Paddy lifted the bottom of the canvas next to where he sat so he could observe the wagon's progress as it rolled parallel to the Central Pacific's tracks. When Stanford's special train came into view, Paddy observed that Braddock's horse and Garcon's mule were tied to what appeared to be a short version of a baggage car. What luck. He'd steal Braddock's horse to ride after he found the spikes. He wouldn't need the horse he'd stolen at Victory anymore. Besides, it would attract too much attention if he tried to untie that horse now from the rear of the wagon.

Paddy slid off the back of the tailgate and lay flat on the ground until the wagon train had rolled on past Stanford's train. Then, he crawled to a large clump of sagebrush near the locomotive *Jupiter* and raised into a crouch to check his surroundings. If he didn't make any sudden movement, the concealment provided by the bushes should keep him safe. He removed his bowler hat to be sure it didn't show above the branches of the brush.

Two men descended from the locomotive and walked back past the tender. The older man had to be the engineer and the younger one the fireman.

"Mr. Booth," the fireman said, "don't you think we should close the subsistence car door? Those golden spikes are on the shelf above the chickens."

"Naw, Murphy. That wagon train's gone on by. They're the only people for miles around, and they aren't a problem now. Besides, Miss Jenny and those two fellows helping her need to keep taking food and wine down to the governor's picnic. And we're invited, so we better hurry down there before we're missed."

"Aw, George, do I have to go?"

"Yes, Murph. Come on."

Paddy's mouth fell open as the engineer and his fireman walked away from the train. They'd called it a subsistence car, they'd left its door open, and they'd told him precisely where to find the golden spikes. He clamped his mouth shut to keep from laughing out loud at his good fortune. To make things even better, Braddock's horse and Garcon's mule were tied to the car.

Paddy waited a couple of minutes before scurrying across the open ground to the subsistence car. He squatted down and peered beneath the car. The engineer and the fireman were making their way toward a tent-fly in the distance, around which gathered a dozen or so well-dressed people. That must be the members of Governor Stanford's party. Farther ahead of the engineer and fireman, a man and woman drew near the fly. They each carried trays. On closer observation, he identified them as Will Braddock and Jenny McNabb. That accounted for everybody except Homer Garcon. Where could that former slave be?

Paddy didn't have time to waste. He had to find the spikes. He climbed into the subsistence car and surveyed the interior. Two saddles lay in the center of the floor. The cackling of hens greeted him from cages along the rear of the car. In front of the chicken cages lay a highly polished railroad tie with a silver plate tacked to its center. He leaned down and read the inscription. Ah, they planned to drive the golden spikes into this fancy tie. A long-handled maul lay propped against the tie. Paddy lifted it and discovered its head was coated with silver. It was too heavy as it was, and he didn't have anything to saw the head off the handle. He dropped the maul onto the floor.

But there, right before his eyes, in plain sight, as the fireman had said, four boxes were lined up on a shelf above the cackling chickens. He lifted the lid of one of the cigar-box-sized containers.

"Wow! Sure, and ain't that something."

Paddy lifted a gold spike out of the box. He weighed it in his hand. My, it was heavy. Must be worth a fortune. He returned the spike to its box and opened the next one, revealing a gold and silver spike. The third box contained a silver spike, and the fourth box another gold spike. Four spikes in all. They should yield a tidy sum in precious metal if they were melted down, but the Central Pacific would pay him a lot more to get them back. He fished into a vest pocket and withdrew a note he'd written earlier demanding ten thousand dollars for the return of the spikes. He'd decided to demand twice the amount of money he had when he'd kidnapped Jenny McNabb. He lay the note on top of the polished railroad tie and secured it in place by positioning the silver-headed maul on top of it.

Paddy found saddlebags affixed to the saddles. He untied one of the bags from the saddle's cantle and dumped the contents of clothing and ammunition onto the floor. Paddy felt a smile crease his lips and wrinkle his scar. Once again he was going to steal Braddock's horse.

He was in the process of cramming the boxes containing the spikes into the saddlebags, when he heard footsteps crunching on the gravel ballast outside the subsistence car. He whirled around to see a familiar, black face looking up at him from the open car door.

"Hey!" Homer shouted. "What's going on in there?"

Paddy flipped the flap up on his holster to draw his revolver. Before he could lift the pistol free, Homer threw a pot at him knocking his hand away from the holster. Paddy quickly drew his Bowie knife from its sheath in his boot and threw it at his enemy.

"Ow!" Homer stumbled back, grabbing his left arm. Blood spurted from between the black man's fingers. The Bowie knife lay at his feet.

Homer dropped out of Paddy's sight, disappearing beneath the subsistence car. Paddy retrieved his pistol from the floor, grabbed the saddlebags, and jumped out the open door. He stooped, cocking his pistol as he did so, and looked under the car. He didn't see Homer, but he did see drops of blood on the ties and ballast. Paddy didn't have time to search. He returned the revolver to its holster, picked up the Bowie knife, wiped the blade across his trousers to clean off Homer's blood, and slipped the knife back into his boot sheath.

Not knowing where the African might be hiding, nor whether he might have a pistol, Paddy decided he didn't have time to saddle. He needed to move. He untied Buck and led him back to the passenger car. He mounted the bottom step and used it to heave himself onto the horse's back.

Paddy would have to ride bareback after all. He balanced the saddlebags across his lap and kicked the horse in the flanks, urging him down the side of the Director's car. He needed to stay away from the gathering of the governor's party down by the lakeshore, as well as the wagon train, which he could see moving farther away to the west. He pulled on the reins, guided Buck across the tracks behind the Director's car, and headed southwest toward the northern edge of the lake.

He jammed his heels hard into Buck and slapped the reins.

CHAPTER 48

Will stomped back up the gentle slope covering the two hundred yards from the picnic tent to Stanford's train in quick order. He gritted his teeth as he walked, shook his head, and muttered to himself. "Do this! Do that! Fetch this! Fetch that! Humph!"

How had he gotten himself roped into helping Jenny with this ridiculous chore of waiting tables on a bunch of Central Pacific dignitaries? He worked for the Union Pacific. What would General Dodge think if he found out Will was catering to Central Pacific folks?

As he drew closer to the Director's car he stopped dead in his tracks. He couldn't believe what he was seeing. Will could swear that was Paddy O'Hannigan who stepped off the car's front platform onto Buck's back and rode off down the far side of the passenger coach.

Will slapped his side. "Dang!" He didn't have his revolver. Jenny had locked it inside the kitchen cabinet. He jumped up the platform steps and jerked open the door of the coach.

"Homer!" he called. "What's going on here?"

Homer wasn't in the kitchen. Where could he be? The subsistence car, of course.

Will hurried back outside and jumped from the platform to the ground. He raced back to the subsistence car and looked in the open door. He peered into an empty space. "Homer?"

"Oh." A moan came from below.

Will squatted and looked under the subsistence car. He saw

no one. "Homer?"

"Will." A scratchy voice called his name from farther away.

Will sidled to his left in a crouch continuing to look beneath the train. He located Homer lying on the ties under the tender. Homer held a hand pressed against his left arm trying to staunch the blood flow.

"Oh, no." Will crawled under the car. "Homer, what happened?"

"Paddy threw his knife at me. I crawled under here to hide."

"So that *was* Paddy O'Hannigan?"

Homer nodded. "I surprised him stealing them golden spikes. He rode off on Buck."

"What's taking so long?" That was Jenny's voice calling. "Governor Stanford's visitors are getting hungry. Where is everybody? Will? Homer?"

"Over here, Jenny!" Will shouted.

Jenny's feet appeared alongside the track on which the tender sat. "Where are you?"

"Down here."

Jenny knelt and turned her head sideways to peer beneath the tender. "What are you doing under there?"

"Help me move Homer out of here. Paddy stabbed him."

"Paddy?"

"Yes. That's not all. Homer says Paddy stole the golden spikes."

Will and Jenny eased Homer out from beneath the tender. They leaned his back against one of the tender's rear wheels with his feet extended before him. Blood soaked the sleeve of Homer's shirt.

"We need to stop the bleeding, Will," Jenny said.

"And who's going to do that?"

"You forget I helped my mother tend wounded soldiers during the war."

"Oh, yeah." Will looked from Jenny to Homer, then back at Jenny.

"Shall we do it here, or take him into the passenger car?" he asked.

"We'd better do it here. We don't want blood all over the Director's car, and we might cause the wound to bleed more if we move him. Wait here. I'll run back to the coach and get a towel to bind the wound."

Jenny disappeared for a couple of minutes, then she was back with a towel and a butcher knife. She knelt beside Homer and Will.

"You're going to ruin that dress," Will said.

"I have other dresses." Jenny folded the towel into a long narrow bandage and used the butcher knife to slit both ends, fashioning ties for fastening the ends together.

"Cut the sleeve off his shirt, Will." She turned the knife in her hand and passed it to him handle first.

Will cut the material around the sleeve of Homer's shirt where it attached at his shoulder.

Homer groaned, still pressing on his upper arm.

"Sorry, Homer," Will said.

"No matter. Jest get it over with. Wish I had passed out like you did when I took that arrow out of your arm that time the Cheyennes ambushed us."

"When I give the word, Homer, you'll have to take your hand away so I can pull the sleeve off. Jenny's going to wrap the towel around the wound as soon as the sleeve's gone."

Homer nodded.

"Ready, Jenny?" Will asked.

"Ready."

"Now!"

Homer lifted his hand away, and Will pulled the cut sleeve down and off Homer's arm. He held Homer's arm up at the elbow while Jenny wrapped the towel around the wound. She knotted the bandage using the cut ends.

"Press on it, Homer," Jenny said, "to stop the bleeding."

Homer groaned as he applied pressure to the wound.

"Don't press too tightly," Jenny said. "It will continue to seep, but I think this bandage will stop most of the bleeding."

"Thank you, Miss McNabb." Homer sighed, and a smile crossed his lips.

"Homer, you can call me Jenny. I think we've been friends long enough."

"Yes, ma'am . . . I mean Miss Jenny."

"Now," Will said, "I have to go after Paddy to get those spikes back before Governor Stanford realizes they're missing."

"I'll ask Dr. Harkness to come up from the picnic area to check on Homer's wound," Jenny said. "My bandaging may be good enough to stop the bleeding, but a doctor needs to stitch that cut. It's deep."

"What are you going to tell the doctor about how Homer got stabbed?"

"Let me tell him," Homer said. "I'll say I come to the subsistence car for food, and when I surprised a horse thief, he knocked me down, and I fell on my knife."

"That's a likely story," Will said.

"It will have to do," Jenny said. "I'll wipe the blade against Homer's soaked clothes to put some blood on it."

"You could get in trouble, Jenny," Will said, "if the governor discovers the spikes are gone. You, Homer, and I were the only ones around when Paddy took them. Governor Stanford might think we helped him."

"Then you'd better hurry after Paddy and get those spikes back."

"If I'd had my Colt with me, instead of locked in that cabinet, I'd have shot the Mick on the spot."

Will looked into Jenny's blue eyes, which narrowed and turned to gray. When that happened, Will knew not to press his point.

"Bring me my rifle and revolver while I saddle Ruby," Will said.

Jenny fished the key out of her apron pocket and hurried back to the Director's car.

Will climbed into the subsistence car, and when he gathered up Ruby's saddle he noticed the scrap of paper under the maul on top of the laurel tie. He picked up the paper and read it.

$10,000 for spikes. Leave money in saddlebags at Monument. Take train back to Victory.

CHAPTER 49

Will cinched the saddle girth tighter on Ruby, who for once did not bray in protest. It was as if she knew she was needed to do something special. Her long ears splayed up and forward. Homer and Will had unsaddled their animals upon arrival earlier that day, but had left the bridles on to use the reins to tie to the subsistence car.

Buck's saddle still lay on the car's floor. Paddy hadn't taken time to place it on Buck. He was riding bareback. Will had seen Paddy struggling with a saddled horse the night the Irishman tried to steal Count von Schroeder's money last year in Wyoming. Will had not been impressed with Paddy's horsemanship.

Will stepped into the stirrup and mounted Ruby. He guided her back to the Director's car.

Jenny stood on the coach's front platform. In her hands she held Will's buckskin jacket, Winchester rifle, Colt revolver in its holster, and haversack.

She handed him the coat, which he quickly put on.

"What do you want next?" she asked.

"The Colt." He buckled the belt and holster around his waist. Then, he lifted the haversack over his head so it hung against his left side with the carrying strap resting over his right shoulder. Finally, he took the rifle and levered a round into the chamber. Holding the rifle in his left hand, he pulled the reins to the side with his right, wheeling the mule back to where

Homer sat propped against the tender.

"Which way do you think he'll ride?" Will asked.

Homer pointed to the west, down the length of the train. "He cut across the tracks behind the train. I 'spect he'll strike for the top end of the lake, then head south."

Will pulled on the reins again, turning Ruby around, and jammed his heels into the mule's flanks. Rider and mule raced down the length of the Director's car in a dozen strides. Will slowed her to cross the tracks behind the car. On the far side of the tracks, hoofprints showed clearly in the salty soil bordering the lakeshore.

"Now, Ruby, run!" Will kicked her flanks and slapped the reins. "Hyah!"

The land between the Central Pacific's tracks off to Will's right and the edge of the Great Salt Lake to his left undulated slightly. In years past, the lake had lapped against a higher shore, and when it retreated it left behind a wide bench of sand and gravel. Salt grass grew in profusion several paces above the lake's edge, replaced with pickleweed nearer the shoreline. A distinct line of dead grasshoppers stretched along the high water mark. A single set of hoofprints marred the surface extending westward. Will would have no trouble tracking Paddy.

Will leaned forward, placing his cheek against the mule's neck. "Good girl. You'll catch them. I know you can." Will alternated Ruby between a trot and a canter as she strode across the soft surface, her hooves sinking moderately into the crusted material.

Fifteen minutes later, Will rounded the northern point of the lake and turned south. A lone rider appeared on the horizon ahead of him. Paddy did not appear to realize Will pursued him. Buck could run faster than what Will now witnessed. Paddy obviously didn't know how to coax more speed out of the horse. Perhaps he feared falling off, since he rode bareback.

Will and Ruby gained a few yards on their prey every couple of minutes.

Finally, Paddy swung his head back in the direction from where he'd come. He jerked upright on Buck's back. He kicked the horse in the flanks and slapped the reins back and forth across the horse's withers.

"He's seen us, Ruby. Let's go!" Will copied Paddy and lashed the reins back and forth across the mule. He jammed his heels into her flanks urging her to a gallop. He didn't want to kick too hard and aggravate her normally cantankerous nature. "Come on, girl! Run!"

Ruby responded. She lengthened her stride. Now, they gained a few yards every minute.

Paddy urged Buck down the lake's western shore. Will remained low over Ruby's neck to reduce wind resistance. Ruby soon had them in a position fifty yards behind Paddy.

Paddy slowed when he approached a depression where a dry streambed entered the lake from the west. This depression near the shoreline provided the advantage Will needed.

"Whoa." Will hauled back on the reins and brought Ruby to a halt. He leaped from the saddle and knelt, propping his elbow atop his left knee and cradling the barrel of the rifle securely in his left hand. He sighted, inhaled, then exhaled slightly and held his breath. Make this a good shot. Don't hit Buck. He squeezed the trigger.

"Blam!"

White smoke engulfed the rifle's muzzle momentarily before the westerly breeze cleared it. Paddy's bowler hat sailed away in front of him. Buck continued forward, descending the slope toward the dry streambed.

Will levered another round into the chamber and stood. He wet his lips, drew a breath, and whistled sharply. *"Tseeeee, Tse, Tse, Tse."*

Buck jammed his forelegs into the ground and stopped, responding to Will's signal. Paddy lurched sideways, grasping for Buck's mane, trying to remain astride.

"*Tseeeee, Tse, Tse, Tse.*" Will whistled again.

Buck reared up. Paddy and the saddlebags slid off the horse. The Irishman crashed to the ground, landing on his butt. Buck whirled and trotted back toward Will.

Will, grasping the Yellow Boy in both hands across the front of his body, strode toward Paddy. When Buck reached him, Will patted the Morgan on the neck and straightened the reins to drop to the ground. "Good boy. Stay here."

Paddy rose to his feet, jerked his revolver from its holster, and snapped off a shot. A spray of dust erupted in the ground where the bullet struck in front of Will.

Will raised his rifle, aimed, and fired. He hit Paddy in the left thigh, the same leg he'd shot twice last year when they'd fought at Green Valley.

Paddy collapsed onto his knees, covering the wound in his leg with one hand. He fired another shot, which flew wide of Will.

"Drop the pistol, Paddy, or I'll kill you. You're not a good shot, but you know I am. I can kill you with this Winchester."

Both young men, now only thirty yards apart, glared at each other.

"Drop it, Paddy!" Will nestled his rifle snuggly against his shoulder and aimed at Paddy's chest.

Paddy raised his revolver and cocked it. "Sure, and ye're a no-good son-of-a-gun, Will Braddock."

The pistol jumped in Paddy's hand when he pulled the trigger. White smoke emitted from the barrel, accompanying the sharp crack of the shot being fired. The bullet whizzed past Will's ear.

Will squeezed the Winchester's trigger. The force of the

exploding powder bounced the barrel slightly in his grip. He continued to sight down the length of the rifle. The breeze cleared the white smoke from the muzzle.

Paddy looked at the hand he now held to his chest. Blood coated his fingers. Then, both arms fell to his side, and he dropped the revolver. His mouth fell open, and he toppled over.

Will approached Paddy, keeping his rifle pointed at the Irishman. When he reached the saddlebags—his own saddlebags—he knelt and picked them up. They were heavy with the weight of the spikes. Will flipped the bags over his left shoulder.

Two steps farther and Will stood looking down at Paddy. Using the toe of his boot, he pushed the Irishman onto his back.

Blood from the chest wound soaked Paddy's shirt and vest. Frothy slime seeped out of the corner of his mouth and slid down his face, puddling along the old saber scar on his left cheek. Paddy struggled to clear his throat, trying to speak, but he only managed a rasping groan.

"Why did you make me do that, Paddy? You didn't have to die. Why did you insist on carrying out your foolish vendetta. Your father brought on his own death. You should have accepted it."

Paddy's eyes bored a hole in Will as he continued to try to speak. His lips opened and closed like a fish on shore. He spit frothy blood from between his rotten teeth. Finally, he uttered a single word. "Mama." He breathed no more. His eyes glazed into a blank stare.

Kneeling beside his one-time enemy, Will used his fingers to close Paddy's eyelids. Will picked up Paddy's revolver and dropped it into his haversack. He slid the Bowie knife from Paddy's boot sheath and added it to the sack. Will noticed the corner of a wrinkled piece of paper sticking out of a pocket in Paddy's vest. He pulled the item from the pocket and unfolded an envelope addressed to: *Patrick O'Hannigan, Lucky Dollar Saloon, Utah Territory.* There was no return address.

CHAPTER 50

"What's going on here?"

At the sound of Governor Stanford's voice, Jenny looked up. She knelt in front of Homer, holding a cup of water to his lips.

"Homer's had an accident, Governor," she said. "I was about to come ask Dr. Harkness for help."

"Dr. Harkness is here with me." Stanford stepped aside, and Jenny saw the doctor. "We came to inquire about why there's no food down to the picnic?"

The doctor moved around the governor and looked at Homer and Jenny. "Homer, is it? That's a lot of blood. What happened?"

"I'se coming out to the subsistence car to get food when a horse thief knocked me down, and I fell on my knife." Homer held up the butcher knife.

Dr. Harkness glanced back at Stanford, then knelt beside Homer. "You fell on your own knife? Now, I've seen lots of accidents in my career as a doctor, but I never knew a grown man to fall on his own knife."

"Yes, suh. That's what happened. Will and Miss Jenny, they bandaged me with a towel."

"Where's Braddock?" Stanford asked.

"He's chasing the horse thief," Jenny answered.

"Hmm. Well, I hope he catches him."

"I do, too," Jenny said.

Dr. Harkness lifted an edge of the towel and examined Homer's wound. "Your bandage has done a good job containing the bleeding, Jenny," he said.

Homer groaned when the doctor probed the area around the wound.

"That's a pretty deep cut," the doctor said, "and rather wide. Fortunately, it didn't cut an artery. I need to put stitches in the wound. Jenny, in the coach you'll find my medical bag. Bring it and three more towels. Also, bring a basin of water."

"I'll be right back," Jenny said.

She hurried to the passenger car, found the doctor's bag, and stopped in the kitchen for the towels and the water before returning to the tender. "Here you are, doctor," she said.

"Homer," Dr. Harkness said, "I want you to bite on this towel." He folded one of the towels a couple of times and slipped it between the black man's teeth. "Good. Now, Jenny, help me unwrap his arm. Leland, you can lend a hand."

Governor Stanford leaned closer. "What do you want me to do?"

"Stand on the other side of him," the doctor said, "so the blood won't fly onto your suit. Support his back with your hand, keeping him away from the wheel so we can unwrap Jenny's bandage."

Stanford squatted on Homer's right side, eased him away from the tender's wheel, and supported his upper back with a hand.

"All right, Jenny," Dr. Harkness said. "Untie the ends of the towel and unwrap it slowly. I'll press this new towel over the wound to contain the bleeding."

It took only a few seconds to remove the soiled towel from Homer's arm. Blood flowed again from the cut.

"Seven or eight stitches will do the job," Dr. Harkness said. "Jenny, you keep this towel pressed against the wound and slide it back along the cut enough for me to apply the next stitch."

Jenny slipped in between Homer and the side of the tender

so she could reach Homer's wound.

The doctor inserted eight stitches, then covered the wound with a gauze bandage he took from his medical bag. With Stanford continuing to support Homer's shoulders, Dr. Harkness wrapped the black man's arm with the third towel and knotted cut ends together in the same fashion Jenny had used in making her temporary bandage.

"Leave that tied around your arm until you can get additional medical help." Dr. Harkness removed the towel from between Homer's teeth. "I assume the Union Pacific has a doctor who can check you over?"

"Yes, suh, they has a good doctor. And, suh, thank you."

"You're welcome." The doctor dipped his hands into the basin of water to rinse off the blood and dried them on the towel he'd taken from Homer's mouth.

"Now, Jenny," Governor Stanford said, "can we get some food down to the folks at the picnic?"

"Right away, Governor," she said.

"I 'spects I can help," Homer said.

"Only if Dr. Harkness says so," Jenny said.

"As long as you're careful," the doctor said, "those stitches will hold the wound together, but not if you put too much stress on them. No heavy lifting."

Stanford grasped Homer beneath his armpits and helped him stand.

Homer blew out his breath and took another deeper one. He winced. "I be fine soon."

When they heard the approach of hooves, Jenny and the others looked down the side of the train. Will rode Ruby up the side of the Director's car leading Buck. He held his rifle in one hand and the reins of both the mule and the horse in the other. Jenny spotted a pair of saddlebags draped across Buck's back.

She glanced sideways at Governor Stanford and Dr. Harkness

and confirmed their attention remained riveted on the approaching Will. She stepped back a pace to get behind the two gentlemen and signaled to Will with both hands to move closer to the side of the train. At least, that's what she hoped she was signaling. When Will looked at her quizzically, she again motioned for him to move to his right.

Will nodded. He had understood. He eased the reins against Ruby's neck and guided her to the right as he rode past the front platform of the Director's car. The move forced the mule to push against Buck, causing the Morgan to step up against the side of the subsistence car. Will halted Ruby in front of Governor Stanford, the doctor, and Homer, effectively blocking their vision of Buck and the saddlebags.

"You obviously caught the horse thief, Mr. Braddock," Governor Stanford said.

"Yes, sir." Will stepped from Ruby's saddle and stood in front of the governor and the doctor.

"Where would a horse thief come from out here?" Dr. Harkness asked.

"That passing wagon train, most likely," Will answered.

"And, what did you do with the thief?" Stanford asked.

"I shot him."

Jenny pursed her lips. "Oh, you shot him? Is he dead?"

Will nodded. "He's dead."

"Pad—" Jenny caught herself before she blurted out Paddy's name.

"What did you say, Jenny?" Stanford asked.

"Sad . . . it's sad," she stammered. "It's sad that Will had to kill a horse thief."

"Horse thieves have it coming," Stanford said. "What did you do with the body?"

"I left him where I shot him. I didn't have a shovel to bury him."

"I'll have Strobridge send some men out there tomorrow to dig a grave. Where do I tell them to find the body?"

"It's probably ten miles away, at the most. Have them follow the shoreline south from the north end of the lake. They'll find him a few paces up from the water's edge where a dry creek enters the lake."

"What happened when you caught up to the thief?" Dr. Harkness asked.

While Will kept the others engaged in listening to his explanation of how he chased down the thief, Jenny slipped between the subsistence car and Buck and retrieved the saddlebags. She tossed them onto the floor of the car and scrambled up behind them. She removed the four boxes from the saddlebags and spread them out across the shelf above the chicken cages.

"What are you doing in there?" Governor Stanford asked.

Jenny whirled around to see the governor staring at her from the open door of the car.

"I'm a . . . I'm a . . . selecting some cheese to go with the champagne." She reached out and grabbed a small wheel of cheese from a shelf and held it up.

"Something's not right about those boxes of spikes," the governor said.

"Sir?"

"That's not the order I left them in."

"Oh, it's my fault if they're not in order, sir. When I was gathering eggs this morning, one of the hens got out of the cage and flew up onto the shelf. I knocked the boxes off trying to catch her."

"Hmm. Oh, well. Let's get on with the picnic, shall we?" The governor turned away from the baggage car, grabbed Dr. Harkness by the elbow, and the two of them headed toward the lakefront. "We need some food down there right away, Jenny," he called over his shoulder. "We're starving."

"Yes, sir, right away. I just need to change my dress."

After Stanford and the doctor disappeared around the end of the train, Jenny plopped down in the open doorway of the subsistence car, her feet dangling outside. She let out a deep sigh. "Whew, that was close. Thanks for bringing the spikes back, Will. But, I'm sorry you had to kill Paddy. I don't mean I'm sorry he's dead. I mean, I'm sorry you had to be the one to do it."

"I do feel sorry for him in a way," Will said. "If only he hadn't insisted on carrying out that stupid vendetta."

"I should have killed him right here at the subsistence car before he rode away with them spikes," Homer said.

"What's done is done," Jenny said. "We're all better off with him dead. But, why do you say you feel sorry for him, Will?"

Will reached into his haversack and pulled out a battered envelope. "This is a letter from his sister asking Paddy to send money for their sick mother's medicine. Kidnapping you, Jenny, and now trying to steal the golden spikes were his way of getting money to help his mother."

"He was a deranged man," Jenny said. "Sooner or later, someone was going to kill him."

"I've been thinking I might send Paddy's mother that extra month's pay General Dodge owes me. There's no return address on this envelope, though."

"That would be admirable," Jenny said. "Unnecessary, but admirable. I suppose if it would help ease your conscience for killing him, Mort Kavanagh can probably give you an address. As I recall, he was Paddy's mother's cousin."

"Good suggestion," Will said. "I'll remember that."

Will lifted the flap of his haversack again and took out a Bowie knife. He grasped it by the blade and held the handle out to Homer. "You gave me the arrowhead that wounded me two years ago. I still use it as the flint for lighting fires. Now, I think you should have the knife that caused your wound. Call it a souvenir."

Homer took the knife and weighed the heft of it in his hand. "I 'spect I can use this where I'se going."

Jenny looked first at Will, then Homer. "Where are you going, Homer?" she asked.

"Well, now. I ain't said nothing to nobody, yet. Especially, I ain't told Mr. Corcoran. I ain't no quitter. So, I'se staying right here until this railroad is joined up proper like."

"You didn't answer Jenny's question," Will said.

"Texas," Homer said.

"Texas?" Both Will and Jenny uttered the word at the same time.

"Like I said. I ain't told nobody about it, yet. But . . . some days ago, I met a man headed to California after his enlistment was up. He been serving down to Fort Clark in Texas with the Twenty-fourth Infantry. Them's buffalo soldiers . . . black soldiers. When I told him my history, he recollected as how there's a laundress working there with the name of Mavis Garcon. And, she has a boy name of Billy."

Will stared at Homer. His friend had decided what he was going to do, and Jenny had decided to return to Sacramento and join her sister. The time had come for him to decide.

CHAPTER 51

Will extended a hand to help Jenny descend from the front platform of the Director's car. The early morning air at Promontory Summit imparted a chill. The rains that had fallen at the basin for the past two days had stopped, but the steps of the coach's platform remained damp.

When she reached the bottom step, Jenny's feet slipped, and she tumbled forward. Will grasped her around the waist as she collapsed against his chest.

"Oh," she said. "I'm sorry."

Will's face was so close to hers he found himself mesmerized by staring into her blue eyes.

She shivered against him. "It's cold out here, Will. But, you're warm."

Will eased her away, but kept his hands on her waist. He wasn't sure what to do. He looked her up and down. "That's a very pretty dress, Jenny. And a nice bonnet, too."

"Thank you. I bought the dress in Sacramento to wear on this special occasion. My sister made the bonnet to match."

She twirled out of his grasp, held her shawl away from her shoulders, spun completely around, and dipped into a curtsy.

"As I recall," she said, "this day is special for another reason."

"What's that?"

"Your birthday."

"Oh . . . yes. I'd forgotten."

"Sixteen years old today. You'll make quite a catch for some woman."

"I—" he stammered. He felt the heat on his cheeks.

"You're blushing, Will Braddock." A smile creased her lips, then she shivered again.

"Do you want to wear my jacket?" he asked.

"No, thanks. That buckskin would wrinkle my dress. I'm fine with my shawl, and once we start walking I'll be warm enough."

Will reached for her hand. "Come on, then. We don't want to miss the ceremony. I thought you'd never finish in there."

"I had to clean the breakfast dishes and put things in order for after the ceremony. Governor Stanford plans to invite the Union Pacific dignitaries on board for champagne and fresh fruit. I couldn't leave a mess."

Will led Jenny up the length of Governor Stanford's train past where the locomotive *Jupiter* huffed and wheezed at the end of the Central Pacific's tracks at Promontory Summit. They paused in front of the engine's cowcatcher to watch James Strobridge supervise a crew of half a dozen Chinese workers in placing railroad ties on the roadbed for a distance of thirty feet to where the rails of the Union Pacific ended in their reach eastward from the opposite direction. This space without rails had been left for the joining of the two halves of the Pacific Railroad. Strobridge directed his crew to remove the center tie in the thirty-foot run.

"That's where the laurel wood tie will be placed," Will said. "Let's go across to the UP side, Jenny."

He held Jenny's hand and guided her around clusters of workers who crowded in closer to the ceremonial area.

"Doc Durant's train is late," Will said. "General Dodge was complaining about it to Uncle Sean earlier."

"Durant's been the cause of a lot of delays," Jenny said. "Governor Stanford isn't too pleased with him, either."

After Will and Homer had helped Jenny serve the picnic food to Stanford's guests the day before, he and his black companion had ridden back to Victory where they'd put Buck and Ruby on Strobridge's work train. At dawn today, the train had carried a full load of the Central Pacific's Chinese and Irish workers up to Promontory so they could participate in the ceremonies.

Will insisted Homer go to the Union Pacific's doctor as soon as they had returned to Promontory. Homer's makeshift bandage was changed for a regular one. Will could tell he was still in pain, but Homer refused to stay in the hospital tent. Homer did not want to miss out on the celebration.

Will guided Jenny through the crowd accumulating around the space between the two ends of track.

"I don't see many women," Jenny said.

"You're one of the few. I know Sam Reed brought his wife and daughter. And Mrs. Strobridge is here with her daughter. But, there aren't many."

"Then, this is a special day for me," Jenny said.

"There's Uncle Sean and Homer with General Dodge," Will said. "Let's join them." He pulled on Jenny's hand and led her through the growing throng.

Clean-shaven Chinese workers spread out along the CP's tracks dressed in blue frocks, their pigtails extending from beneath woven straw hats. Bearded Irishmen, Germans, and assorted other nationalities wore suits and ties, which didn't do much to enhance their appearance. Their heads covered with bowler and slouch hats, the Caucasians crowded in from the UP's tracks. A battalion of the Twenty-first Infantry, on their way to the Presidio of San Francisco, adjusted their alignment along the west side of the ceremonial area. Their crisp, blue uniforms, and the gleam of their bayoneted rifles, added a semblance of order to the pending proceedings.

"Hello, Miss McNabb." General Dodge doffed his hat and

bowed slightly. "Nice to see you."

"Nice to see you again, too, General."

Will dropped Jenny's hand, returning his own to his side. He saw her glance at her now abandoned hand. She looked back up at him and grinned. He felt himself blush, again.

"Ah," Dodge said, "here comes Strobridge and Montague."

The two Central Pacific supervisors approached from the CP's construction train he and Homer had ridden earlier that day.

Jenny nudged Will with her elbow. "I recognize Mr. Strobridge. Who's the other gentleman?"

"Samuel Montague," he answered. "I met him last year in California. He's General Dodge's counterpart for the CP."

"I thought Strobridge was."

"No, he's General Jack's counterpart."

Will, Jenny, and Homer stepped back a ways, but remained within hearing distance, while Strobridge and Montague shook hands and exchanged greetings with Dodge and Will's uncle.

"Where's Charlie?" Dodge asked.

"Crocker went back to Sacramento," Montague answered. "He said he had his celebration when he finished laying the ten miles of track."

Dodge laughed. "Yes, he got us on that one."

"And where's Brigham Young?" Strobridge asked. "I expected to see the Mormon leader joining the festivities."

"I think he's still smarting over the railroad bypassing Salt Lake City," Dodge said. "He claimed to have business elsewhere in the state and sent Bishop John Sharp and some others to represent the Mormons."

"Interesting," Strobridge said. "Sharp would probably have been here anyway. Doesn't his company do grading for the UP?"

"Yes," Dodge answered with a smile.

A long, wailing whistle from the east caused all heads to turn to observe the approach of Durant's train. The military band accompanying the Twenty-first Infantry struck up a march. Will watched several Irish workers raise bottles to their lips. They sipped the liquor, then elevated the bottles in a salute to the arriving Union Pacific train. Will glanced in the direction of the Central Pacific's gathering. The Chinese stood silently, isolated in their own group.

As soon as the march music ended, the Tenth Ward Band from Ogden broke into a lilting waltz. The shouting and cheering from the Union Pacific's crowd drowned out the music as Engine No. 119 hissed to a stop at the end of the UP's track. Doc Durant and his accompanying dignitaries had arrived.

"Look, Will," Jenny said. "That's Mr. Russell stepping off the train, isn't it?"

"Yes. He'll be photographing the ceremonies for the UP, like Mr. Hart will be doing for the CP. Let's go, Jenny. I can lend him a hand setting up his camera." Will grabbed Jenny's hand again and led her in the direction of Durant's train.

Another whistle announced the arrival of a second Union Pacific train. General Jack Casement's construction train eased to a halt behind Durant's Pullman palace car. More workers streamed from the construction train's cars and swelled the crowd to even greater numbers.

"There must be five or six hundred people here, Jenny. Hold on to me. We don't want to become separated. I might not find you again." Will gripped her hand tighter and pulled her along behind him. They fought their way against the surge of men who moved in the opposite direction intent on getting closer to the area separating the two ceremonial locomotives.

"Mr. Russell!" Will waved a hand and tried to shout over the cheering congregation of tracklayers and graders who flowed past Jenny and him. "Mr. Russell!"

Andrew Russell finally looked Will's way from the rear platform of Durant's special coach and raised a hand in greeting. "Ah, Mr. Braddock . . . and Miss McNabb."

"I'm flattered you remember, sir," Jenny said.

"I've been known to recall the names of pretty girls." Russell touched the brim of his hat and gave Jenny a broad smile as he stepped down from the platform.

"Can we help you set up, sir?" Will asked.

"Why, that would be nice. Certainly."

"Oh, look, Will." Jenny tugged on his arm to attract his attention and pointed around the rear of the passenger car to the opposite side of the tracks. "There's a Wells Fargo mud wagon. Duncan's riding in the driver's box, and Butch Cartwright's driving. I'm glad she came. But, where's Papa? Oh, there he is, inside the wagon. They've come to see the celebration."

The mud wagon rocked to a stop next to a small tent bearing a sign for Wells, Fargo & Company. Jenny's brother stood up in the box and waved frantically. Duncan had spotted her.

"Will, I'm going to go over to them."

"You sure you'll be all right in this crowd?"

"I'll be fine. It's only a few yards on the other side of the tracks. Most of the crowd has gone past us already. As soon as Papa finishes his business over there, I'll bring them all back here."

"Be careful. Don't let any of the drunks knock you down."

Jenny leaned up on her tiptoes, pecked a kiss on his cheek, and dashed across the tracks. Will felt his face turn warm. He forced himself to close his mouth.

"Are you ready to start?" Russell winked at him.

Will knew his face must be red. "Yes, sir."

Before Will and Russell could mount the steps into the coach, Doc Durant, wearing a black, velvet jacket, emerged from the rear door. He descended from the platform and brushed past

271

Will without speaking. He paused when he saw Russell.

"Be sure you take good photographs of all the events, Mr. Russell. This is an historic event, and the Union Pacific will want it recorded for posterity."

"Certainly, sir. I will do my best."

"See to it that you do." Durant removed his low-crowned, brown hat, and ran his hand up across his forehead and back through his graying hair. "I have a splitting headache, and the noise from this crowd isn't helping. I hope this ceremony doesn't take long. I want to get back on board."

Will noticed Russell shake his head as Durant moved away. John Duff, Sidney Dillon, and Silas Seymour appeared on the rear platform. Will and Russell stepped aside again to let the two directors and the consulting engineer descend and follow after Durant.

"I think the way's clear, now, Mr. Braddock. Let's gather up my gear."

Twenty minutes later, Russell ducked his head beneath the black curtain at the rear of his camera to make necessary adjustments. Will stood to one side holding a wet plate ready to hand to the photographer.

"Will, I'm back . . . as promised." Jenny's voice drew his attention to her approach. Her father, Duncan, and Butch walked up with her.

"Hello, Will," Jenny's father said. "She told me how you and Homer helped her serve the picnic. Thank you for that. I'll bet that was a sight to see . . . white jacket and all."

Will smiled when Alistair McNabb laughed heartily.

"I hope I don't have to do that again any time soon," Will said. "Welcome to the ceremonies, Mr. McNabb."

"Looks like they're about ready to start, Pa," Duncan said. "That's Mr. Shilling, the telegrapher from Western Union's

Ogden office. He's set up a special telegraph line next to the locomotives. I'd like to go see how he rigged it."

"Go ahead," McNabb said. "Be careful, though. You don't want to be trampled by that noisy throng."

Duncan ran off to where a single pole had been erected beside a table on which a telegraph key could be seen. A wire led from the pole to the main telegraph line on the other side of Engine No. 119. Another wire led from the telegraph key to a sledgehammer propped against the table. Some brave soul climbed the pole, stood on the cross bar, and tied an American flag to the top. The stiff breeze drove the fly horizontal, revealing thirty-seven white stars in the blue canton.

A trumpeter with the Army band blared a flourish. From where Will stood near Russell's camera, he could see that members of the group of dignitaries assembled in the space between the two facing locomotives were addressing the gathering. The noise from the crowd precluded him from hearing the words being spoken.

Duncan raced back to rejoin his family, and Will listened to Duncan explain what was planned.

"Mr. Shilling has wired his key to the head of that sledgehammer. The telegraph line has been cleared between here and Washington City, so President Grant will know immediately when the railroads are joined. Mr. Shilling will tap out three dots when they begin driving the spike, then the hammer will automatically signal each blow to the spike."

Will assumed the dignitaries were now listening to a prayer, because they had removed their hats and bowed their heads. The roar from the crowd continued to make it impossible to hear.

A couple of minutes passed before the hats were returned to the heads of the group of men standing between the locomotives.

"What are they doing, Will?" Alistair McNabb shouted his question.

Will turned his head back toward McNabb and raised his voice to be heard. "That's Mr. Reed and Mr. Strobridge placing the laurel tie. I saw it on Governor Stanford's train. It has holes already drilled in it to accept the four special spikes."

As soon as Reed and Strobridge stepped away from the special tie, a Chinese team dropped a thirty-foot iron rail into place and an Irish team dropped the opposite one. Then, both tracklaying teams moved back into the crowd.

"That's Dr. Harkness," Jenny said, "presenting the two golden spikes from California to Doc Durant."

Durant bent and slid the spikes into holes in the tie on each side of the near rail.

"Who're those men, Jenny?" Will asked. "I recognize them from the picnic, but I don't know who they are."

"The one on the left is Mr. Tritle. He's one of the government's railroad inspectors. The other man is Governor Safford of Arizona. They're presenting the gold and silver spikes from Nevada and Arizona to Governor Stanford."

Stanford knelt and slipped the remaining ceremonial spikes into the predrilled holes on either side of the far rail. Stanford lifted the silver-headed maul and touched the tops of each of the four precious metal spikes. He passed the hammer to Durant, who repeated the process.

Both engineers blew their respective locomotive's whistles and clanged their bells. The spectators tossed hats into the hair, slapped one another on the back, and shouted louder.

A worker extracted the special spikes and placed them back in their boxes, while a couple of workers removed the laurel tie and replaced it with a regular pine tie. Two other workers dropped ordinary iron spikes into holes that had been drilled into the regular wooden tie.

"Here's where the telegraph will signal the driving of the final spike," Duncan said.

Stanford lifted the wired sledgehammer and swung at the spike. He missed. A roar of laughter emerged from the crowd nearest the ceremony. Those farther away could see nothing. Next, Durant picked up the hammer and took a swing. He missed. A louder roar of laughter erupted. Reed and Strobridge stepped forward with their own sledgehammers and took alternating swings at the spike, driving it home.

"I was watching Mr. Shilling," Duncan said. "When they missed hitting the spike, I saw him tap out D-O-N-E on his key."

"So," his father said, "the fancy wiring job didn't work?"

"No, sir," Duncan answered, "but the word was sent anyway."

Will saw Alistair McNabb pull his pocket watch from his vest pocket, flip open the face, and check the time. "Twelve forty-seven p.m.," he said.

The engineers on both locomotives blasted their whistles and rang their bells repeatedly. The crowd opened up while the *Jupiter* backed away a few feet and Engine No. 119 moved forward to cross the final tie. Then, the two locomotives reversed the action and the *Jupiter* crossed the joining. With final, mutual whistle blasts, both engines eased forward to touch pilots over the final tie. The tracklayers shouted, jumped, and yelled.

"Now, Mr. Braddock," Andrew Russell said, "take this plate—"

Before Will could grasp the plate, a drunk staggered against the photographer causing him to drop it. The glass plate shattered.

"Oh, no," Russell said. "That was the shot of Stanford swinging at the spike."

Will bent to retrieve the remains of the photographic plate.

"Leave it," Russell said. "Can't save it. We'll set up a better shot. I want to expose a couple of this one, at least."

General Jack Casement, swishing his riding crop, cleared a swath in front of Russell's camera. Russell coaxed Samuel Montague to represent the Central Pacific and Grenville Dodge the Union Pacific and placed the two chief construction engineers clasping hands in front of the two locomotives. While Russell made final adjustments to his camera settings, locomotive engineers George Booth of the CP's *Jupiter* and Sam Bradford of the UP's Engine No. 119 climbed onto their respective cowcatchers and extended champagne bottles toward each other across the intervening space. Before Russell could expose his plate, dozens of workers crowded back into the picture.

"Oh, that will make a great picture," Jenny said. "I'll want a copy of that to show my children someday."

"Your children," Will said. "Are you getting married?"

"Well, not right away. No one's asked me."

CHAPTER 52

Following the ceremony of driving the final spike, Will found himself wandering around alone. Jenny had returned to Stanford's train to serve a champagne luncheon to the dignitaries. Will had helped Russell haul his camera equipment back on board the train and had said goodbye to the photographer.

The throng of workers thinned quickly, many of the Irish drifting back to the row of tents and shanties offering libations and entertainment. The noise had diminished only slightly, simply coming from a different direction. Will searched the dissolving crowd of Central Pacific workers for Chung Huang. He found him preparing to board Strobridge's work train for the trip back to Victory.

"Chung Huang!" Will waved his slouch hat above his head.

His Chinese friend heard his call and turned back to meet him. "Will Braddock, you come with me to China to build railroads?"

Will pushed his windblown hair out of his face and returned his hat to his head. "No. I would like to build more railroads, but I won't be going to China."

Chung Huang smiled. "I not thinking you would. But I glad you want to build railroads. There be much need."

"Yes, I agree. The Pacific Railroad is only the first of many that will cross this continent, as there will be many to cross China. I must say goodbye and wish you good luck."

"I preased to have met you, Will. I say goodbye, too."

The locomotive attached to the work train sounded two short blasts of its whistle signaling depart time.

"Board! All aboard what's going." A conductor shouted the call from the rear of the train.

Will shook hands with Chung Huang, and his friend ran to climb onto one of the flatcars loaded with workers dressed in similar blue frocks and straw hats. The CP's Irish workers were not visible. They undoubtedly had seats in one of the passenger coaches.

Will walked to where Alistair McNabb stood with Duncan and Butch near Durant's train. "Jenny not back yet?" Will asked.

"No," McNabb said. "Durant, Dodge, and several others entered the Director's car on Stanford's train some time ago. Hopefully, they won't be much longer."

"What will you do now, Mr. McNabb?" Will asked.

"Wells Fargo has offered me an office position in Sacramento. I've decided to accept. It will be better than being a one-armed farmer." McNabb laughed.

Will did not feel comfortable joining Jenny's father in laughter. He wasn't sure how sensitive the former Confederate cavalry officer was about losing his arm during the war.

"California was the original destination for our family," McNabb said. "We will finally reach there, although it didn't quite work out the way we'd planned when we left Virginia two years ago. We'll make the best of what we have and be thankful. Jenny and Elspeth will have work in their millinery shop. Duncan can enroll in a regular school. But, before we can head farther west, I have to go put the mail on one of the Central Pacific trains and close Wells Fargo's Promontory station."

"What are your plans, Butch?" Will asked.

"I'm staying in Utah. Wells Fargo will be running feeder lines north and south all along the length of the railroad. I'm going to work the line from Ogden up into Idaho and Montana.

There's still work for a stagecoach driver."

"Good luck to you, Will." Alistair McNabb extended his hand. "It has been a pleasure knowing you."

"Good luck to all of you, too," Will said. He shook everybody's hands, and McNabb, Duncan, and Butch crossed the tracks, back to the small tent that served as Wells Fargo's station.

A clatter of hooves attracted Will's attention. A detachment of cavalry approached with Lieutenant Luigi Moretti riding at its head. Trotting alongside Luey rode Will's mixed-blood Cheyenne friend, Lone Eagle. Will raised his hat and waved it, allowing the stiff breeze to ruffle his long hair again.

"Ho!" called Moretti. The detachment halted in front of Will. "Sergeant Winter!"

From the rear of the column, Moretti's sergeant rode forward. Sergeant Winter halted and saluted. "Sir!"

"Take charge and find food for the men and the horses, then make camp away from this rowdy place. We'll be heading back in the morning."

"Yes, sir," Winter said. He nodded to Will and smiled before he swung his mount around and issued orders for the detachment to follow him.

Moretti and Lone Eagle dismounted. Moretti twisted the ends of his mustache to sharpen their points.

"Welcome to Promontory Summit, Luey," Will said. "You missed all the excitement."

"I was afraid of that. General Casement's train didn't have room for our horses, so we had to ride from the big cut."

"I'm sorry you missed the ceremonies. What are you going to do now?"

"Our job is finished. All I have to do is report to General Dodge and turn this detachment around. As soon as I can find transportation for the horses, we'll return to Fort Fred Steele. From there I imagine I'll go to chasing hostile Indians."

"And you, Lone Eagle?" Will asked.

"I will stay with Lieutenant Moretti. Perhaps I can help the Army tell the difference between a good Indian and a bad one. Save a few lives at least." Lone Eagle smiled. "Besides, Butterfly Morning will have the baby soon, and I need a job to take care of the family."

Will's conversation with his friends was interrupted when a group of men approached from Stanford's train. Will recognized General Dodge, Doc Durant, the Casement brothers, Silas Seymour, John Duff, and Sidney Dillon.

"That was some luncheon," Durant said. He walked past Will, Luey, and Lone Eagle without acknowledging them. "But all that champagne didn't help my headache. It's worse than ever. I'll be glad to get back aboard my own car and be on my way home."

"I'll be there in a few minutes," Dodge said. "I have to give some instructions to my men before we leave."

Durant waved a hand to indicate he'd heard Dodge. Seymour, Duff, and Dillon followed Durant in silence down the length of his special train.

Dodge stopped Jack and Dan Casement and shook their hands. "You go on, General Jack. You'll have to get your train on the way before Durant's can move. I wish I could ride with you, but unfortunately, I have to go with Durant to Omaha."

The Casements shook hands with Dodge and Will and returned to their work train.

"Luey, you're late," Dodge said.

Luey explained about the necessity for his detachment to ride from the *big cut*, resulting in their late arrival. He explained about his orders to return his men to Fort Fred Steele.

"Very good, Luey," Dodge said. "Thank you for all your good work. It helped me keep my sanity knowing you were close at hand to protect me, if necessary."

Luey saluted. He and Dodge then exchanged handshakes and Luey extended his hand to Will. "I'll say goodbye for now," he said. "Be sure to look me up when you pass through Fort Fred Steele the next time."

Luey and Lone Eagle turned to leave.

"Lone Eagle," Will said. "Can you wait a minute? I'd like a word with you, and Jenny would like to see you before you leave, I'm sure."

Lone Eagle looked to the lieutenant. Luey nodded his approval and led his horse in the direction they'd seen Sergeant Winter take the detachment.

Homer and Will's uncle walked up. A broad grin on the black man's face confirmed that Will's uncle had accepted Homer's reason for leaving the team. Will had told his uncle about killing Paddy O'Hannigan. Along with Homer and Jenny, now four living people knew what had almost caused the ceremony to take place without the special spikes.

"General Dodge," Will's uncle said. "What are your instructions for the survey inspection team? What's left of it. Homer's decided to head to Texas to search for his family. That leaves me . . . and Will, of course." His uncle reached out a hand and clasped Will on the shoulder.

"I'd like you to draw up plans for what General Jack has constructed here at Promontory, then come to Omaha. I want to plan for the expansion of the Union Pacific. First, we'll head up across Oregon from here and strike the Pacific Ocean without having to share the route with the Central Pacific. After that, it's hard to tell what we might build."

Jenny hurried over from General Stanford's train. She held the strings of her bonnet to keep the breeze from lifting it off her head.

"Ah, Miss McNabb," Dodge said. "That was certainly a nice luncheon you served. Even Doc Durant was impressed."

"Thank you, General," Jenny said. "I'm glad you enjoyed it. I came to say goodbye. I only have a few minutes. Governor Stanford is anxious to start back to Sacramento."

Lone Eagle stepped out from behind the others where he had stood in silence.

"Oh, Lone Eagle," Jenny said, "I didn't see you there. What a pleasant surprise."

Lone Eagle nodded, but did not speak.

Engine No. 119's whistle blasted twice, indicating Durant's train prepared to depart.

"Now, I have to go," Dodge said. "Durant's in a hurry to get away from here, too. But, before I go, I have a question for Mr. Braddock."

"Sir?"

"What do you plan to do with the rest of your life, Will?" Dodge asked.

Will looked at his uncle, then he looked at Jenny. Neither spoke.

Will faced Dodge. "Ah . . . I . . . ah, I want to build railroads, General Dodge. I don't mean as a hunter for a survey party. I want to do something more important."

"How about becoming a surveyor?" Dodge asked.

"I don't have the education, sir. I only went through the eighth grade. I haven't gone to college like Uncle Sean."

"You don't have to go to college. We can put you in an apprentice program."

"Become an apprentice?"

"Not like that blacksmith apprentice program you ran away from when I first met you. I would not have liked the confinement that implied, either. We put candidates through an apprenticeship that entails working in the field alongside a trained surveyor. The apprenticeship doesn't have to last seven years, either. It can end as soon as you learn the trade. I'll even assign you to your uncle . . . if he'll have you?"

Will's uncle nodded. "I would be delighted to train a family member."

"Do you accept?" Dodge asked.

"Yes, sir! I accept."

"Done." Dodge shook Will's hand. "Now, I must be on my way. Sean, walk with me to the coach."

Will's uncle and General Dodge headed toward the Pullman palace car of Durant's train.

Will turned to Jenny. "You know Lone Eagle's wife is going to have a baby?"

"Yes. Where is Butterfly Morning now, Lone Eagle?"

"She is with her family on the Shoshone Wind River reservation. After the baby is born, I will take her and the baby to Bullfrog's cabin on the North Platte. It is a good place to raise a child."

Jenny reached beneath the neck of her dress and pulled out a rawhide thong. A single eagle talon hung from it. She lifted it over her head and stepped in front of Lone Eagle.

"Please give this eagle talon to your baby. It is lucky. It saved my life once, as you well know. I want to return it to your family."

Jenny raised the thong, Lone Eagle bent his head, and Jenny dropped the rawhide necklace over it.

"Thank you, Jenny. Our baby will cherish it. Now, I must go find the lieutenant. We are returning to Wyoming tomorrow."

"Goodbye, for now, Lone Eagle," Will said. "I know I will see you again."

"Goodbye, Will. Goodbye, Jenny, Goodbye, Homer. Thank you all for being my friend." Lone Eagle walked away.

"You have a tear in your eye, Will," Jenny said.

Will swiped a finger across his cheek beneath his eye. "We're all going in different directions," he said.

"Miss Jenny," Homer said, "you and Will must excuse me. I needs to feed Ruby and Buck and pack things up for Mr. Corcoran and Will to go to Omaha."

"Of course, Homer. Good luck on your trip to Texas. I hope you find your family."

Homer nodded and headed back to the row of tents used by the UP workers for temporary living quarters.

Following the celebratory party, George Booth, the *Jupiter*'s engineer, had turned the governor's special around using the Union Pacific's new wye track. Two blasts from the locomotive's whistle sounded the alert for the departure of Stanford's train to Sacramento.

"I must go, Will," Jenny said.

"I'll walk you back."

He held her hand, and they headed toward the Director's car.

"Will," Jenny asked, "have you decided whether you're going to see Mort Kavanagh?"

"Yes, I plan to stop there on my way back through Corinne."

"I think that will help you find peace."

At the bottom step of the passenger car's front platform, she stopped and looked up at him. He stared into her pale blue eyes. He saw no hint of gray.

"If you come to California, be sure to see me. Elspeth's millinery shop is right across the street from the depot in Sacramento."

"I'll do that."

Jenny stood on her toes and kissed him firmly on the lips. She turned away, climbed the steps onto the platform, and grasped the handle of the coach's door. She removed her bonnet and allowed the evening breeze to blow her long, black tresses across her face and float around her shoulders.

"You're blushing, Will Braddock." She opened the door and

disappeared.

Will touched his fingertips to his lips. Hopefully, the apprenticeship wouldn't take too long.

HISTORICAL NOTES

In *Golden Spike,* Will Braddock encounters the following historical characters:

Grenville M. Dodge, Union Pacific's chief engineer

Ulysses S. Grant, President of the United States

Jack Casement, Union Pacific's construction contractor

Dan Casement, Union Pacific's construction contractor
(partners with his brother, Jack)

Thomas "Doc" Durant, Union Pacific's vice president &
general manager

"Colonel" Silas Seymour, Durant's consulting engineer

Samuel B. Reed, Union Pacific's engineer of construction

Jacob Blickensderfer, former Department of Interior railroad
inspector working for Union Pacific

Brigham Young, Mormon leader

James Strobridge, Central Pacific's construction superintendent

Hanna Marie Strobridge, wife of James Strobridge

Samuel S. Montague, Central Pacific's chief engineer

Charles Crocker, one of the "Big Four" Central Pacific founders

Andrew J. Russell, Union Pacific's official photographer

Colonel John Stevenson, Fort Fred Steele commanding officer

Governor Leland Stanford, one of the "Big Four" Central
Pacific founders and its president

Sidney Dillon, Union Pacific director and head of Crédit Mobilier

John Duff, Union Pacific director

George Coley, Central Pacific's foreman on team that laid ten miles of track in one day

Sam Bradford, engineer on Union Pacific locomotive No. 119

Cyrus Sweet, fireman on Union Pacific locomotive No. 119

George Booth, engineer on Central Pacific locomotive No. 60, *Jupiter*

R. A. Murphy, fireman on Central Pacific locomotive No. 60, *Jupiter*

Watson N. Shilling, Western Union telegrapher

Jenny McNabb encounters the following historical characters traveling in the director's car on Governor Stanford's special train from Sacramento to Promontory Summit. These persons, first named in Chapter 40, do not represent all of the passengers making the journey:

Eli D. Dennison, Central Pacific conductor

Governor Anson P. K. Safford, newly appointed governor of Arizona Territory

J. W. Haines, Federal Commissioner of Inspection for the Central Pacific

Frederick A. Tritle, Federal Commissioner of Inspection for the Central Pacific and candidate for governor of Nevada

W. G. Sherman, Federal Commissioner of Inspection for the Central Pacific and brother of General William T. Sherman

Judge Silas W. Sanderson, Chief Justice of the Supreme Court of California

Alfred A. Hart, Central Pacific's official photographer

Dr. Harvey Willson Harkness, *Sacramento Press* editor and publisher and Stanford's physician

E. B. Ryan, Stanford's private secretary

All other characters are fictitious.

In 1869, the community of Wahsatch was spelled differently than it is today and from how the Wasatch Mountains have always been spelled.

References to the day and date about the agreement reached between General Grenville M. Dodge of the Union Pacific and Collis P. Huntington of the Central Pacific as to the location for the meeting of the two railroads differ. Maury Klein in *Union Pacific, Volume 1,* states that "late in the evening on April 9 a bargain was struck." Stephen E. Ambrose in *Nothing Like It in the World* writes "So, on April 9, Dodge met with Huntington in Washington." David Haward Bain in *Empire Express* claims "On the evening of Sunday, April 8, Huntington met Dodge in Washington . . ." In fact, April 8 is a Thursday. It appears that the meeting between Dodge and Huntington commenced on the evening of April 8 and was concluded the next day, April 9, Friday. On the night of April 9, Congress met in a late session and issued the joint resolution specifying the joining of the railroads would take place at Promontory Summit, Utah. The wording in Chapter 33 of a telegram from Dodge to Samuel Reed announcing the agreement is the author's invention.

The tracklaying record set by the Central Pacific described in Chapter 39 was never beaten by traditional tracklayers. There is no record that Doc Durant ever paid the bet he lost.

Over twenty newspaper reporters attended the ceremony joining the two halves of the Pacific Railroad. Following the festivities they evidently kept the telegraph line busy transmitting their stories. As described in Chapter 51, most of them could not hear what the dignitaries said, so the "facts" vary considerably. Three persons also wrote about the ceremony in their diaries, and four people, including General Grenville Dodge, later wrote articles about their participation. Like the newspaper reports, their versions of the events are different. As the author, I chose what I considered to be the most interesting "facts" and included them in *Golden Spike*.

The Golden Spike is on display in the museum at Leland Stanford Junior University in Palo Alto, California. Nevada's Silver Spike is also on display at Stanford University, as is the Silver-Headed Maul. Arizona's Gold and Silver Spike is on display at the Museum of the City of New York. The Second Golden Spike and the Laurel Wood Tie apparently were lost during the San Francisco earthquake and fire of 1906.

ABOUT THE AUTHOR

Award-winning author **Robert Lee Murphy**'s *Eagle Talons,* the first book in *The Iron Horse Chronicles,* won the 2015 Bronze Will Rogers Medallion Award for younger readers. In 2016, the second book, *Bear Claws,* received the Silver Will Rogers Medallion Award for younger readers and was awarded First Place for Fiction by the Wyoming State Historical Society. *Golden Spike* concludes the trilogy.

Murphy devoted years of research to ensure the historical accuracy of the timeline his characters encounter. He traveled the route of the transcontinental railroad, walked the ground where the scenes take place, and visited all the museums and historical parks along the way.

Prior to becoming an author, Murphy worked with international organizations on all seven continents, including Antarctica, where Murphy Peak bears his name. Murphy is a member of the Society of Children's Book Writers & Illustrators, Western Writers of America, the Wyoming State Historical Society, and the Railway & Locomotive Historical Society. Visit the author at his website: http://robertleemurphy.net.

The employees of Five Star Publishing hope you have enjoyed this book.

Our Five Star novels explore little-known chapters from America's history, stories told from unique perspectives that will entertain a broad range of readers.

Other Five Star books are available at your local library, bookstore, all major book distributors, and directly from Five Star/Gale.

Connect with Five Star Publishing

Visit us on Facebook:
  https://www.facebook.com/FiveStarCengage

Email:
  FiveStar@cengage.com

For information about titles and placing orders:
  (800) 223-1244
  gale.orders@cengage.com

To share your comments, write to us:
  Five Star Publishing
  Attn: Publisher
  10 Water St., Suite 310
  Waterville, ME 04901